OAK LAWN PUBLIC LIBRARY

3 1186 00833 9087

18

W9-CCP-573

Through
the
Skylight

Through
the
Skylight

Ian Baucom
Illustrated by Justin Gerard

MAY 1 6 2013
OAK LAWN LIBRARY

A Atheneum Books for Young Readers
atheneum New York London Toronto Sydney New Delhi

Wendy and our children inspired this book and lent it every contour of its writing.

Justin Gerard drew it into richer light than I could've imagined. Sonia Chaghatzbanian, Ariel Colletti, Jeannie Ng, and all the brilliant team at Atheneum have each given it the priceless care of the bookmaker's art. Above all, Caitlyn Dlouhy believed in it and quickened it, patiently, into life. For all those gifts, my deepest thanks.

—I. B.

ATHENEUM BOOKS FOR YOUNG READERS • An imprint of Simon & Schuster Children's Publishing Division • 1230 Avenue of the Americas, New York, New York 10020 • This book is a work of fiction. Any references to historical events, real people, or real places are used fictitiously. Other names, characters, places, and events are products of the author's imagination, and any resemblance to actual events or places or persons, living or dead, is entirely coincidental. • Text copyright © 2013 by Ian Baucom • Illustrations copyright © 2013 by Justin Gerard • All rights reserved, including the right of reproduction in whole or in part in any form. • ATHENEUM BOOKS FOR YOUNG READERS is a registered trademark of Simon & Schuster, Inc. • Atheneum logo is a trademark of Simon & Schuster, Inc. • For information about special discounts for bulk purchases, please contact Simon & Schuster Special Sales at 1-866-506-1949 or business@simonandschuster.com. • The Simon & Schuster Speakers Bureau can bring authors to your live event. For more information or to book an event, contact the Simon & Schuster Speakers Bureau at 1-866-248-3049 or visit our website at www.simonspeakers.com. • Book design by Sonia Chaghatzbanian • The text for this book is set in Scala. • The illustrations for this book are rendered in pencil. • Manufactured in the United States of America • 0213 FFG • First Edition • 10 9 8 7 6 5 4 3 2 1 • Library of Congress Cataloging-in-Publication Data • Baucom, Ian, 1967– • Through the skylight / Ian Baucom. — 1st ed. • p. cm. • Summary: Living temporarily in Venice, three American siblings uncover a mystery surrounding magical objects, an Arabian Nights book, and animals that can walk in and out of paintings. • ISBN 978-1-4169-1777-9 • ISBN 978-1-4424-6079-9 (eBook) • [1. Mystery and detective stories. 2. Magic—Fiction. 3. Brothers and sisters—Fiction. 4. Americans—Italy—Fiction. 5. Venice (Italy)—Fiction. 6. Italy—Fiction.] I. Title. • PZ7.B3248Ve 2013 • [Fic]—dc23 • 2012010642

For Camden and Tristan,
waiting all the way
—I. B.

Lagoon of Venice

To Mestre

Ponte della Libertà

Ghetto

Grand Canal

Santa Lucia
Railroad Station

St. Mark
Basilica

Ponte
dell'Accademia

Gallerie dell'
Accademia

Giudecca Canal

La Giudecca

N

Cemetery

Venice

te di
alto

Apartment

Arsenal

Piazza
San Marco

Doge's Palace

Isola
San Pietro

Canale di San Marco

Sant'
Elena

0   MILES   1.5

CONTENTS

1
The Leather Bag

Jared figured it was now or never. They'd been in the old Italian church for an eternity. So the minute his mom was finally done talking about the painting of the saint with his hands tied behind his back and all the arrows sticking through his chest, he headed down the center aisle, hurried past the pews where old women were kneeling, and grabbed his skateboard from the entrance to the gloomy *chiesa*. The white-haired signora selling postcards at the entryway slid her glasses down her nose and squinted at him disapprovingly as he hopped onto the deck of his board, pushed through the velvet curtains, and burst out into the open space of the Venetian square.

It was a week till Carnevale, Venice's huge costume party, and everywhere Jared looked, people were already wandering around in fancy getups.

"Whoa! Whoops! Sorry!" he called out to a woman in green face paint standing on a box, where German tourists dropped coins into a basket at her feet. The back wheels of his skateboard had knocked her basket flying. She glared at him, the Medusa-like lengths she'd woven her hair into quivering. Behind her, Jared could see his sister Shireen hurrying out of the shadowy entrance to the church and onto the square. She was about his size. They had the same brown eyes and thick black hair. Sometimes people mistook them for twins, and that drove him crazy—she wasn't like him in any other way, and plus, he was a year older.

"Jared!" he could hear Shireen yelling as he whizzed past a café table ringed with girls in voluminous ball gowns drinking cappuccinos and texting on their cell phones. He crouched low on his board, ignored his sister, and sped toward the embankment fronting the deep waters of the Venetian lagoon.

"*Jared!*" Shireen shouted again. "Mom! Tell him to stop!"

But he'd had enough. They'd been in the church for an hour. And tomorrow they'd go to another one to look at *more* paintings. And the day after that, another. He dropped his heel and pushed again. Up ahead he saw a lumbering vaporetto force its way between crowds of bobbing gondolas.

"*Ja-red!* Stop! That's the wrong boat!"

He glanced over his shoulder as the wheels of his board spattered a knot of pigeons with a spray of lagoon water that had spilled over at high tide. Shireen was forcing her way through the crush of people milling around. His mother and his youngest sister, Miranda, were a few steps behind, Miranda craning her neck back to get one last look at the Medusa lady on her box.

"The number eighty-two, Jared!" Shireen was pointing furiously at a vaporetto docking one platform farther down. The breeze had caught her dark hair, wrapping its ends around her face.

"We need to take the eighty-two! The number one takes forever!"

Jared turned his back on Shireen, pulled his ski cap lower, and eased his weight on the board. He'd reached the wooden ramp stretching out to the vaporetto stop. With one hard kick of his heel he popped his skateboard into the air, tucked it under his arm, and maneuvered through a thicket of luggage-toting grown-ups exiting the boat. "MOM!" He heard Shireen's protest lifting through the air as he pushed through the doors of the vaporetto cabin and grabbed a seat, grinning to himself.

The drizzle started falling as the vaporetto crept down the curving length of the Grand Canal, pulling in at every stop. Now Shireen was really steaming.

"You're such an idiot," she hissed to Jared. "How long have we been here? And you still don't know the difference between the number eighty-two and the number one?"

Jared looked up at the route board screwed above the cabin door. He hated to admit it, but Shireen was right. The number one *did* take forever. Eleven stops down. Seven more to go. He spun the wheels of his skateboard against his hand and gave her a sheepish "Sorry."

"Not good enough!" Shireen frowned back. "What if it's closed? It's Wednesday, remember?"

It took him a second. Wednesday? Then it hit him. Wednesday in Italy wasn't like Wednesday in America. Stores here closed at all sorts of weird hours. On Wednesdays they were barely open at all. Ugh.

Miranda looked from Shireen to Jared. "Mom?" She leaned forward in her seat to catch her mother's eye. "Is the bookstore closed already? It can't be closed. It's the only one in Venice."

Meaning, Jared thought, the only *English* bookstore in Venice. Miranda and Shireen had been making lists for a week, ever since their mother told them about it. He couldn't blame them. Italian TV was awful.

"We'll see," their mother answered, her lips pressed a bit tight. His sisters glared at him. He pulled his skateboard in to his chest and slunk down in his seat as the vaporetto went chugging down the canal.

Three-quarters of an hour later, no one was any happier. The vaporetto had finally let them off, and then there were fifteen minutes of turning down skinny little side alleys, climbing over canal bridges, and angling across tiny *campos* rimmed by shuttered stores. Jared couldn't even skate. It was pointless. The drizzle had turned into a cold, hard winter rain, so it would be suicide to try to ollie up the steps of the bridges. Half an inch of water was sluicing across the alleyways. They were getting drenched.

Their mother pulled them up to shelter in the

tunnel of a long covered alley running alongside a wide *campo*. Jared could just barely make out the name of the square painted on the wall of a building on the far side: GHETTO NUOVO.

"We're here!" he announced happily. His sisters looked at their mother expectantly. She pointed word-lessly at a storefront off to the right. There were no lights on inside. A metal shutter had been drawn over the door. The English bookstore was closed.

A wind gust swirled down the sheltered *calle*, rushing freezing pages of rain over them. They scurried back.

"Thanks a lot!" Shireen fumed at Jared as she wiped the water off her face.

Then Miranda saw it. "Mom, look!" She pointed at a glimmer of light that was shining through the win-dows of the store next to the bookshop. "That one's open. Maybe we can go in there while we wait for the rain to let up."

Their mother sized up the distance across the exposed square. Another swirl of rain-chasing wind from the back of the *calle* made up her mind.

"Right," she said, grabbing Miranda's hand. "Let's go."

"*Mi dispiace,*" their mother apologized to the old man sitting behind the wooden counter of the shop as the bell-tinkling door closed behind them. Water was dripping from the ends of their scarves and pooling on the marble floor.

"Prego." He smiled. "Welcome." He had a white beard. A pair of little round glasses perched on the end of his nose. Behind the wire-rimmed lenses his blue eyes gleamed with pleasure at the sight of the children. A black cat curled at his feet blinked at them as they stood there awkwardly. The shopkeeper disappeared briefly into a back room and came back out holding a towel. "Please." He smiled again, handing it to their mother. "For the children." She took it from him and briskly toweled Shireen and Miranda off. Jared held his hand out for the towel before she could do him. He wiped his face and dried off his skateboard.

"Thank you," their mother said, handing the towel back to the man. "You're very kind."

"No," he responded, "it's nothing. The rain is bad." Jared noticed that he seemed to be studying them intently over the rims of his glasses, like he was trying to work something out. Well, it wasn't the first time that had happened, though it still bugged Shireen if people were too obvious about it. "We're adopted, okay?!" she'd blurted to a cashier in a Kroger Food and Drug at home when she caught the lady staring at them as they stood together in line: Miranda, a blond, blue-eyed, round-faced miniature version of their mother; she and Jared with their black hair, brown eyes, brown skin. "Me and him! We're adopted. From India. Get it?" But it didn't really bother Jared anymore. People got used to it. After a while, they forgot. And besides, no one at the skate park cared. So he just folded his wet ski cap into his coat pocket, propped his skateboard in a corner by the door, and was turning to check out the contents of the shop when he realized something.

The old man wasn't looking at them as though he thought they were an odd grouping—it was more like he'd been waiting for someone exactly like them. Like he'd been expecting them.

The old man caught Jared eyeing him and gave him a quick wink, then turned back to their mother. "So, signora, can I help you with anything?"

"No," she admitted, "we're really just escaping from the rain." She gestured out the window to the torrential downpour.

"*Prego,*" he said again. "Stay as long as you want." With another welcoming nod of his head, he returned to the book he'd been reading at his counter.

It was one of those dark little shops they'd seen all around the back neighborhoods of Venice, jammed full of masks for a Carnevale of fifty or a hundred years ago: lion-faced masks, jesters' masks, and simple black-ribboned masks for hiding your eyes. The shelves were stacked with brass candlesticks; embroidered scarves; velvet slippers; big blue bowls of mismatched, multicolored glass Murano beads; and really old portrait paintings of ancient bearded Venetian men in bright cloaks and red skullcaps. The doges of Venice, Mom had taught them, were like dukes, and were the only ones who wore those caps. Stacks of musty books were piled in every corner. The wall behind the old man's desk was covered with framed maps of Venice drawn in black ink on yellowing parchment. At the opposite end there was a statue made of blue porcelain, almost life-size, holding a fraying leather bag.

"Marco Polo!" Miranda exclaimed, looking to their mother for confirmation. "Look, Mom, that's Marco Polo, right?"

She studied the statue for a few seconds and nodded. It *was* Marco Polo, the thirteenth-century explorer who'd spent years crossing half the world from Venice to Asia until he'd finally arrived at the court of the Great Khan. He'd been the first person they had to study in their homeschool class on Venetian history when they'd arrived in Italy back in January. After Marco finally came home to Venice, he'd written a book about all the things he'd seen: the strange animals; the horse-riding warrior clans; the spicy, steaming food.

But what had captured Jared's attention now wasn't history—it was the leather bag clutched in the statue's hand. Something was flashing inside it. He waited until their mom had wandered off to flip through a pile of maps, then crossed over to the statue. He quickly peeked over his shoulder to make sure no one was watching, then reached inside the leather pouch.

There! There it was again!

"Shireen, Miranda," he whispered, "come on, take a look!" The coast was clear: The storekeeper was over with their mother, talking to her about the maps she was paging through.

"What is it?" Miranda asked, standing at his elbow.

"Treasure!" he answered. He widened the mouth of the bag to get a better look. It was full of rings, coins, oddly marked dice, gold-colored balls, little stoppered glass vials, writing nibs, and other stray things.

"Hey, cut that out," Shireen whispered furiously,

glancing back at their mother. "You'll get us in trouble."

"Hang on," Jared said, digging his hand deeper into the bag. "I saw something in there."

"What? It's tourist junk!"

"No, I saw a light!" He tipped the bag to show his sisters—and there! He was sure he'd seen it again! Somewhere deep inside the trove of coins and dice and cold glass balls, a golden light was gleaming. And there it was again! And there! Coming from two or three corners of the leather sack. Jared had started to scoop the top layer of treasures out when he heard a voice behind him and stiffened.

"What have you found?" It was the shopkeeper. He'd left Mom studying a map he'd suggested and come over without their noticing. Jared blinked dumbly at the old man, the heat rising in his face. His hand was frozen in the bag. He knew what it looked like. He was aching to just grab his skateboard from the door and get out of there before he got into more trouble. But he was trapped.

The look on the old man's face wasn't angry, though. "Come, *ragazzo*," he said, looking Jared in the eye. "I know you are not a thief. It is only . . ." He paused, and it seemed like he was weighing his words carefully. "You are drawn to these things. Yes, you are drawn to them." He was giving Jared that strange look again. "Very well," he finally announced. "I make this agreement with you: You may have one thing from the bag. No charge. Each of you. But first you must tell me what the statue holds."

The words were out of Miranda's mouth before she had thought about them. She wasn't trying to win anything from the bag. She just loved answering questions, especially when she thought she was right. "It's Marco Polo's treasure. He brought it back from China."

"No, it's not," Shireen interrupted. "That stuff would be worth a fortune." She pushed her wet bangs out of her eyes. "It's got to be in a museum some-where. Not here."

"You are right." The old man turned to Shireen. He didn't seem put out by her response. "Your little sister made a good guess, but it is true, I don't sell such pre-cious things. So what do *you* think it is?"

"Kid stuff," Shireen answered, narrowing her eyes at Jared. "It's for children to look at while grown-ups shop for real things."

"That is half right," the shopkeeper said slowly. The black cat had stalked over and was eyeing them all curiously. "These things are just for children. Just for *kids*," he added, as if amused by the word. "But they are real. Very much real. Still, I think you have guessed it close enough. You may pick. But I think maybe you shouldn't look. It would be hard to choose. Just reach in, and whatever you pull out is yours." He paused again. "Yes, that is best. Let us see what the bag gives you."

Shireen frowned. He was acting too mysterious. It was just a bag of tourist junk.

Miranda wasn't waiting, though. Before her siblings could say anything else, she closed her eyes, reached inside the leather bag, and pulled out the first thing she touched. Jared couldn't believe it. It was a ring, and it was gleaming. Or, at least, it was when she pulled it from the bag. He could see its bright light as she plucked it out. But the moment it was free of the bag, the light went out, as though cold water had been thrown on it.

This time, though, Shireen had seen the flash of light. Her eyes widened.

"You see," the old man said gently. "What is in the bag is real. Quick, now—your mother will be finished with the maps soon, and like I say, these things are just for children. Now you must take your turn. And the boy, too. *Subito.* Quick. It is our secret."

2
The Most Powerful
Thing of All

Jared couldn't believe it. Shireen had snagged one too. She'd stepped up to the statue, darted a cautious look across the store to make sure Mom was still busy, then pulled out another ring. This one had some kind of emblem or design on its crown, and it also glowed briefly with light before growing dim. Shireen closed it in her hand, a look of amazement in her eyes.

Now it was his turn. Jared plunged his hand into the bag, but no matter where he reached, he couldn't find a ring. His hand was starting to sweat. The coins and dice he touched were slithering away. Any moment now, their mother was going to look over and see what they were up to. He groped around desperately. There was no way he was going to let his sisters beat him at this. And then he felt it! A perfect circle of cold metal. But as he tried to take it, the ring slipped out of his fingers. His hand was too sweaty. He was about to give up—he'd rather have nothing than pull out some worthless writing quill or marble—when the old man reached into the bag and said, "Here, let me help you." He guided Jared's hand to the very bottom and said, "There, it is there; take it." Jared's fingers closed on something, and he pulled it from the bag without knowing what he'd picked. He took a breath and unclenched his fingers.

It was a dull brown wooden cube. One of the dice. He dropped it back in the bag in disgust.

"No, *ragazzo*, no," the old man whispered in his ear. "Look again." Deep in the leather pouch, the wooden die was teetering on its edge against a slide of coins and tiny perfume bottles. For a second it lit up with an amber light, as if a minute lantern had been switched on inside it. Then it rolled over and the glow extinguished. But Jared had seen the light. He grabbed the die.

And then time ran out. Their mother was holding up a map, calling the shopkeeper over. The kids stuffed their treasures into their pockets and hurried over to join her, grinning crazily.

"What is it of?" Shireen asked, trying to act nonchalant as she looked at the map her mother had spread out on the countertop. It showed a green countryside bordering on the sea. A gray path stretched across the green land from one side of the map to the other. There were numbers on the path, inked in a medieval-looking script, from one to thirty-seven, and beside each number, colorful drawings: a castle, a monk sitting by a well, a water mill, a strumming troubador, a knight on a horse, lots of churches.

"It's one of the pilgrim routes to Santiago de Compostela, in Spain," their mother answered, a smile lighting her face as she gently touched the old parchment. "See? It starts here, in France." She pointed to the drawing of a walled town beside the number one. "And it ends in Santiago, at the cathedral. Every number is a place to stop along the way. People have been performing the pilgrimage—walking this route—for more than a thousand years."

"Cool," Shireen said.

"But why do they do it?" Miranda piped up.

"Because the body of Saint James, one of the

apostles, is supposed to be buried at the Cathedral of Santiago de Compostela, and some people think it's holy. A relic. What do you think? The shopkeeper recommended it. Will Dad like it? I'm thinking of getting it for his birthday."

"Yes," Shireen answered. "Definitely. He'll love it. It's beautiful."

Their mother paid the shopkeeper. He was going to have the map framed and delivered to their apartment in time for Dad's birthday next week. They were about to head off—the rain outside had finally let up—when the old man stepped into a room at the back of the store. He came out holding an ancient-looking leather-bound book.

"For the children," he said, handing the slim volume to their mother. "A souvenir."

"Oh!" she exclaimed. "Are you sure?"

He nodded while she opened the cover. The pages were made of yellowing parchment, covered in a fading handwritten script.

"It's in Latin," she said. "The kids don't read Latin. Well, not much. My husband's teaching them, but they're just beginning." She sized him up a little uncertainly. "I don't know what we'd do with it. Isn't it valuable? A book this old?"

"You will find a use," he answered quietly. "Please, signora, take it for the children. You will make an old man happy."

By the time they got back to the apartment, Dad was home. He'd spent the day at the university on San Servolo, one of the islands scattered across the Venetian lagoon. Back in the States, he taught history at the college in their hometown. But now he'd taken a job as a visiting professor in Venice for a semester while he worked on a book about the doges, the ancient dukes of Venice.

It had seemed like a cool idea at first. Dad had promised to take them to an Italian soccer match every couple of weeks. Cruising around everywhere on boats instead of being thrown in the back of a minivan definitely sounded like an upgrade. And Italian gelato was supposedly the best ice cream in the world. But after two months Jared had had enough. His cell phone didn't work in Italy. His parents had made him leave his Xbox at home. They didn't even have a laptop in the apartment to Skype with their friends in the States. Worst of all, he had to share a bedroom with Shireen and Miranda.

"You're kidding!" he'd blurted out when they'd first

arrived and he'd realized that the apartment had only two bedrooms. Mom and Dad were dropping off their suitcases in one of them and steering him and his sisters into the other. He'd begged them to let him stretch a sheet across the living room and live in a corner with his skateboard and a sleeping bag, but they'd refused.

No question about it. Venice was a bust.

Until today.

Jared slipped his hand into his pocket while Dad gave Mom and the girls kisses and then waved them all into the kitchen, where pasta was already boiling. The die was still there, deep in his pocket, hard and angular against his fingertips. Had it lit back up? He was aching to take it out to see. But not now, not with his parents around. He'd have to wait until later, after bedtime, when he and his sisters could get a serious look at what they'd found.

After supper Dad started flipping through the book the old man had given them. He squared his glasses on his nose and concentrated on the script. His lips moved silently while he translated the Latin in his head. "It's a story," he finally said, "about the

Arabian Nights. You know—Aladdin, Sinbad, all those tales. It's about a bookseller from a really long time ago who got his hands on a copy of the Arabian Nights and set off on an adventure with his nephew." He paused. "Are you sure the shopkeeper said we could keep this? It looks pretty rare to me. It has to be worth something. Maybe we should take it back."

"You can't take it back!" Miranda broke in, her eyebrows furrowing.

"Excuse me?" Dad answered.

"It's ours! The old man gave it to us, me and Shireen and Jared. You can't take it back!"

"Miranda." He gazed firmly at her. "Your mom and I will make that decision. Not you. What were you doing there anyway?" he asked. "I thought you were going to the English bookstore."

Jared frowned across the supper table at Miranda. Why was she making such a big deal out of the book? The book was not important. The last thing they needed was for their father to start asking too many questions about what they'd been up to at the store.

"We were just killing time while the rain blew over," their mother called out from the sink. "Right, kids?" she added, giving them one of those remember-we're-a-team looks.

Shireen blinked at her. Why was she covering for them? And then she remembered: Dad's birthday present. Mom wanted to keep it a secret.

"Maybe the shopkeeper just gave us the book because we didn't buy anything," she volunteered. "He wanted to make us think he had interesting things in his shop. So we'd come back. You know, kind of like advertising. I bet Mom told him you were a professor. He's probably got tons of old books like that in the back of his shop."

"Boxloads," Jared chipped in. "I saw them."

"No, you didn't!" Miranda interrupted. "We spent the whole time over at the . . . Ouch! He kicked me!" she yelled. "Jared kicked me!"

"Didn't," Jared lied.

"Yes, you did!" Her eyes narrowed angrily. "Mom! Dad!"

They were in the bathroom, brushing their teeth. Jared had timed the kick just right. The squabbling had gone on for five minutes, until Mom and Dad had had enough and sent them off to get ready for bed. There'd been no more questions about what they'd been doing at the store.

"I wasn't going to tell them," Miranda muttered as

she put her toothbrush away. "I'm not stupid."

"Sorry," Jared said with a shrug. "We couldn't take the chance."

Miranda made a face at him and stalked off to the bedroom, slamming the door behind her.

"Pretty cool, huh?" Jared turned to Shireen.

"What?"

"Oh, come on. You know, our stuff—your ring, my die. Don't pretend now like you don't care! You saw how they lit up. Maybe we can figure out what they are after lights-out."

Shireen smiled to herself but didn't say anything. She took a minute to put her long black hair in a ponytail, eyeing her reflection approvingly in the bathroom mirror. "So maybe you're not such an idiot," she said as she brushed past Jared. "At least, not all the time."

The bedroom was just big enough to squeeze three beds into. One to the left of the door; one against the far wall, where the ceiling sloped down almost to the floor; one opposite the walk-in closet. That was the best bed, because there was a skylight above it. At night, when the sky was clear, you could lie under it and look right up at the stars, listening to the church bells tolling over the roofs and towers of the city. Jared had been the first one to claim that bed after their mom and dad had turned down his idea of camping out in the living room, but Shireen and Miranda had protested. So now they rotated, each one getting it for a week at a time. Tonight Miranda had it, and when Jared and Shireen came in, she was already tucked in under the covers, staring up at the skylight expectantly, as if she was waiting for something to happen. Their father followed a minute later and made space for himself to sit down next to Miranda. He had the book from the store in his hands.

"I thought I'd read some of it for you," he announced.

"We can keep it?" Miranda asked excitedly, pushing herself up to a sitting position.

"For now, yes," their father affirmed. "Your mom and I talked about it."

Jared groaned. How long was *this* going to take? Over on her bed, Shireen was mouthing something to him while their dad opened the leather binding to the first page and took a minute to get the Latin straight.

What? Jared mouthed back.

Act sleepy, she mouthed, miming a yawn.

Jared grinned in agreement. Okay, so she *was* just as curious as him, no matter how superior she acted.

Dad rubbed his palm against his bearded cheek, and began. "On the thousand and first night, when Scheherazade had told the emperor her last tale—"

"Scheherazade?" Miranda asked. "Who's she?"

"The princess whom the emperor was going to marry. She knew that he was crazy. He'd been married lots of times, and the day after each wedding he always had his new wife put to death. So when Scheherazade found out that she was next, she made a deal. Every night she'd tell the emperor a story. If she could keep him interested for a thousand and one nights, he'd spare her life. That's where the real title comes from—it's not really called the *Arabian Nights*; it's *One Thousand and One Nights*."

"And it worked?" Shireen asked fake-dozily, opening her mouth in an enormous yawn.

"Yes," he replied. "It worked. Are you tired?"

"A bit." She yawned again.

"Me too," Jared added, giving a tonsil-baring yawn himself.

"Hmm." Dad gave them a quizzical look. They never went to sleep this early. He found his place in the book and started again.

"On the thousand and first night, when Scheherazade had told the emperor her last tale, the great ruler clapped his hands and summoned his court scribes. 'Write them down,' he commanded. 'Every tale. Make me a book of all these stories. Send copies to every corner of my empire. I wish all the world to know that Scheherazade, my empress, is the queen of storytellers.' When the work was done, the copies of the books, each stamped with the emperor's seal, were loaded aboard sailing ships, packed in camel bags, slipped into the carrying satchels of the fastest horse-riders of all the empire, and sent off, north, west, east, and south, one to each city of the emperor's vast realm. Now one of these books was sent across the Mediterranean Sea, to the city of Almeria, in al-Andalus—"

"Al-Andalus?" Miranda interrupted again. She had her hands behind her head, elbows out, and was staring dreamily up through the skylight into the winter night.

"Spain," Dad explained. "It was part of the Islamic empire for hundreds of years, all through the Middle Ages."

Jared took advantage of the break to yawn hugely again. "Man, oh man, I am so exhausted!"

Their father ignored him. "Now, one of these books," he translated, "was sent across the Mediterranean Sea, to the city of Almeria, in al-Andalus, where after many years it fell into the hands of the famous book merchant, Mounir al-Mari. Mounir had traveled every quarter of the Mediterranean, buying and selling books, from Alexandria to Marseille, Istanbul to Tangiers, but never had he seen so precious a manuscript. 'We shall sell it for a mountain of gold,' he told his nephew, Rashid, the day they boarded a ship to set out on their newest bookselling voyage—"

"All that running around in the rain," Jared broke in. "I'm wiped."

"Jared?" Dad said, putting the book down. "Are you trying to tell me something?"

"We're just tired, Dad." Shireen smiled sweetly.

"I'm not!" Miranda objected.

"Well, we are!" Shireen snapped back, staring daggers at her sister. Jared was right, she thought. Did they have to share a room with a nine-year-old?

Their father closed the book. "Okay," he said, "I'll read more tomorrow. Miranda, we'll start earlier." She started to protest, but he hushed her. "No arguing. Now, it's time to pray. Miranda, why don't you do it tonight?"

She was about to object when a gleam lit her eye. She snuck a mischievous glance at Jared and Shireen, folded her hands over her chest, and prayed: "Dear God, thank you for the cat. Amen."

"The cat?" Dad asked.

"Back at the old man's store," Miranda explained. "The cat. He spoke to me."

"Oh," said Dad, looking over at Shireen and Jared for an explanation. They shook their heads in confusion. Who could tell with Miranda? "What did he say?" he added.

"'Hello.'"

"And did you say 'hello' back?"

"No."

"Why not?"

"I said 'miaow,'" Miranda explained.

"I suppose you did," he answered with a chuckle. He bent down to kiss her. "Now go to sleep, little cat." After kissing Shireen and giving Jared a good-night pat on the head, he switched on the night-lamp, turned off the overhead light, and closed the door.

"The cat? You prayed about the *cat*?" Shireen demanded incredulously once she was sure that their father was safely gone.

"Yes. Maldini, that's his name." Then she added mysteriously, "You'll see."

Shireen rolled her eyes and Jared shook his head in

disbelief. They had some seriously strange Venetian treasures in their coat pockets and Miranda felt the need to go with some make-believe nonsense. What was wrong with her?

But who cared? Jared could hear the noise of the TV coming on down the hall. At last! Mom and Dad were settled in for the night. He pushed back the covers, bolted to the closet, and recovered his die from his coat pocket. Shireen followed, and after a minute so did Miranda.

Miranda slipped her ring over her finger and held it out for her siblings to see. A picture was carved on its crown: an etching of a man and a tree with the smallest of little birds sitting on its branches. The man seemed to be listening to them.

Shireen's ring also had an image carved on it, but it was less clear than Miranda's. The lines seemed fuzzier, as if they had been worn away or hadn't settled into a final pattern. As best they could tell, the lines were cut in the shape of a shield, with something vague in the middle. A dragon? An eagle? A flying horse? None of these seemed quite right to Shireen. But even if she had to hold back from saying it to Jared and Miranda, right now that actually made it better. Not knowing. It felt amazing to be clutching a mystery so tightly in her hand on a winter night in Venice.

And Jared's wooden cube, or die? It was the most mysterious of all. On two of its sides they could see the outline of a faun and a dragon. On three of the remaining surfaces were a book, a map, and a man holding what looked like a round guitar or mandolin. The sixth side was blank. Jared had no idea what to make of it.

"It's from a game," Miranda announced as he held it up to the shaded light from the sole night-lamp they were allowed to keep on.

"But how do you win?" Jared asked, raising his eyebrows.

"You don't win," Miranda decided firmly. "It wins."

Jared didn't know what the heck that meant, but for the moment he didn't care. Miranda was wrong. He knew it. He'd won. He'd captured the most powerful thing of all. Why else would the old shopkeeper have taken the trouble to make sure that *he* got the die? He turned it to study each side before settling at last on the blank surface. What could that mean? Why had it been left bare?

And why wouldn't it light back up? For that matter, why didn't the rings light up either?

Shireen must have been wondering the same thing. She was over on her bed, rubbing and twisting her ring. But it just sat there on her finger. She started to frown at it, like she'd been tricked. Like maybe it was just kid stuff after all.

Miranda was the only one who wasn't concerned. She'd crawled back under the covers and was lying on her back again, her ring snug on her finger, holding it up to admire against the fall of moonlight coming through the skylight. "Don't worry," she called out from her bed. "They'll come back to life."

"How do you know?" Jared demanded.

"The cat told me."

"The *talking* cat?" Shireen asked.

"Yes. Maldini, that's his name."

Jared and Shireen stared at her in exasperation.

But for now, there was nothing more to discover. Maybe they'd think of something tomorrow that would help them find out how the treasures worked. So they all settled down with their own thoughts. As she was drifting off to sleep, having finally given up, temporarily, on getting her ring to come back to life, Shireen looked over at Jared. He was blowing on his die and rubbing it, hoping that might have some effect.

"Cut that out," she instructed him. "Nothing's going to happen."

"It might!" he countered angrily.

"Not if it's up to *you* to make it work. Now just put it away somewhere safe."

"Nope," Jared answered. "Why should I? You and Miranda aren't putting your rings away."

"That's different. They fit on our fingers. You'll probably lose it, knowing you."

Jared shook his head again and turned his back on her, clenching his fist around the die. Nothing ever changed. Even when something amazing—something *magic*—happened, she still had to tell him what to do. Well, not this time.

Before long, though, much sooner than he would have guessed, he'd also fallen asleep. Miranda was the only one still awake, her eyes fixed on the skylight, waiting patiently. The cat didn't disappoint her. Just as the bells of Santi Giovanni e Paolo were ringing ten o'clock, he slipped across the red ceramic tile of their roof, padded onto the glass of the skylight, and stretched his furry black body out, looking down at her.

"Miaow," said Miranda from her bed in the room below, looking up at him as the ring on her finger began to glow.

"Good night," purred the cat from his spot on the skylight. He lifted one paw to his mouth and began to clean it with his neat pink tongue. Miranda closed her eyes happily and tumbled into her dreams.

3
Something Missing

The next morning, right at seven o'clock, just as the distant sound of a church bell was ringing the hour, Jared jerked awake. Something was shining in his eye, something sharp and bright. He scanned the room to see what was causing it. The room was shrouded in winter-morning gloom. The light wasn't coming from the skylight—the sun wasn't anywhere near high enough yet. So what was making it? His sisters were still sleeping. He swung out of bed and there it was, on the floor, beaming at him. His die! The light was coming from his die! It must have fallen out of his hand while he was sleeping. One of its sides had kindled fiercely to life.

Jared snatched up the die and angled it away from his face to get a better look at it without being blinded. A square-edged cone of light was coming from the side with the outline of a book cut into its surface.

"Shireen! Miranda!" he whispered urgently. "Wake up! Look!"

Before they'd blinked their eyes open, Jared heard footsteps approaching from the other side of the door. He spun and dove back into bed, stuffing the lit die under his pillow.

"Kids," their mother called, pushing open the door. "Come on, time to wake up. Dad's gone to pick up *frittelle* from the pastry shop."

The two girls dragged themselves out of bed, stretching as their mother headed back down the apartment hall. Jared started to pull the die out from under his pillow to show them what had happened. But then he thought better of it. Why tell them? Shireen would just make fun of him for not being able to hold onto it. And besides, he didn't need their help. He could figure it out on his own. *Then* he'd let them know what was going on.

As soon as Shireen and Miranda filed sleepily past, he tucked the still-shining die in his pajama-pants pocket and followed them.

Their mother was whisking a pot of milk for coffee. Dad had just come bustling back into the apartment with a bundle of pastries. "Help yourselves," he said, holding out the ribbon-tied package. He had a fleck of sugar on his beard. He must have already gobbled up his share at the *pasticceria*. The kids greedily unwrapped the package and tore into the sugarcoated rolls. Puffs of steam came wafting out of the doughy insides as they broke the *frittelle* apart with their fingertips. When they were finished, Jared was still hungry, so he poured himself a bowl of cereal. Dad swallowed a gulp of coffee and hauled out their Latin grammar book.

"Right," he said, flipping to an earmarked page. "Predicate nominatives!"

Jared groaned. Okay, so Dad was a professor, but did he have to treat everything like a classroom? Even breakfast! But Miranda's eyes were lighting up. She liked Latin, as long as Dad explained everything carefully.

"Jared," Dad continued cheerily, "how do you say 'Bears are wild animals'?"

Jared looked down into his cereal bowl, hoping that the floating Rice Krispies might magically arrange themselves into the required letters and words. He was actually pretty good at Latin; he just couldn't see the point. Now Elvish, he thought as the floating puffs drifted into odd, runelike shapes, if Dad could teach them Elvish, or one of the other languages from Middle Earth, *that* would be worth learning. Maybe the rings had hidden runes on them, he suddenly thought. They'd just need to put them in a fire to find out! As his mind churned, he didn't notice Miranda, on her side of the table, silently mouthing out the answer to him. Before her father could raise Jared from his reverie, she blurted it out.

"*Ursae bestiae sunt! Ursae bestiae sunt!* Bears beasts are! Right?"

"Yes, Miranda, that's correct," her father said, "but the question was for Jared. You need to wait your turn."

Miranda closed her eyes angrily and crossed her arms.

And on it went until, finally, their father glanced at his watch, realized that he was late, gathered up his book bag, and hurried off to catch the boat to the university. As his steps rang on the marble-topped staircase leading down from their second-floor apartment, their mom told them to put on their coats. They were going to start today's art class with a visit to the Accademia, Venice's main museum.

Jared looked at his mother in dismay. A museum! Churches were bad enough, but at most they only had five or six paintings to study. A museum had hundreds. It would take forever! At this rate he was *never* going to get a chance to figure out what was happening with his die. There was no arguing with her, though, so minutes later they were in their coats and heading down the *calle* outside their building.

As if to make everything take even longer, their mother decided to make a stop at an Internet café along the way. The kids tried to follow her in, but she made them wait outside. "I just need to check my e-mail. If you get online we'll be here for an hour. This afternoon, after your lessons are done . . . I'll think about letting you come back then."

So they waited by the door while Mom settled down in front of one of the computers. Jared was pop-kicking his skateboard in frustration, making it flip. Shireen watched her mother idly through the glass front of the Internet café for a while. Sure enough, she wasn't just checking e-mail. She'd logged onto Facebook so she could catch up with all her friends back home at once. It was totally unfair. Shireen looked on jealously for a minute, then glanced around. Where was Miranda? She'd wandered off somewhere.

Shireen spotted her after a few seconds, down at the far end of the *calle*, bending over a stray cat, stroking its fur. Shireen headed down the *calle* to see what she was up to, edging her way past a group of old women milling around an outdoor fruit and vegetable stall. The cat looked familiar. Then she recognized it: It was the cat from the old man's store. What was it doing here? The Ghetto Nuovo was on the other side of Venice.

Miranda, meanwhile, was talking earnestly to the cat. She must have recognized it too, Shireen decided.

And then she saw.

Miranda's ring was glowing! Each time she ran her hand down the cat's spine, the golden band on her finger cast a sharp beam through the shadows of the *calle*. Shireen froze. Her heart started pounding. A second later she had her own ring out. Was it doing the same thing? No. Nothing. Disappointed again, she quickly stuffed it back into her pocket. So why was Miranda's ring lit up? What had made it do that? What was so special about her? And what if someone saw it?

She had to get that ring off Miranda's finger before someone noticed. She'd pull it off if she had to.

"Miranda!" she hissed. "Take off your ring! Quick!"

"I don't need to," Miranda replied merrily. She checked for confirmation with the black cat, who glanced up at Shireen.

"Yes, you do! Now, before someone sees it!"

"No one can see."

"Of course they can see!" Shireen grasped her sister's arm. "Everyone can see it!" She pointed frantically around the crowded street—women busy at the vegetable stand, friends strolling arm in arm, a man dressed as Casanova in soft velvet shoes and white tights. "It's like you've got a laser on your finger!"

"No," Miranda replied calmly, "only kids can see our things. Adults can't. Except the old man. And he's special. Maldini just told me." She reached down to stroke the feline's smooth fur. "Look," she said, and before Shireen could stop her, she'd bolted down the *calle*, past Jared, and through the glass door of the Internet café. Shireen scrambled after her, but it was too late.

"Her ring!" Jared blurted, grabbing Shireen's arm. "It's glowing!"

"I know!" Shireen replied. "She won't take it off!"

"Mom'll see!"

"I know," she repeated, joining him at the window of the store and pressing her face up against the glass. She felt sick. There was nothing they could do. Miranda had sidled right up to their mother and was pointing at the screen of her computer. Her ring was less than a foot from their Mom's face, boring its light into her eyes.

They got to the Accademia museum a long tromp later. Their mother bought the tickets, made Jared check his skateboard at the front desk, and ushered them upstairs to the Carpaccio gallery on the second floor. "They're about Saint Ursula," she said, pointing at the wall of elaborately framed paintings.

Miranda was the only one paying attention. Shireen barely listened as their mother told them the complicated story about the young British princess Ursula, who hadn't wanted to marry the prince who'd come all the way from Armorica to ask for her hand, but then she changed her mind and ended up getting slaughtered on her way to the wedding—which was why she was a saint. Shireen was too busy following the glow of Miranda's ring and stealing glances at the other grown-up visitors in the gallery to see if they were as blind to its light as their mother had been back at the Internet café. It had looked like Miranda was trying to stab her in the eye with the light from her ring. Mom hadn't even blinked.

Jared wasn't tuning in to their mother's words either. First his die, now Miranda's ring. What was making them light up? On the way to the museum he'd let Shireen and their mother walk ahead so he could ask Miranda what she thought. His sister pointed to the cat, who was still padding along at her side. "I think it's Maldini. Tell him," she said. The great arch of the Accademia bridge was ahead of them, crowded with tourists leaning over its wooden railing and snapping photos of the Grand Canal. But the cat didn't respond. "Maybe later?" Miranda suggested as they started climbing the bridge. "I don't think Maldini's ready to talk to you and Shireen yet," she said. "But he can tell you later. Once the others have joined us."

"The others?" Jared asked, his heart taking a little skip. They'd reached the top of the bridge. Off to either side, the curving rank of Venice's water-hugging palaces stretched as far as he could see.

"Just wait," Miranda responded as they crossed the platform at the top of the bridge and started down the other side. "Maldini told me all about them. You'll see."

The others? Jared was still wondering as he circled the Carpaccio gallery in the museum, scuffing the heels of his canvas Vans against the marble floor. What others? And Miranda's cat? Had it really been talking to her?

When they were done with the Saint Ursula room, their mother steered them down a long hallway to the next gallery. There were two or three other visitors in the room, studying the paintings appreciatively. One of the museum guards stood in front of a massive canvas, his arms crossed over his chest, his head cocked to one side. He stayed there for a good half a minute before stepping out of the room and calling out for someone. In moments two more blue-uniformed guards joined him. Now they all stared at the painting intently and started to whisper to one another.

"Mom, what's going on?" Shireen asked in a low voice.

"I'm not sure," she answered, now studying the painting herself. She checked the brochure she was holding to see what it said about it. "It's called *The Miracle of the Relic of the True Cross at the Rialto Bridge*," she read. "It's also by Carpaccio."

The kids turned back to the painting to see if they could figure out what was bothering the security guards.

On one side of the canvas, Carpaccio had painted the Grand Canal crowded with black gondolas. Old-fashioned gondoliers in striped tights were neatly balanced on the sterns of their silver-tipped boats, rowing their wealthy passengers and calling out to one another. In the middle of the painting, a procession of monks in white hooded robes was crossing a rickety old wooden bridge spanning the canal. On the other side of the canal, more white-robed monks were gathered on the balcony of a palazzo. That was the part of the painting where all the uniformed guards were pointing. The monks on the balcony were kneeling down. Just in front of them, another monk in a black habit was extending his hand to a group of men who had come out to meet him. Everyone on the balcony was looking at what the black-robed monk held in his hands. Their faces were full of awe.

The museum guards were getting more agitated. At first they'd just been muttering at one another, but now they started shouting, waving their arms and gesticulating at the painting until one of them noticed the crowd their angry voices had drawn to the room.

He whispered something sharp to the other guards and they quieted down for a bit. But not for long. A minute later they were snapping at one another and jabbing their fingers at the section of the painting where the black-robed monk had his hand held out. More and more people were crowding into the room to see what was going on. One guard ran from the room.

Miranda had an idea. She took the brochure from her mother, peered at the printed image of the Carpaccio painting in her hand, studied the canvas on the wall, and looked at the pamphlet again. "Oh!" she exclaimed.

"What?" Jared demanded.

"There's something missing," she answered, pointing to a spot on the pamphlet. Their mother started nodding her head. She'd seen it too.

"See that monk with his hand stretched out?" Miranda whispered. "He's supposed to be holding something. A piece of Jesus's cross. A relic."

"So?" Jared asked.

"It's not there," she said. "It's missing from the painting."

She handed them the pamphlet. Jared and Shireen examined it, then looked back at the painting. Where the piece of cross should have been, there was nothing. It wasn't like a hole had been cut in the canvas. The monk's hand was just empty.

A troupe of museum officials had entered the room. One of them, a round-bellied balding man in a gray suit, gave the painting a long suspicious look before walking over to an alarm box on the wall and pulling the lever.

A loud bell began to clang over and over.

"Avanti! Avanti!" The official waved his beefy hands at the crowd of astonished visitors. "Outside, everyone outside! *Avanti!"*

4
Followed

J ared got pushed to the back of the exiting mass, way behind his mother and sisters who were being swept along at the front of the wave of visitors trying to get out of the building.

The whole museum was clearing out. Jared picked up his pace to catch up. But then the long expanse of marble floor opening in front of him gave him another idea. This was too good to pass up. He needed something to clear his head. Something clean and simple. And fast. He could figure out what was going on with Miranda's ring, his die, and that weird cat once they got back to the apartment. Right now he just needed some fun. He kicked off his Vans and broke into a dead sprint. Twenty paces down the hall he jumped up, extended his arms like he was surfing, and hit the slick marble floor at high speed. Paintings zipped past him on either side as he slid down the hallway. He planted his back foot for another push when—*wham!*—he lost his balance. He was tumbling face-first onto the floor. His die popped out of his pocket and rolled across the polished surface. It skittered, skidded, and finally came to a stop at the foot of a large painting.

And immediately another side of the wooden cube began to glow.

Jared couldn't believe it. He'd done it again. He shook off the throbbing in his palms and knees and darted over to the die, glancing nervously up and down the hall. There was no one but him and the glowing cube in his hand.

Okay, no one had seen.

He scooped it up and began to study the new side of the die that was glowing. But then a quiver of motion at the corner of his eye caught his attention.

He looked, then looked again in disbelief. It couldn't be, but it *was*—his eyes weren't lying. Something was moving around *inside* the painting in front of him. He stepped backward for a better look.

It was a forest scene. A ring of five or six women was dancing around a clearing. Two shaggy-legged and pointy-hooved fauns were holding hands with the women, dancing with them.

Until just a second ago. Right now one of the fauns was moving toward him. *Moving!* Jared's jaw went slack in shock.

The faun had dropped the hands of the dancing women and begun to cross the forest clearing, a surprised expression on his goateed face. As the faun advanced on the foreground of the painting he grew bigger and bigger, and more and more real.

Jared took one look at the approaching creature, stuffed the glowing die back in his pocket, snatched his shoes from the floor, and fled.

By the time he'd grabbed his skateboard from the front desk and gotten outside, the square was swarming with people. A police boat was just pulling up to the edge of the canal, its blue light flashing. A brace of *carabinieri* leaped out of it, vaulting easily from the running board of their cruiser onto the paving stones of the *campo*. They pushed their way through the crowd and stormed inside.

Jared scanned the crowd for his family. He spied

his sisters by a newsstand just outside the museum. That black cat was back, and Miranda was squatting down, saying something to it.

Jared took a deep breath to calm his pounding heart, then dashed over to them. "Where's Mom?" he asked Shireen.

"Over there." She pointed toward the excited mass of people on the far side of the square. "Looking for you." She took in his flushed face. "Where've you been? Are you okay?"

He started to answer—she'd never believe what had just happened—but then it dawned on him. He had just seen the most incredible thing *ever* . . . and he'd bolted like a chicken. How could he tell Shireen that? *Like she wouldn't have done the same thing,* he fumed, avoiding her eye, *if she'd seen something come to life inside a painting and start coming after her!*

But that was the problem, and he knew it. The faun hadn't looked dangerous. Just curious. Why'd he taken off so fast? What if he'd stayed? Now he'd never know. He wanted to kick himself. After all this lame time in Venice, something had finally happened and he'd run away from it! Pathetic.

"You sure?" Shireen pressed.

"Yeah." But he wasn't okay. He was disgusted with

himself. He turned to Miranda before Shireen could probe any more, patting his hand against his pocket to make sure the die was still there.

"Maldini's worried," Miranda informed him. She was tickling the little spot between the cat's ears.

"Come again?" Jared asked, forcing his ski cap down over his head. He looked the animal over suspiciously. It wasn't showing any signs of understanding a word they said. "What do you mean, the *cat's* worried? It's not really talking to you. *Is* it?"

Before Miranda had a chance to respond, their mother hurried back.

"Where were you?" Her eyes narrowed at Jared. "I've been looking all over for you."

"Um, getting my board." He held it up hopefully.

She shook her head in exasperation.

Another troop of *carabinieri* came down an alleyway into the square. They had their little notebooks out and were starting to question people.

"Okay," Mom said, "time to go home. Or we'll never get out of here." They turned and started climbing the big wooden bridge across the Grand Canal. Behind them, the alarm bell was still clanging away deep inside the building.

As Mom led them along, Shireen noticed that her sister's ring was no longer glowing. Miranda hadn't seemed seem to register that it had gone out. She just kept peering down every cross alley they passed as if expecting to find something waiting for her. What was she looking for? That cat that kept showing up? Well, she was out of luck. Shireen had seen it padding off a few *campos* back. And then she realized that that's when Miranda's ring had dulled. Right after the cat had taken off!

So was it the cat that was making it light up? Whenever it was close by?

Would that work for her ring too? The cat had brushed past her before it had disappeared. Maybe it had left some little spark behind, something to bring her ring to life. She felt it itching in her pocket, urging her to put it on, to give it one more chance. Okay, so it was a dumb idea, but she couldn't stop herself from trying. She stuck her hand in her pocket, took a deep breath, and slipped the ring over her finger.

Nothing happened. She should have known better. It was time to stop acting like a little kid. But still, her mind went on whirring: If it had worked for Miranda, couldn't she at least feel *something*? Some heat or tingle when the metal slid on? The world was *so* not fair.

The *calle* T-junctioned ahead, and she grudgingly followed the others onto the Fondamenta de l'Osmarin, a narrow embankment flanked by an uneven line of houses on one side, a green canal on the other. Behind the window of the shop to her right, rows of Carnevale masks grinned at her.

"Hello, little girrrl!" a low voice growled.

Shireen staggered to a halt, stunned. Her ring! Suddenly it *was* blazing with light. The voice was calling out again, "Hello, little girrrrl!" She tore her eyes away from the bright golden band and glanced at the storefront. But that wasn't where the sound was coming from. Just as her mother and the others turned the corner ahead, she heard it again, a deep rumbling animal voice, calling down at her from somewhere up above.

"Hello, little girrrrrl!"

She looked up. For a second she still couldn't pin down exactly where the voice was coming from, even as it continued its low, gravelly purring, sounding the words out as if pleased and a little astonished to hear itself speak. "Hello, little girrrl! Little girrrrl. Hello!" Then her jaw dropped.

Two stories above her, on the opposite side of the canal, a small white lion, about the size of a bear cub,

was pacing along a balcony railing. She shook her head. What the heck? Wasn't he made of stone, just like the railings? Still, there he was, up above her, *moving!* Three other little statue lions sat next to him on the balcony. Shireen managed to walk forward a few more steps, not taking her eyes off the pacing lion, and as she passed each statue, it shook itself into motion. "Hello, little girrrl! Hello, little girrrl!" they were soon all calling down to her in their deep cattish voices. Shireen ground to a standstill, gaping. All at once, it was too much. She gave the prowling, growling pride of little lions one last astonished look and took off around the corner after her family.

As she disappeared, the first three rumbling creatures gave little grunts of disappointment and returned to their posts, their bodies hardening again. But the fourth one, the smallest, kept moving. He leaped down from the balcony, splashed into the canal, swam across its narrow breadth, pulled himself up onto the paving, shook the water off his stony fur, and padded after her.

As the family arrived at the door to their building, Miranda hesitated, casting a quick glance up and down the *calle* as if looking for something before following the others inside. The door closed behind them with a loud click.

As their footsteps clattered up the internal staircase, the little lion that had been following Shireen turned the corner of the *calle* and padded forward. A moment later the clattering of hooves rang out against the paving stones.

"Well, come join me, then," the lion growled, shivering the length of his back to shake off the last splashes of canal water. He turned his maned little head and gestured to the faun, who trotted up to where the lion stood, studying the door to the building.

"Ah," the faun responded in a friendly tone. "How did you know I was here?"

"I scented you," the lion responded haughtily. "You have quite a smell. You've been following us."

The faun had, in fact, followed them all the way from the museum, his goaty head twisting quizzically to the side as he tried to make sense of the dark-haired boy who had freed him from the painting. He was used to humans, of course. He'd seen them every day, off at the far edge of the clearing in the woods, peering in at him and his brother fauns and their dancing partners, and the fat god Bacchus lolling on the grass beside them. The humans rarely stood watching them for long. They soon wandered out of sight, leaving room for someone else to come sauntering into view to look in on the dance. He'd often wanted to invite them into the glade in the woods, to come join the merriment. But they never seemed to hear him when he called out. The boy, though, was different. There had been that sudden burst of light that had caught the faun's eye, and then he'd looked over and seen the handsome lad standing there, dark eyes wide. He'd walked over to greet him and invite him to join the fun, but the boy had bolted off.

And here was the strange thing: When the faun had taken another step forward, he'd walked right out of the forest and found himself in a long hall filled with paintings! "Vulcan's forge!" he'd muttered, looking around. "Where am I?" But the boy wasn't around to answer, so he'd decided he'd best follow him to find out.

He'd made it out of the museum only seconds before the doors were closed. He'd been slowed down by the sound of feet approaching at a furious pace and confused shouting voices coming at him from the far end of the hall. Each time that had happened, he'd ducked into a side gallery and watched, unseen, as a troop of men in blue pants and jackets had gone sprinting by. When the path was clear, the faun had hoofed to the entrance just in time to see a woman leading the boy and two girls away.

Crossing the square, he'd caught a few curious looks. But with the clanging of the alarm bell, the flashing lights of the police boats, and the general confusion, he hadn't drawn any prolonged attention. He looked like another person in costume. There were scores of people wandering around in strange disguises. One man had even shouted, "Great getup, buddy!" What a "getup" was, he couldn't imagine; but as it was great, that was fine by him. So he'd kept going. *That lad will want to meet me*, the faun had decided. *Yes, yes, by Jupiter, so he will. Everybody loves a faun. I'll need to introduce myself.*

At this very moment, however, he wasn't thinking about the boy. A smell? he wondered, sniffing at himself. Did the lion say he had a smell? He'd never noticed it before, but, well, yes, there was a musky odor wafting from him. All those years in the woods, he reflected. All that dancing. Makes a faun sweat. Healthy, though, by Bellona. It was a vigorous, lively scent he carried on him. No need to apologize for that. So he trotted up to the watching lion.

"Caius Marcus Silvanus," he introduced himself, bending down and offering his hand. "But you can call me Silvio. All my companions do."

The lion wrinkled up his nose, shooting Silvio a disdainful look. Declining to lift his paw, he responded,

"I am Lorenzo il Piccolo. You may call me Lorenzo il Piccolo."

"Il Piccolo?" Silvio answered, raising his tufted eyebrows and appraising the lion. "The 'little one'? Well, yes, I can see why. Nothing to feel bad about."

"Because of my *father*," the lion corrected him, his stone eyes hardening. "Lorenzo il Magnifico. Lorenzo the Magnificent. My name is in honor of him. It has nothing to do with my size."

"Oh, yes," Silvio responded, chastened, "because of your father. Il Magnifico."

"Exactly," the lion affirmed, turning his attention back to the door behind which the children had disappeared.

"Try it," he instructed the faun, though he knew it wouldn't open. His sharp ears had heard a key turning as the door closed.

Silvio twisted the knob, but the lion's ears hadn't deceived him. It was locked.

"Now what?" Silvio asked after a pause.

"Now we wait," Lorenzo il Piccolo answered. "At the end of the *calle*. It's dark there. We won't be seen." He stalked off in the direction he had indicated, twenty paces beyond the door, where the *calle*, which dead-ended onto a canal, was covered overhead. He was right: It was deeply shadowed down there.

"What are we waiting for?" Silvio asked as he joined the lion.

"Our chance," Lorenzo il Piccolo responded curtly. Wasn't that obvious?

"Ah, yes," Silvio replied. "Just what I was about to recommend."

5
A Noble Oath

Inside the apartment, Jared decided that keeping what had happened back at the museum a secret wasn't going to get them anywhere. He needed to spit it out. It was time to swallow his pride. But not here, not with their mother around. He caught Shireen's attention, pinched his thumb and forefinger together as if he was holding something small and sharp, and mimed stitching his lips together.

Shireen's eyebrows shot up. Jared must have something serious to say. The stitched-lips sign was her idea, and it was for rare occasions. Jared had only used it once in the last year—back home in America, when one of her friends at school had told Shireen that she'd seen him kissing Emily Chandler at the eighth-grade dance. He'd grinned goofily and admitted it. That was the deal with stitched lips. If you agreed, you had to tell the truth. But it was completely secret, and no matter what you revealed, there couldn't be any teasing. So what did Jared want to talk about? Had he seen the talking lions up on the balcony? That was it! He'd seen the lions! Well, it was a good thing he'd done stitched lips. She was going to have to tell him about it sooner or later, and this way he couldn't make fun of her for taking off like a wimp before she could find out what the lions wanted from her. And neither could Miranda. They just needed to be sure their little sister accepted the rules before Shireen told her and Jared what had happened.

"Not here," Jared whispered. "Mom."

He was right. So where could they go? She thought about it for a second, and then she remembered.

"Mom," she called, ducking into the kitchen where their mother was putting away the plates from the lunch she'd just made for them. "The Internet café? This morning you told us we could go. It's been ages and we need to check in with our friends."

Her mother thought about it for a few seconds,

then nodded. "Okay. Anyway, I'm feeling tired. I could use a nap. Just don't be gone long. And only e-mail and Skype; no other Internet." She handed Shireen a five-euro note and headed for her bedroom.

The kids put on their coats and started off. But just as the older two stepped through the door, Miranda started causing problems.

"I'm not coming," she announced from the doorway. "Go without me."

"Miranda," Jared answered sharply, "you need to come. I have to tell you something!"

"Nope," she answered, shaking her head. "I'm staying." She leaned out and swiped the key from Shireen's hand, then hopped back inside, closed the door, and twisted the dead bolt, locking them out.

Jared and Shireen stared at each other in astonishment.

Jared started pounding on the door.

"I'm not opening it," Miranda told them. "Ring the buzzer when you get back. I'll let you in." They could hear her feet climbing the steps inside.

Jared hammered on the door again.

"Oh, leave her alone, Jared. It doesn't matter," Shireen said. "We can fill her in later. So, did you see?" she added, lowering her voice. "On the way home?"

"What?" Jared asked, turning from the door.

"The lions! Didn't you see them? The talking lions? And look, now my ring's glowing!" She reached into her pocket, slipped the ring back on, and showed him.

Jared's heart jumped. He pulled out his shining die.

"Yours too?" she asked.

"It brought something to life." He grinned. "A faun! You're right. Forget about Miranda. But I get to go first. Then you can tell me about the lions."

Five minutes later Miranda crept back down the stairwell and nudged open the door of the building. There was no sign of Jared or Shireen. The coast was clear. She looked toward the covered end of the *calle*. She could just make out two figures huddled in the shadows.

She bunched her hands in her coat pockets and stood there for a moment, collecting herself. She was a little nervous, but the cat had told her not to worry. They would be friendly. She gathered up her courage and headed toward them.

As she approached, the lion and the faun scrutinized her. Silvio had been squatting down, his arms wrapped around his furry shanks for warmth, but now he stood up. Lorenzo il Piccolo gave his stone mane a brief shake and prepared himself to greet her.

"Hello," Miranda said, pulling up in front of them. She began rocking from one foot to the other in excitement.

"Lorenzo il Piccolo at your service," the lion responded gravely, bowing his head a fraction.

"Silvio," the faun introduced himself with his friendliest voice. He was charmed by the sight of the small human child. She looked like a woodland elfling. "Delighted to meet you. What is your name, child?"

"Miranda," she informed him, taking his hand and shaking it. She stood there for another moment, grinning, not quite sure what to say next. Then she couldn't help herself from blurting it out. "Are you real?"

Lorenzo il Piccolo looked offended. "Real?" he echoed incredulously. "Is the sun real? Is the moon? Are duty, honor, and courage real? Why do you ask such a thing?"

"It's just . . . I've never met a talking lion before," Miranda explained. "Or a faun," she continued, looking up at Silvio. "That's what you are, right? A faun? The cat—Maldini, that's his name—Maldini told me you'd be nice. He knew that you'd be coming. His friend, the old man at the store, told him."

Silvio and Lorenzo il Piccolo weren't quite sure what to do with this rush of information. They all stood eyeing one another silently. Then Miranda remembered what she was supposed to do.

"Oh!" she exclaimed. "Come inside. Quick, before Shireen and Jared get back."

"The dark-haired boy?" Silvio asked.

"The girrrl with the ring?" Lorenzo il Piccolo inquired at the same time.

"Yes, they're my brother and sister," Miranda said, nodding. "You'll get to meet them later. But first I need to get you inside, so you can find somewhere to hide. I want to surprise them."

She tugged on Silvio's hand and he followed her. The lion trailed after them, muttering under his breath, "'Are you real?'! Ma Donna!"

As they reached the apartment door, Miranda put her fingers to her lips. "Shh!" she said. "My mom's napping." The apartment was quiet, so she led them in.

"Where are we going?" Silvio asked, tippy-hoofing as quietly as he could across the marble floor.

"To our bedroom," Miranda whispered back.

The lion had taken the lead. He was following the

scent of the clothes hanging in the children's bedroom closet. Silvio brought up the rear, his sense of merriment increasing. He'd spied a great glass-fronted cabinet filled with bowls, plates, pitchers, and wine glasses. The sight of wine glasses had given him a warm feeling about the place.

Lorenzo il Piccolo nudged open the door to the kids' room with a paw, and Miranda and the faun followed him inside. "Now what?" Silvio asked, taking in the beds, the sloping ceiling, the closet, the jumble of games, and the red armchair with one look.

"Find a place to hide," Miranda answered. She was about to suggest some spots when the apartment's buzzer rang. Shireen and Jared! "Quick!" she said, rushing out of the bedroom. "Hide!"

Lorenzo il Piccolo showed no signs of haste. He padded about the room in search of a nice warm place to curl up for a nap. He was used to standing guard on his balcony all day, surveying the canal and *calle* below. The tromp across the city had tired him. Finally he found a pile of soft blankets stacked in the bottom of the bedroom closet. He pushed them about with his stone paws until he had made a pleasant nest and settled in. He asked Silvio if he would shut the closet door so the children wouldn't have a fright when they came in, and advised the faun to do as Miranda had said.

Silvio nudged the door closed and looked around. Easy for the lion to tell him to hide. That was simple when you were little larger than a fox. But Silvio was huge, close to seven feet when he stretched up on his shaggy goat haunches, and he was barrel-chested, with wide powerful shoulders. Quite a specimen, if he did say so himself. But where was he to stash himself? He lifted one edge of Miranda's bed. There was lots of stuff beneath it—books that had fallen to the floor, crayons, a scarf. But he'd never fit under it, so he settled the legs of the bed on the floor and looked around again. He was about to give up, thinking that maybe he could push open the skylight and squat on the roof until the children came back, when he spotted a crayon drawing taped to the wall. Looking it over, Silvio made out a stand of trees, a grassy clearing, and a bright blue sky. That would do. Almost. It just needed one or two more touches.

He reached under the frame of the bed and kicked out several of the discarded crayons with his nimble hooves. Red or white? he wondered as he settled the bed back into place and picked a crayon from the floor. Red, he decided, pleased by the deep plum tone of the crayon in his hand. In a few quick motions he sketched out four bottles of wine and set them against the bottom of one of the crayoned trees. Much better. He reached through the plane of the drawing and pulled himself in, shrinking to just a few inches in height as he walked into the crayon forest and uncorked the first bottle of wine.

If the wait until bedtime the day before had been terrible, today it was nearly impossible. Their dad took forever coming home from work, then, at supper, he wanted to hear the story about the vandalized painting at the Accademia over and over again. After that he insisted on keeping his promise to Miranda and getting in an extra long stint of reading from the book the old man had given them. He pulled it out while they were eating dessert at the kitchen table.

"Right, where were we?" He scanned the page for a few seconds. "Okay, yes. The bookseller and his nephew, Rashid. They were heading out on a voyage with a copy of Scheherazade's stories. Here we are.

"After many weeks at sea, their vessel steered through a narrow strait and entered a wide, green-watered lagoon. In the distance a line of bell towers was etched against the sky. All around the steepled towers, palace walls and great vaulted churches were climbing right up out of the water. The city appeared to be floating. . . ."

"Venice?" Miranda cut in. "Rashid and his uncle, they came to Venice?"

"It looks like it," Dad answered, and kept on reading.

Jared and Shireen could barely pay attention. All they could think about were the secrets they'd exchanged. They'd been so stunned by each other's news that they'd completely forgotten about going to the Internet café. Instead, they'd headed back to the *calle* leading off from the Fondamenta de l'Osmarin and peeked around the corner to get a look at the balcony where Shireen had seen the prowling lions. "They were really talking and moving around?" Jared had whispered as they'd peered up at the stone creatures crouching on their banisters. "Just like the faun in the painting? So awesome!

"Hey," he'd added teasingly, "didn't you say there were four lions? I only see three up there now. Maybe one of them followed you."

"Shut up!" Shireen had answered, shivering.

"Listen," he'd said more seriously as they headed home. "Do you think, tomorrow, we could get Mom to take us back to the museum? You know, to investigate a little?"

He was already plotting it out as he sat at the table half-eating his dessert. This time, if the faun was still roaming around in the canvas, Jared would be ready. He wasn't going to run off again.

Meanwhile, even Miranda seemed distracted as their dad read on and on. She kept sneaking glances in the direction of their bedroom. She'd just remembered that Mom or Dad would be going in there later to say good night. Lorenzo il Piccolo and Silvio better have done a good job hiding themselves, she thought.

But their father was too absorbed by the story to notice, and their mother seemed wrapped up in it too. Rashid and his uncle had been met by one of the bookseller's friends when their boat had docked. He was a book merchant too. He had a shop in the Ghetto were they'd be staying. First, though, he'd arranged an audience with the doge, to show him their books. It was there, in the doge's palace, that things started to go wrong. Rashid had a secret. He knew something about the Scheherazade book that he hadn't told his uncle. He couldn't let him sell it to the doge.

Jared looked up from the sculpture he'd been making with his tiramisu, startled. The Scheherazade book? What had his dad said about the Scheherazade book? All at once the image was coming back to him: that morning, his die shining on the bedroom floor, the etching of a book cut into one of its sides burning brightly.

Was there some connection? Is that why the old man had insisted they take the book his dad was reading? Was it a clue?

"What was the secret?" Jared asked.

"Hunh?" His father looked up from the book.

"The secret. You know, that part you just read? Rashid knows something about the book with all the princess's stories in it. What's the secret?"

His father flipped a few pages ahead. "Interesting," he said, raising an eyebrow.

"What? Come on, Dad!" Jared insisted.

Shireen was giving him a quizzical look. She'd have to wait; he'd explain it later. Now he wanted to hear what his father had to say. Rashid's secret. Scheherezade's book. His die. Maybe even the faun. There had to be something holding them all together. He just knew it!

"You'll have to wait to find out." His father closed the book with an ironic smile. "I'm glad we finally found a book you all like. Now come on, I've been reading for a long time. It's hard work translating this as I go along. *And* I've got papers to grade. Time for bed."

Jared started to object, but then he stopped himself. If he pushed too hard, Dad might get suspicious. Maybe tomorrow, while he was at the university, they could get a look at the book on their own. They had a dictionary. Maybe Miranda could translate it. Then he thought wryly, *Nothing like having a sister four years younger than you be better than you at Latin.*

Prayers were done. Their parents were gone. They had the bedroom to themselves. Shireen had retrieved her ring and slipped it back over her finger. The light was still shining. Jared, meanwhile, was starting to tell his sisters what he'd guessed about the book, but Miranda put a shushing finger to her lips. She wasn't taking any chances. She positioned herself behind the red velvet armchair in the far corner of the room, set her hands against its back, and began to push.

"What are you doing?" Jared demanded as the clawed feet of the chair squeaked across the floor. Miranda's cheeks were puffing out with the effort.

She ignored his question and kept pushing. When the armchair was finally lodged under the handle of the door, she flashed him a grin.

"Okay," she said. "Now we can count."

"Count?" Shireen asked, looking up from the glowing band around her finger and taking in what her sister was up to.

"You know. To twenty," Miranda replied. "So they know we're coming. They did a great job. I was worried that Dad would see them. But they're totally hidden." She faced into a corner, put her hands over her eyes, and began to sound off the numbers.

Jared watched, baffled. Shireen rolled her eyes. *Genetics*, she thought, watching Miranda's ponytail bob against the collar of her flannel pajama top as she called out each number. *Thank you, genetics!* If she and Miranda had shared the same gene pool, maybe she'd be a weirdo too. Sometimes it totally paid to be adopted.

"Ready or not," Miranda announced, spinning round excitedly, "here we come."

"What are you doing?" Jared insisted again as Miranda started looking around the room, poking her head under the beds, pulling unmade sheets off the mattresses.

"Looking," she answered.

"For *what*, exactly?" Shireen asked.

"Shhhh!" Miranda answered. She cocked her head, cupping a hand behind her ear as if listening for some tiny sound. "Did you hear that buzzing noise?" She finally fixed her attention on the wall by her bed and then bolted across the floor.

Then they heard it too, a kind of *prrrpp-prrrrpp-zzzzz* noise, barely audible but definitely coming from somewhere near Miranda's bed.

Miranda was looking all around, befuddled. Suddenly her eyes lit up and she burst out laughing. She climbed on the mattress and banged her fist against the drawing taped to the wall. "It's okay, Mr. Faun," she called out. "You can come out now."

"Faun?" Jared echoed. "Did she say 'faun'?" He grabbed Shireen's elbow and steered her over to the drawing.

"Is that him?" Shireen asked Jared a long, stunned twenty seconds later. He could only nod. It was definitely the faun from the museum. There was no doubt about that. Except the faun wasn't in the museum anymore. He was *in their bedroom*. In a drawing taped to the wall. Curled up at the base of a tree with a bunch of empty wine bottles scattered around him. Snoring. To be specific.

Jared gave the dozing faun a hard stare. Was it alive? Really, truly alive? Inside a crayon drawing taped to their wall? Another snore rattled from the faun's tiny lips. Evidently, it was alive.

Now that he had a good chance to study him, the faun didn't look threatening at all. Actually he was more, kind of . . . dopey. Jared gingerly reached a finger out to give the faun a poke to see if he could wake him up. He was only a couple of inches long. How dangerous could he be?

But when he made contact, he could only feel creased paper against the tip of his finger.

Shireen rounded on their sister. "Miranda, what the heck is going on?"

When Miranda didn't answer—watching Silvio sprawled out on the grass of her crayon forest, the buzzing snores rolling off his lips, was too funny—Shireen grabbed her by the shoulder. "Miranda! What have you been up to? How did the faun—?" But another noise caught her attention: a creak from the closet door. For the second time that day, Shireen's heart jumped. Lorenzo il Piccolo had emerged from his nest in the blankets and was padding across the room to pay his respects.

"Hello, Mirrranda," the lion growled, bowing his head to her. "Hello, Jarrred," he added, bowing again. "Hello, Shirrrrrreen," he concluded, regally oblivious to the dumbstruck look she was giving him.

"I told them your names," Miranda informed her gaping siblings before returning the lion's bow with a neat little curtsy. "Silvio's sleeping," she informed Lorenzo il Piccolo, pointing to the snoring faun in the crayon forest.

"Ah, yes," said the little lion. "He would be." He hadn't taken his eyes off Shireen, and now he leaped up onto her bed to get a better look at her. He fixed his unblinking stone gaze on her face as if memorizing her bit by bit: her stunned dark eyes; her brows arching in astonishment; her long black hair, falling in a wave over her shoulders; the gaping O of her mouth as thoughts flashed through her head.

Jared had been right. The lion *had* followed her!

"May I?" he inquired gravely. One of his heavy paws was pointed at her gleaming ring.

"What?" Shireen replied, startled.

"Your ring," he answered.

She didn't understand at first, but then a vague memory from some movie she'd seen came back to her and she extended her hand to him, a broad smile suddenly widening her mouth. The lion touched his muzzle to her hand and gently pressed his lips against the ring. She could feel hot little puffs of breath on her skin.

"My lady," he said, "Lorenzo il Piccolo at your service. May the sun shine upon you in the morning and the moon light your path at night. May the orchards bring forth their fruit for you and the mountains their springs. May the Father, His Son, the Virgin, and the blessed Apostle extend you their favor. So long as Venice flies the banner of Saint Mark, I am yours." He gave her ring another kiss, offered her an elaborate rolling bow of his shoulders and head, then laid himself lazily down on her bed, tucked his hindquarters elegantly beneath himself, extended his forelegs, and settled his features into a rather vain and aristocratic expression, heartily pleased with himself.

6

"The Ones We Have Been Expecting"

Shireen had no idea how she was supposed to respond to Lorenzo il Piccolo's vow of loyalty. All she could manage was a breathless "Thank you."

For a minute none of them could think of what to do next. And then the questions poured out. Who was Lorenzo il Piccolo? How had he come to life? Was it Shireen's ring? Would it work with other lions? How about the faun? Were they old friends?

"And the Scheherazade book?" Jared asked, quickly filling his siblings in on what he'd guessed. "What about the book? Is that part of what's going on too?"

But to all their questions, Lorenzo il Piccolo gave

only an elegant shrug. He knew nothing. He had his lady to protect and his code of chivalry to honor. Beyond that the details didn't trouble him. So it was a good thing that as the lion was giving the children his last indifferent "Who can say? It is in God's hands, and the hands of his Apostle," Miranda heard a purring voice calling down to her from the skylight. It was Maldini the cat.

She gave him a wave and asked Jared and Shireen to help let him in. *He* could explain things. The older two were through arguing with her. Like it or not, she knew something about what was going on.

It took some doing. Jared put a chair on the bed and Shireen held it in place while he balanced himself, reaching up to loosen the latch of the skylight and push the glass pane clear of its molding. The cat squeezed through and leaped onto the bed below. Lorenzo il Piccolo gave him a look of languorous contempt, then returned to cleaning his paws with his broad stone tongue.

"Typical," said the cat, matching Lorenzo il Piccolo's look of disdain with one of his own. "Please excuse these two brutes," he said to the kids, indicating the lion and the faun he'd just spied snoring in the drawing on the wall. "I expect they're rather ignorant."

By this point Jared and Shireen were beyond surprise. It felt like anything amazing could happen, and then did. Miranda introduced her siblings to Maldini. It seemed that as long as she was wearing her ring, all of them could talk to him. That was enough to get them started all over again with questions.

It didn't take long to figure out that Maldini was a great mine of information. He took a purring pride in answering each question, casting scornful glances at the haughty lion as he spoke. He'd been living with the old man in the little shop in the Ghetto for years. During the long hours between customers, his master would fix him a plate of sardines and read to him from one of the ancient leather-bound books they'd seen him browsing through. In that way Maldini had learned many things, including the story of how the rings and the die had first come to his signore's shop.

"They have been there for hundreds of years," Maldini purred as Miranda ran her hand over his black fur. "A traveling merchant brought them late one night, centuries ago. He had pushed through the door of the shop and startled my signore's noble ancestor, Signor Isaac. The merchant reached into a hidden pocket of his cloak and pulled out the die and two rings. 'They are enchanted,' he had said 'What will you give me for them?'"

"Our things?" Shireen stared at the cat in amazement. "They've been in the store for hundreds of years?"

"Yes," Maldini answered.

"And your master's ancestor," Miranda asked, "Signor Isaac, he bought them from the merchant?"

"No," Maldini purred. "He said he had no interest in magical objects. It was not wise, in those days, to possess such things. Particularly for a Jew."

"But he must have changed his mind." Jared interrupted. "Right?

The cat nodded.

"Why?"

"Because the merchant told him something else. He said Rashid had sent them."

"Rashid!" Jared exclaimed. "Rashid from the story my dad's reading?"

"Yes," Maldini affirmed.

"He was real? He really lived? Centuries ago? It's not just a story?"

"No. He was a real boy."

I was right! I was right! Jared was thinking excitedly. The old man *had* given them the book as a clue.

"Signor Isaac?" Miranda spoke up. She was thinking back to what their father had read earlier that night. "Wasn't he the bookseller who met Rashid and his uncle at their boat when they arrived in Venice?"

"Yes," Maldini answered. "That is why Signor Isaac had changed his mind when the merchant gave Rashid's name. There was a mystery, you see: Rashid had disappeared. He vanished from the doge's palace the day he arrived in Venice, the day Signor Isaac took him and his uncle to show the doge their books. There had been no sign of him since. His uncle had spent weeks and weeks searching the city for him, until he'd finally realized that he had to sail back to Spain to tell Rashid's parents what had happened and bring them back to Venice to start looking again. The treasures were the first evidence that Rashid might still be alive."

"So *then* Signor Isaac bought our things?" Miranda asked, still not quite following the story but wanting to get at least this part straight.

"No," Maldini answered. "He tried. But once the merchant knew that Signor Isaac truly wanted the die and rings, no matter what Signor Isaac offered, it wasn't enough. Finally, though, the merchant proposed a wager. They'd roll the die and bet on which side rolled to the top. If Signor Isaac guessed right, the merchant would give him the rings and the die. If he bet wrong, he'd have to give the merchant all the books in his shop."

"And he agreed to do that?" Miranda asked. A whole bookshop! Would she risk losing a whole bookshop for her ring?

"Yes," Maldini answered. "Signor Isaac thought it was his fault that the boy had vanished. He was the one who had taken Rashid and his uncle to the doge's palace. If it was true that Rashid had sent these things, then he had to have them. They might give some clue to what had happened. So he bet everything on a roll of the die. Signor Isaac picked the map. And it rolled to the top."

"Did it light up?" Jared asked, looking at his die.

"No," Maldini answered. "The merchant had kept one thing secret. Signor Isaac did not find out until after he left. The die is like the rings: It is only enchanted in the hand of a child. Only then can it come alight. Signor Isaac never saw it glow. And neither have I, until you came into our store. May I see it?"

Jared set the cube on the bed between Maldini's paws. The cat examined it carefully, nudging it with the tufted pads of his paw to turn it over until he had seen each of its faces. He had a puzzled expression in his eyes.

"What is it?" Miranda asked. "Is something wrong?"

"The book," Maldini purred uncertainly, tapping one sharp claw against the surface with the image of the book cut into it. It was still burning fiercely. "The faun, I had expected the faun." He tipped the die back over to the glowing side embossed with a tiny etching of a goat-man. "My signore told me there would be a faun. But he did not tell me that the book would come alive so soon. I do not know if he foresaw this." Maldini fell silent, the golden pupils of his eyes narrowing in concentration. "You see how it works," he finally purred, setting aside his worry and gesturing at the faun side of the die again. "Jared, when the die fell out of your pocket in the gallery, that is the side that landed facing up. Yes?"

"I don't know," Jared admitted. "I didn't have time to see."

"But it fell at the base of the painting of the faun?"

"Yes."

"And it began to glow?"

"Yes."

"And the faun came to life?"

"Yes," Jared said again, sensing where all this was leading. "So that means I can summon another beast?"

"Yes," Maldini answered. "What?"

"A dragon!" Jared breathed, turning the die to that image. "And these sides," he added, turning the cube as he spoke. "There's a map, and, here, a guy with a weird guitar."

"A troubador," Maldini corrected him, "with his lute."

"I can call them, too?"

"Yes. But it must match, you understand? If you find a painting of a dragon, but the die rolls the troubador or any other side, nothing will happen. If you find the wrong map, it will not matter if the die turns that image up. Nothing will happen. And there is something else," he continued quietly, "something secret. See, where the sixth side is blank?"

Jared nodded quickly—he had been wondering about that unmarked surface since the moment he first held the die. But that wasn't the question at the top of his mind. "What about the book?" he asked excitedly. "If that side of the die's shining, then what did it bring to life?"

"I do not know," Maldini answered, a slightly

ominous tone in his voice. "My signore did not tell me that part. He told me there would be a faun, and that Shireen's ring would summon a lion. But I did not know that the book he gave you would come to life so soon."

"Is that . . . bad?" Shireen asked.

"I do not know," Maldini purred again, gravely. "You must ask my signore. He will explain it."

"But it's Rashid's story?" Jared demanded. "That's the book my die brought to life? It woke up something from Rashid's story?"

"Yes, I think so."

"What?"

"I told you: I do not know."

"Something scary?" Miranda whispered worriedly.

Maldini didn't respond. Shireen darted her brother a reproachful look. Jared might be too dim to pick up on it, but she'd noticed the sudden change in Maldini's mood. The cat had seemed so confident and in charge until he'd seen the etching of the book glowing on Jared's die. She wasn't quite so sure about all this.

"It's okay," Miranda broke in. "Even if Jared's die woke up something really bad, Lorenzo il Piccolo will protect us. Won't you?" She smiled encouragingly at the stone beast. "And Silvio's big; I bet he'll help out too, if he ever wakes up. And maybe Shireen's ring can call some other animals too. It can't just be good for lions, can it, Maldini?"

"Just good for lions?" Lorenzo il Piccolo rumbled angrily. "Just good for lions! I daresay a lion is a pretty fine companion when your other choices are a drunken faun and a pet cat!" He rose to his feet, a challenging look in his eyes, as if daring anyone else to repeat Miranda's insult. "Just good for lions! Ma Donna!"

Maldini glared at him. But it seemed Lorenzo il Piccolo was just trying to provoke him. His lips were curled in a snide grin beneath his bristling whiskers. "Lions!" The cat sighed. Had no one ever told them that kings were just for show these days—tourist attractions? The idiot beasts still thought it was the Renaissance or the Middle Ages. But what could he do? The old man had told him to keep an eye on the children. And if that meant suffering the company of this haughty lion, Maldini would just have to tolerate him as best he could. So he restrained himself and responded to Miranda's question.

"Shireen, look at your ring again. What do you see?"

She extended her fingers to get a good look at it,

then answered hesitantly, "A shield. And inside the shield, a lion."

"Was it always a lion?" Maldini asked.

She furrowed her brow. "I don't know. When I first looked at it, the lines inside the shield were fuzzy."

"Why?" Maldini asked.

Her furrow deepened, but she couldn't come up with an answer.

"Lion?" Maldini asked. "Can you enlighten her?"

Lorenzo il Piccolo turned his head away.

"You don't know?" Maldini goaded the lion, unable to restrain himself. "No, I suppose you don't. I shall have to explain it. The shield is a standard. What is inside it changes, depending on where you are. In Venice, the lion is the symbol of the city, so here, when you are wearing the ring and are near a lion, you have power over him and he must come to you if he can. And he must serve you and obey you," Maldini added with relish. "Like a pet."

Lorenzo il Piccolo turned back toward them, flexed the muscles of his powerful chest, and extended his claws. His ears tensed and dropped. It looked as if he were about to spring at the cat.

But before he could leap, his sharp ears were startled by a tiny but very distinct hiccup, immediately followed by a plaintive groaning. It was coming from somewhere inside the room. He swung his maned head around. Was there peril? Did his lady need defending?

"Oh, by Jupiter, Juno, and all the gods of Mount Olympus!" a faint, wobbly voice croaked. "What was that, vinegar? Oh, by Bacchus, it has given me a dreadful headache!"

Jared looked immediately at Miranda's drawing on the wall. The faun! He was rolling around on the floor of the forest in the drawing, clutching his belly with one hand and his skull with the other. Shireen and Miranda leaned closer for a better look. Even Maldini and Lorenzo il Piccolo seemed to have forgotten their quarrel in the presence of Silvio's pathetic writhing.

"Hey, faun?" Jared muttered awkwardly, tapping on the drawing to get its attention. "You okay in there?"

But Silvio didn't seem to notice. He just kept whimpering, his hands pressed to his belly. "Oh, by Mercury and Jupiter! I'm poisoned! I'm poisoned! Crayon wine! Why did no one warn me about crayon wine?" Then he suddenly jerked halfway up, released a rolling volley of burps, collapsed back on the ground, and fell asleep again.

Jared stared at him for a long time.

Miranda had a genius cat. Shireen had a lion. He had some kind of mystery book no one knew anything about—and a burping goat-man. It was so not fair! It was typical that *he'd* get stuck with this whimpering doofus.

He could feel them all looking at him, so he shrugged like it was no big deal and turned his back on the stupid faun.

"Why us?" he asked the cat quickly. Right now he didn't really care about the answer. He just needed to change the topic so they'd all stop staring at Silvio. "If Rashid's treasures have been in your signore's store for hundreds of years, and there's some big riddle about how he disappeared in the first place, why'd your signore let *us* have them?"

"Because you are part of Rashid's story," Maldini purred quietly. "We have been waiting for you."

"For us?" Jared blurted.

"For us?" Shireen echoed.

"The book, Rashid's tale." Maldini's golden eyes flashed intently. "Your names are in it. I do not know the whole story—my signore never read it all to me, only parts—but I know that your names are written in the book, and your descriptions: 'a girl with hair the color of wheat and eyes the shade of the morning sky; her brother and sister, with skin like cocoa and eyes like black pearls.' Why else do you think my master allowed you to pick from the leather bag? Do you think it is an accident that of all the things in there, you chose Rashid's treasures? No. My signore knew. And I did too. As soon as you walked in the door, we knew the long wait was over. You are the ones we have been expecting."

It was late. The bells of Santi Giovanni e Paolo had long since sounded midnight. They'd made Maldini repeat it all over again. And then one more time. But it still didn't make any sense.

How could their names be in the book? It was hundreds of years old.

Maldini couldn't say. But he was able to tell them a bit more about the book itself. The merchant who'd come to Signor Isaac with the die and the rings hadn't brought it. The book had come later, arriving from a convent in Spain, with a mysterious note: *This is Rashid's tale. Keep it until the time is right.* From that day, year after year, generation after generation, century after century, the book and Rashid's treasures had been passed down from one owner of the shop to the son who followed him, until at last they had come into the possession of Maldini's signore. But how the siblings' names and descriptions had found their way into the ancient volume, Maldini couldn't say, no matter how many times they asked. All he knew was that it was true.

They'd fallen silent. They couldn't think of any more questions to ask. They'd agreed to start again tomorrow. Shireen had given Lorenzo il Piccolo permission to return to his nest of blankets in the closet to sleep. Silvio was still snoring away in his drawing. The kids were starting to head to bed too. Maybe things would be clearer in the morning.

But Maldini had one last thing to add. "Children," he said. His whiskers were twitching. "There is something else you must know. I have told you, as soon as you came into the store my signore saw that the time had come. So he gave you the book. To help you."

"Help us do what?" Shireen asked suspiciously.

"To help solve the robberies," Maldini purred gently.

"The robberies?" Jared echoed. "What robberies?" Then he remembered the commotion at the Accademia. "You mean at the museum? That piece of the cross that went missing from the painting? That's connected too?"

"Yes," Maldini nodded. "How, I do not know. But

that is what my signore told me. When the robberies begin, be on your guard and on the lookout. That is the sign that everything is in place, that it has started.

"Still," he added after a pause, "I do not understand it. I did not think the robberies were supposed to happen yet. Not until later, after my signore had explained everything to you. We must be very careful. Something is wrong. It is too soon. But it *has* started."

7

The Signore Calls

The alarm clock went off at six thirty the next morning. Jared woke up startled, still in a fog of sleep and not sure why the alarm was beeping so insistently. Then he remembered and scrambled out of bed to turn it off. They had to get the lion and the cat hidden before their mother came in.

He woke his sisters. Looking around, they saw that Maldini was gone. He must have slipped back through the skylight while they were sleeping. Shireen opened the door to the closet and told the lion to stay hidden until she came back for him. He obeyed without offering the growls of protest she'd worried he might raise.

But in fact the warm bed he had made for himself at the base of the closet was a marked improvement over his old balcony post. No wind or rain or bad weather of any sort could get in there to eat away at his body or smudge the perfection of his sharp lines.

Now there was only Silvio to secure. Jared thought about it for a second and then gathered a handful of crayons. He quickly sketched a neat little brown house with a yellow thatch roof in the clearing where Silvio was still dozing. Switching from crayon to pencil, he traced out a sheet of paper at Silvio's feet and wrote in tiny block letters: PLEASE GO INSIDE HERE WHEN YOU WAKE UP. DO NOT COME OUT. PS NO MORE WINE!

Heading to the kitchen, they ran into their father pushing through the apartment door, a bag of pastries in one hand, the Venice newspaper in the other.

"Take a look!" he exclaimed as the kids tucked into the *pane dolce.* He was pointing at the newspaper headline. "It's happened again. Someone robbed San Marco!"

The kids exchanged worried glances. Another robbery? At San Marco?

"They what?" Mom asked.

"A robbery in the basilica," Dad said, sitting down and helping himself to one of the pastries. "There's that room off to the side of the apse where they keep old silver plates and chalices for communion and all sorts of relics in gold boxes. Well, someone stole one of the relics."

They'd all visited the giant church on Saint Mark's Square way back in January, the day after they'd first arrived in Venice. When they were done making the gloomy circuit of the nave with all the other tourists, Dad had led them through the door of the treasure room. There were display boxes full of all the stuff you'd expect: jewel-encrusted dishes, ancient silver cups, elaborately finished gold boxes. But there were other things too. In one of the cabinets, Shireen had seen what looked like human bones. And that's exactly what Dad had said they were. Saints' bones. From the Middle Ages. "People think they're holy," he'd explained. "They're called relics. They're supposed to have special powers—for healing, things like that."

And now someone had stolen another relic? Was this one of the robberies the cat had warned them about? It had to be.

"Did anyone get a look at who did it?" Miranda asked nervously.

Dad took another look at the paper. "Yes," he said.

"It says that a priest keeping a prayer vigil heard noises coming from the treasure room. When he went to investigate, he found three thieves taking a relic from one of the cabinets."

"They got away?" Mom asked.

"Yes," Dad answered, checking the page again. "They threw some kind of exploding powder at the priest. When he could see again, they were gone."

"So what did they take?" Jared asked.

"A bone from Saint George's arm," Dad answered. "The saint who killed dragons. Strange—they didn't touch any of the silver or gold. Why would they just want that bone?" he mused. "The other things have to be much more valuable."

"It *is* strange," Shireen said, narrowing her eyes at her brother from across the litter of pastry crumbs dotting the table. "Jared, what do you think?"

"Um, I don't know," he answered, avoiding her look. "But listen, Dad," he continued, determined to change the subject. His father set the newspaper aside with a puzzled shrug and hauled out the Latin grammar book. "I had a thought. For Latin today."

"Yes?"

"The story you've been reading us. About the book-seller and his nephew. Why don't you let us try to translate the next bit of it? You could leave the book with us and we'll read to you tonight."

"*You* want to *translate* it?" his father asked, looking at Jared over the rim of his glasses as if he had a fever or something. "On your own?"

"Yeah," Jared said, forcing himself to sound enthusiastic—but not *too* enthusiastic. "It'll be a challenge."

The buzzing of the doorbell gave Jared the chance he'd been looking for. The book Maldini's signore had given them was spread open on the table; the passage their father had picked out for them to translate was lightly marked with pencil. They'd been working at it for about half an hour, ever since he'd headed off for the university. But it was impossible, no matter how often they checked the dictionary or asked Miranda. They'd barely started learning Latin.

Their mother went down to see who was at the door.

"Thanks a bunch, Jared!" Shireen snapped as soon as the apartment door closed behind their mom's back. "Like we don't have enough going on! Now we have to translate the book!"

Jared ignored her. He grabbed the book and was flipping speedily through the pages. "Come on, quick, Miranda, help me out. Shireen, guard the door!"

"What are you doing?" Shireen demanded.

"Our names," Jared muttered hurriedly. "Looking for our names."

Shireen's eyebrows shot up. "Oh!"

"Here! Look!" Jared cried. Miranda was already crowding over his shoulder. Shireen grudgingly came over too, resentful that she hadn't thought of it first. Jared set his finger down on the line he'd found. There it was, in among a thicket of Latin mumbo jumbo, firmly marked out in the ancient handwriting: *Jared et Shireen et Miranda*. There they were, in this crazy old book! Jared and Shireen and Miranda.

Maldini had been telling the truth!

They looked at one another uneasily. It was one thing for the cat to tell them about it; it was something completely different to see their names staring back at them from the pages of a book someone had handwritten hundreds and hundreds of years ago.

A shiver ran down Shireen's spine.

The sound of their mom's returning footsteps rang on the stairwell. "Quick!" Miranda urged. "Mark the page!" Jared hurriedly scribbled down the page number and slammed the book shut while Miranda and Shireen scurried back to their seats.

Their mother came into the room, carrying a large

parcel wrapped in brown paper. She eyed them suspiciously. "Hey, where are your pencils? Have you been playing around?"

"No, Mom." Miranda smiled brightly. "We finally figured some of it out. I think it'll get easier if we keep working at it. Maybe you could ask Dad to let us finish it on our own. You know, for his birthday? Oh, what have you got?"

Their mother clearly wasn't sure about the birthday translating idea. But she was out of breath from going down and up the apartment stairs. And she had that kind of tired-queasy look on her face again, like when she'd had her nap yesterday, so she simply said, "Okay, I'll think about it," and put the parcel down on the table to unwrap.

"It's Dad's map," she told them as they gathered to see what she'd brought in. "The shopkeeper finished having it framed and sent it over with a delivery man."

As she lifted the map up to get a better look, Jared noticed a small handwritten note tucked away inside the paper wrapping she'd laid on the table.

Ragazzi, it said on its outside cover.

He plucked it out before his mother could see it and stuffed it in his pocket.

Their lessons went on and on, but finally Mom told them they were done. She'd made them lunch and headed back to her bedroom for another afternoon nap.

"Shireen, Miranda," Jared whispered as her bedroom door closed. "Look!" He pulled out the note that had been hidden in the map's wrapping paper and unfolded it. "Jared, Shireen, Miranda, dear children," he read. "Come see me. I must talk with you."

Jared made up his mind in a flash. "Mom?" He knocked on the bedroom door. "We're going out to the Internet café. They've got better Latin dictionaries online. Okay?"

There was silence behind the door. She must already be asleep. That was all right. They'd told her. It counted. Just to be sure they were covered, Jared wrote her a note and left it on the dining room table. Then he headed for the front door, pausing to grab his skateboard. "Come on!" he whispered urgently to his sisters. "Let's go to the old man's store!"

Shireen measured him up for a second. "Okay, we'll come. But leave the skateboard. You can't be trusted on that thing. It's what got us into this mess. If you hadn't been in such a rush, we'd have gotten on the right vaporetto and then none of this would have happened!"

He frowned at her. But she wasn't budging. So he slammed his board down in disgust. "Happy now?"

"Happier." She smirked. "Okay, Miranda, let's go."

They hopped a vaporetto (the *correct* one—Shireen had double-checked) at a boat stop on the Fondamenta Nuove, the long walkway running the length of the northern side of the city. Beyond the *fondamenta* lay open lagoon water, and farther out, the walled cemetery island where all the really ancient Venetian families went to bury their dead. Jared figured they had an hour and a half, maybe two hours at the most, to get to the store and back. That's how long Mom was napping these days. The vaporetto would get them to the Ghetto quicker than walking.

With Carnevale just five days away, all the water buses were jammed with people flooding in for the giant costume party Venice had been throwing off and on for more than seven hundred years. Getting on board the vaporetto was like being crammed into a sardine can. And today was worse than usual. Every scarf-wrapped adult on the boat had a newspaper snapped open between their jutting elbows. It was bitterly cold. The freezing banks of fog blowing off the water of the lagoon didn't help. Nor did the blaring headlines and photographs of the Accademia and the San Marco treasure room shouting from every newspaper's front page. Shireen didn't have to be fluent in Italian to imagine what the newspaper stories were saying: *Thieves!* She looked around the crowded deck uncomfortably. Who could tell? The robbers could be right there on the boat, mixed in with all the other passengers.

Miranda nudged her in the ribs. "Look," she whispered. "Silvio."

Shireen's heart jumped. The faun? He'd followed them?! She looked around wildly but couldn't spot him.

"The newspaper," Miranda whispered again. "At the bottom of the page."

Shireen took a closer look at a newspaper clutched in the hands of a signora with thick black stockings and a rolling wicker cart filled with grocery bags. Sure enough, there he was, photographed in a small inset box toward the bottom of the page, whirling around with the other dancers in his painting, with a big question mark over his face. Someone must have noticed that he'd vanished from his painting in the museum.

"Just great!" she whispered to Jared, pointing out

the grainy photo. "If anyone ever finds him, in *our* bedroom, they'll think *we're* the thieves!"

"No, they won't," Miranda corrected her. "They'll think we're wizards."

Jared grinned at Miranda. She was right. Whatever happened, this was a thousand times better than being stuck in the apartment doing schoolwork. Now that they were outside and there was cool air in his lungs, everything was feeling great again. How many kids had the chance to have an adventure like this? So what if they didn't understand everything that was going on? So what if his faun was still curled up snoring on the floor of the crayon forest? So what if there were some thieves out there? He had a magic die in his pocket and his sisters had magic rings hidden in theirs! It was fantastic!

"Listen," he told them. "The old man's going to explain everything to us, just wait and see. Everything's going to be fine, okay? I promise." He looked around to get his bearings on how much farther they had to go. The weather wasn't cooperating. To their left, the white facade of a church was gliding past them, barely visible in the fog. Up ahead, the banks of misty cloud floating on the surface of the lagoon were growing even thicker. Too thick.

Suddenly the vaporetto's horn blared and they were steering into a pontoon, then the conductor was directing everyone to disembark. *"Chiuso,"* he was calling out firmly. *"Chiuso per la nebbia.* Closed for fog, ladies and gentlemen. Please, off the boat. It is too dangerous; the pilot cannot see."

Shireen gave Jared a dirty look. But he just shrugged. They were going to have to run for it. He recognized a gelato place up ahead. Their mother had taken them there once. He tried to picture where the Ghetto was from here, made up his mind, and set off at a sprint down a narrow slick-stoned *calle,* shouting back for his sisters to follow him.

"Hold up, Jared! Hold up!" Shireen was panting angrily twenty minutes later. "We've been here before! Ten minutes ago!" Over to her side, Miranda was doubled over, her mittened hands on her knees, taking deep breaths.

Jared looked around. They were in a small square. There was a compact church on the far end. Its walls were covered in pink and green rectangles of marble. Drifting gray banks of mist were wrapped all around its bell tower. Shireen was right. They'd been through here ten minutes earlier.

"We're lost?" Miranda asked.

"No, we're not," Jared answered. The breath was coming out of his mouth in sharp white puffs. "We just . . . kind of . . . doubled back."

"Uh-uh, Jared." Shireen was hugging her hands round her chest to keep warm. "We're lost. L-O-S-T. Lost. Got it?"

"Like you could have done any better!" he snapped back.

"I could have. If I'd been in the lead."

A pair of elderly nuns in black-and-white habits and heavy gray winter cloaks frowned at them as they brushed past and started climbing the bridge spanning a narrow canal. Miranda waited until the nuns were out of sight and grinned wickedly. "That's okay," she said. "I can help. See?" She peeled off her mittens, exposing the glowing ring on her finger. Shireen could have choked her. On their way out of the apartment, they'd promised not to wear their rings outside. Just in case. She was keeping hers safe in her coat pocket. Even if Mom and Dad couldn't see its glittering light, there was no way she was going to chance wearing it and waking up every lion statue they passed. Miranda, though, had done her own thing. Typical!

"Take that off!" Shireen insisted. "How's it supposed to help anyway?"

"You'll see," Miranda answered. She scooted over to a metal trash container and started digging through it until she pulled something out triumphantly: a crust of bread.

"Thanks, Daniela! Thanks, Miss Pigeon!" Miranda shouted gaily as the bird went wheeling off fifteen minutes later.

Shireen hated to admit it, but her sister had known what she was up to. All it had taken was crumbling up that bread, and a dozen pigeons had come fluttering down at her feet. Miranda instantly began jabbering away at them and this one, a pebbled gray one with a flirty manner named Daniela, had volunteered to guide them through the foggy maze of alleys and canals. Kind of like a personal pigeon GPS system. Every time they'd been about to make a wrong turn she'd come winging back down, cooing away in that feather-ruffling throaty Italian voice of hers: "In fifty meters, *carini*, turn left. . . . After the bridge, *piccolini*, turn right. . . ."

Before they knew it, she'd gotten them to the right spot. The old man's shop was less than twenty yards away. Miranda gave the pigeon one last shout of thanks as they hurried across the square with the four leafless trees. But instantly Jared saw that something was wrong. The lights were off inside, and a broad wooden plank had been nailed across the doorway of the shop. Taped onto it was a large sheet of paper with a message written on it in hasty, sloppy-looking letters: CHIUSO! Closed.

Closed? How could it be closed? Maldini's signore had just sent them a note telling them to come see him. He wouldn't have boarded up his shop. It didn't make any sense.

They pressed their faces up against the window. At first it was too gloomy to make anything out, but then a ray of cold sunlight broke through the fog, briefly lighting up the square and shining through the storefront.

Jared drew in his breath. "Look!" he whispered.

Someone was moving stealthily through the back corner of the store, over by the Marco Polo statue. They saw a pale face crouched over the bag in the statue's hand. And then another. And another. There were three of them, pawing through the leather sack. Suddenly one of the intruders looked up—a girl, about the same age as Jared and Shireen. She looked them

right in the eyes and whispered something sharp to her companions, who also turned to glare. Jared could make out a younger girl's face, and beside her a green-eyed boy who looked a year or so older than himself. They were filthy. Their skin was smeared with grime. And they were wearing strange clothes. The girls had brown capes draped over their shoulders and white scarves wrapped over their hair. Sparkles of green and blue light glinted from their scarves, as if jewels had been sewn into them. The boy was dressed in a tattered vest and billowing pants that gathered up at his calves. A faded turban was wrapped around his head and a shining silver pen hung from a chain around his neck.

But it wasn't the sight of their odd clothing or their dirty hair that made Jared start back. It was the look in their eyes as they crouched there. A sharp, fierce, desperate look. The boy seemed to snap something at the two girls, and suddenly they all darted away from the statue toward the back room of the store and disappeared.

"C'mon!" Jared called out sharply, grabbing his sisters' arms. "We need to go." The girls didn't need to be told a second time. They stumbled away from the shop window and took off at a run.

8
At the Palace
of the Doge

They'd made it back to the apartment just in time, covered in sweat and feeling jumpier than ever. Their mother was still sleeping, but they'd barely had a chance to shrug out of their coats when their father came through the door. He went in to check on Mom, and when he came out of the bedroom he told them she wasn't feeling well. So he cooked supper, which wasn't all that good: mushy noodles with a sauce he'd poured out of a jar. Jared kept sneaking glances at his sisters to see how freaked out they were by what had happened. But they were avoiding eye contact. It wasn't like he really wanted to look himself in the face either. This was the second time he'd run away. Why was he such a wuss?

"You're a quiet group tonight," Dad observed as he followed them to the bedroom after they'd helped with the dinner dishes. "How was the translating?"

"Um, okay, I guess," Jared answered, settling on his mattress. "We didn't get very far. But we want to keep going," he rushed on before his sisters could stop him. He'd made up his mind. Those thief kids back at the store *had* been frightening. But still, he'd bolted twice now. He definitely, absolutely wasn't going to do it again. "Maybe if you just read some more of it, that'd make it easier. If we knew where the story was headed, maybe we'd have a better idea of what to do next. Um, you know, the next time we're . . . translating."

He gave his sisters his best encouraging grin, and Miranda nodded silently in agreement. But Shireen refused to look his way. Her eyes were on the book their father was already spreading open, trying to figure out how long it would be until he got to the page with their names on it. She couldn't decide if she wanted him to find out or not. If he did, they'd have to spill the beans about everything that had been happening, but then, at least, they wouldn't be on their own. She slipped her hand into her pocket, feeling around to make sure her ring hadn't fallen out while they'd been sprinting home. What would happen to Lorenzo il Piccolo if she'd lost it? Would he turn back into stone and be trapped forever in their closet? Okay—she breathed easier as her fingers touched the cool gold band—it was still there. Lorenzo il Piccolo would still be waiting for her. He'd vowed to keep her safe. She tried to keep her mind on that thought as her father began to read.

Whatever else happened, his uncle couldn't sell the book. Not the Scheherazade book. Not yet. Not after what had happened on the ship. If Rashid knew nothing else, he knew that much. So he had taken his chance. While the gondola was carrying them to the doge's palace and his uncle and Signor Isaac were deep in conversation on the cushioned bench in front of him, he'd edged open the lid of one of the book-filled trunks and secreted the volume out. In a second it was inside the pouch pocket of his loose shirt. He could feel the corners of the book against his stomach, just below the silver pen dangling from a chain around his neck.

The gondola drifted in to rest against a line of docking poles outside the doge's palace. Golden paint ran in spirals around the poles, whose tops were mounted with miniature

carvings of flying gold lions. As they stepped out of the gondola, Rashid could see a double line of flaming braziers lighting the way to the doors of the palace.

The palace guards examined the papers Signor Isaac handed them, uncrossed the spears they'd been holding in front of the doors, and waved the booksellers in. A vast courtyard lay ahead. As they crossed the open square and began to climb a giant stairwell on its far side, Rashid started to sweat. A dozen guards were following behind them, carrying the book-filled trunks. What had he been thinking? There was no chance that his uncle wouldn't notice that the Scheherazade book was missing! He'd barely spoken about anything else on their long voyage across the Mediterranean Sea.

"Just wait, Rashid," he'd boasted proudly as he stood at the rail of the ship, salt foam spattering his tanned face and his flowing white robes, eagerly searching for the first sight of Venice's towers climbing up against the horizon. "Wait until the doge sees what we have brought him!"

"But why is it so special?"

"Here," he'd answered, unwrapping the book from its oilskin covering. "Read for yourself."

That's when the trouble had started. Rashid had taken the book back to their cabin under the deck and started reading. Once he'd started, he couldn't stop. Late that night, long after his uncle had fallen asleep, Rashid was still stretched out in his narrow bunk, vaguely aware of the waves slapping against the hull of the ship. He'd come to the tale of Ala ad-Din.

The memory vanished as they turned the corner at the top of the giant stairway and Signor Isaac directed them through a molded archway and up another row of steps leading to the highest floor of the palace. Rashid blinked. The walls and ceiling were paneled with gold—thick sheets of pure gold molded into scenes of Venice's triumphs over its enemies. He'd never seen anything like it. Behind him he could hear the tromp of the guards' feet as they strained against the weight of the book-filled trunks. Another contingent of armed men was up ahead, examining Signor Isaac's papers again. How powerful was this doge? And what would *he* do when he found out that someone had stolen the prize book Uncle Mounir had sailed all the way from Spain to sell to him?

Rashid slipped his hand guiltily into his pouch pocket and touched the edge of the leather binding. Was it too late to sneak it back into one of the chests?

The soldiers up ahead were waving them forward, and a courtier had appeared at Signor Isaac's side. "The doge has been expecting you," he breathed in an undertone. He ushered them into an enormous audience chamber. A man in a rich red cloak and an oddly shaped velvet cap was standing at a wall of mullioned windows overlooking the lagoon.

"Ah, Signor Isaac," he said, turning, "I see you have come. Guards, you may set the books there." He pointed at a table running nearly the entire length of the chamber. There were two girls at his side. They were wearing simple ankle-length dresses and capes. Their hair was tied up in matching lace scarves that shot out little gleams of light, as if precious stones had been stitched into the lace. One of them looked to be about Rashid's age. Her dark eyes were clear and steady. The other girl was younger—maybe eleven or so. She dropped her gaze shyly and inched closer to the man.

"My lord," Signor Isaac responded, bending his knee. Rashid's uncle followed suit and a second later, with his uncle's hand gently pressing on his shoulder, Rashid bowed too. But his mind was racing. How much longer did he have to return the book?

"So," the doge said, drifting to the trunk-laden table, opening one of the chests, and idly paging through a volume or two. "This is a generous gift."

"A gift!" Rashid's uncle exclaimed.

"And you, my lord, are fabled for your generosity," Signor Isaac said. He flashed a hushing glance at his friend.

The doge ran an evaluating eye over Rashid's uncle. "Did you have a question?"

Rashid could see his uncle swallowing hard. There was a humorously calculating look in the doge's eyes.

"No, my lord," Uncle Mounir finally spoke through clenched teeth.

The doge smiled. "Ah, then I was mistaken. Signor Isaac," he continued in a low, silky voice, "I believe you have met my wards, Maria and Francesca?" He indicated the two girls.

"I have, my lord. It is a pleasure to see them again."

"And who have you brought with you?"

"My friend and fellow bookseller, Mounir al-Mari of al-Andalus, and his nephew and apprentice, Rashid."

The doge inclined his head slightly. The two girls were staring at Rashid and his uncle. "So," the doge said to Signor Isaac and Uncle Mounir. "Join me. Let us see what you have brought."

That was it. Time had run out. Rashid shuffled over reluctantly in his uncle's wake, holding one hand awkwardly over his stomach to hide the outline of the book. A gift! The doge was treating the books like a gift! So now he hadn't stolen from his uncle. He'd robbed the doge of Venice! He glanced hastily around the chamber to see if there was some way out. It was hopeless; there were guards at every door.

He could feel the heat rising in his body. The silver pen stung like ice against his burning chest. Why had he picked it anyway? Of everything he could have chosen, why had he picked the stupid pen? What he needed now was the magic lamp, with its wish-granting genie. That would get him out of this mess.

Signor Isaac and Uncle Mounir were at the doge's side, telling him about each book as he pulled them one by one from the trunks. Rashid could see his uncle studying the emptying chests with a confused look. Then it hit him. Of course! Of course! Why hadn't he thought of it before? But he had better move fast. "Um, Uncle Mounir?" he called out. The doge turned, arching one eyebrow. He was not accustomed to being interrupted. Signor Isaac and Uncle Mounir didn't look much happier. "Uncle?" Rashid said again. He started shuffling his feet and crossing one leg tightly over the other.

"What is it?" Uncle Mounir said in a strained voice.

"I have to go."

"Go?"

"Yes, you know, go. . . . I haven't been since we got off the boat."

The two girls' eyes widened in shock. Signor Isaac was studying his feet. Uncle Mounir looked like he was about to explode. But the doge burst out laughing. "Every day, something new." He chuckled. "Come, Maria, Francesca, show this pup the way to what he is looking for." He laughed again and returned his attention to the next trunk of books.

That was all the chance Rashid needed. The moment the chamber door had closed behind them he bolted down the golden stairwell, raced along the balconied landing overlooking the courtyard, and started down the final flight of steps. All he needed was a few minutes to himself.

"Rashid," the older of the two girls called after him. "Where are you going? That is the wrong way."

He ignored her. With two more bounds he was in the courtyard. He sat down on the bottom step and glanced up nervously across the moonlit rectangle to the lighted windows on the third floor, where he'd left his uncle and the doge. Then he plucked the book out of his pocket and began to read.

"Rashid," one of the girls called again. "What are you doing?"

"Nothing. Reading. Leave me be!" he shouted back. His eyes were zipping across the page, looking for the right place. There! There! He'd found it. The passage he'd been reading in the cabin when everything began. Would it happen again? He reread the lines. Ala ad-Din was climbing the steps down into the enchanted cavern. The evil wizard was outside, waiting for him to come out with the magic lamp. Everywhere he looked there were glittering piles of treasure, heaped with tumbles of gold coins and flashing jewels. Rashid's eyes drank the words. "Please! Please!" he was muttering desperately. "Hurry up!" But it wasn't working. The words were just words. The book was just an open volume in his lap.

He took a deep breath. He was trying too hard. He needed to relax. He reached up to touch the silver pen. It was real—even if it wasn't what he should have grabbed that first time on the boat, it *was* real. If it had happened once it could happen a second time. But touching the pen wasn't enough. He needed to see it. He slipped it out from under the collar of his white shirt and lifted it up toward the moonlight. He pressed the tip of his finger against the fine, delicately split nib, let the pen fall back down inside his shirt, and started to read again.

All at once, he was there! The jagged rock walls of the cave were rising all around him. Piles of golden coins lay scattered at his feet. Rubies, emeralds, and diamonds winked and glittered their red, green, and crystal light. Everywhere he turned he saw shining rings, crystal balls with shadowy blue flames dancing in their depths, tumbles of glinting gold, pouches full of sparkling dust. But the lamp? Where was the lamp with the wish-granting genie that would get him out of this mess? He plunged forward, kicking over piles of treasure, grabbing everything he could, anything that might help.

A cold, sneering voice cut through the air.

"So, boy, what have you found?"

Rashid looked up, startled. Ala ad-Din's magic cavern evaporated in the air. He was back in the courtyard of the doge's palace. A dark, cowled figure was striding toward him from the direction of the palace gates, a company of personal guards trailing after him. "Come, boy," the hooded monk repeated. "Open your hands. Show me what you have!" Rashid shrank back. One flight of stairs above him the two girls, Maria and Francesca, were staring down in amazement. Their faces were pale in the moonlight. The monk closed the gap and stooped over Rashid, his black robes swirling. He forced Rashid's hands open. The book fell to the ground at his feet, and then so did the other things Rashid found himself holding: a clutch of jewels, a pouch full of sparkling dust, two golden rings, and a wooden die.

Jared bolted up in bed. "Um, Dad, could you read that part again?"

"What part?" his father asked, putting the book down in his lap.

"That last bit," Jared said. He could feel his heart pounding. Over on their beds, Shireen and Miranda were just as stunned. "I kind of drifted off while you were reading. Could you just read that last part again? What did Rashid pull out of Aladdin's cave? It is Aladdin, right? Ala ad-Din is Aladdin?"

Dad nodded and read the last paragraph again.

They'd said their prayers and Dad had gone back to the living room, closing the door behind him. They had the bedroom to themselves. But none of them knew what to say or do next. Their treasures—Rashid had pulled their treasures out of *Aladdin's cave*? The Scheherazade book came to life when Rashid read it, and he'd pulled the die and rings out of Aladdin's cave! But that wasn't the weirdest part. The weirdest part was Rashid and those two girls, Maria and Francesca: their descriptions fit, identically, the thieves they'd seen prowling through the old man's store! The boy with a turban and a silver pen hanging from a chain around his neck; the girls with flashing jewels in their head scarves. They were the thieves?! Rashid and Maria and Francesca? How could that be? And yet, the similarities were too exact. But they were alive hundreds of years ago. And now they were awake and alive from the pages of the book? No way. It was totally impossible. *Unless that's who my die brought to life,* Jared finally said to himself.

And if that was right, then what else had it woken?

Shireen spoke up. "You know . . ." She was twisting her ring anxiously on her finger, pulling it on and off again. "Maybe it's time to tell Mom and Dad."

Jared blinked at her. Tell Mom and Dad? But if they did that, then they'd never—

A scratching noise against the skylight broke into his thoughts. It was Maldini. Miranda helped Jared balance the chair on the mattress and open the sky-light. Maldini leaped down with a satisfied look on his face.

"Where have you been?" Miranda asked, wildly relieved to see him again.

"Feasting," Maldini purred. His pink tongue darted out to lick his lips. "At the fish market. I went to see my signore this morning at first light. I asked him about the book, and the side of Jared's die with its image coming to light, and the robberies beginning too early. He told me to be patient. 'In time, everything will be clear,' he said. We only need to wait. He will be with us when the time comes, to explain everything. In the meantime he told me to enjoy myself for the day before finding you again. So I prowled the fish market and took my chances where I could."

"Then you don't know?" Jared asked.

"Know what?" The cat's ears tipped forward alertly.

"About your signore's shop? It's closed. He sent us a note this afternoon. He said it was urgent. We needed to come see him. But when we got there . . ." Jared's voice trailed off.

"What?" Maldini asked, his tail beginning to switch. "What has happened?"

"The shop was boarded up," Jared answered. "And there were some kids inside."

"Scary kids," Miranda added, her voice quavering.

"We think we know who they are," Jared went on. "They were the kids from the book. Rashid's one of them. And the girls, Maria and Francesca. We think they were trying to steal something."

"Wait! Slow down!" Maldini interrupted. "Tell me exactly what has happened."

Jared quickly filled him in on what they'd seen, and read.

"So that is it," Maldini said when Jared was done. The golden coins of his eyes had narrowed to angry slits. "That is who was called from the book. Rashid and the girls. And now they have broken into my signore's store?" His tail switched back and forth furiously. "I must go. My signore is in danger—I never should have left him. I will come back to tell you what I find." Before they could say a word to stop him, he leaped all the way up to the open jamb of the skylight and sprang off into the cold winter night.

9
Into the Fog

No one noticed the faun loping out of the thatched crayon house. They were still looking up to the skylight, wondering what Maldini was going to run into once he got back to the old man's store. But the moment Silvio thrust his hoof through the surface of the drawing and began climbing into the bedroom, there was no missing him. His huffs and puffs grabbed their attention, and then it was like watching a giant balloon inflate. As he clambered awkwardly into the room, poking one hooved leg through, then the other, Silvio's body grew back to its supersize proportions.

"Don't mind me," he said, giving them all a conspiratorial wink and hustling past them before they had time to say a word. "I'll be back in a moment, faster than the wings of Mercury." He pushed through the bedroom door and hurried down the hall, walking a little awkwardly on his clicking hooves, as though he had a cramp in his stomach.

"What's he doing?" Jared demanded incredulously, looking to his sisters. "Where's he going?" He sprang over to the door of the bedroom to see what on earth the lunatic faun could be up to. At least the door at the end of the hall was closed. Still, for all he knew, Silvio was about to go blundering into the living room where their parents were watching television. That would sure put an end to things. Just wait until their parents caught sight of him! But the faun hadn't turned down the hall in that direction. He'd hustled into the bathroom to the right and closed the door behind himself.

"He's going to the toilet!" Miranda snickered. "He has to go!"

Jared stood staring at the bathroom door. He wasn't sure how much more he could take. It wasn't even embarrassing anymore. It was humiliating. But Miranda was obviously right, as the groaning and sighing and sounds of muttered oaths on the far side of the door made clear. "Aeolus's winds, that's a relief!" they could hear the faun muttering. "Neptune's trident, that feels better!" They heard the sound of flushing and the spill of tap water, and then Silvio was back in the bedroom, his goateed face a little flushed but glowing with pleasure at the sight of them. He nodded familiarly to Miranda and bent over to get a better look at Shireen and Jared.

"Delighted to meet you! Delighted to meet you!" He extended his hand to both of them in turn. "Caius Marcus Silvanus is my name. But you may call me Silvio—all my friends do. Delighted to meet you! Have you any wine? Not that crayon vinegar I had last night. Real wine, made from grapes. Perhaps out there somewhere?" He waved hopefully in the direction of the living room and kitchen. "I did see glasses, you know, when I came in. There was a cabinet full of them. Perhaps you have a barrel or two of wine stored away somewhere? Or a flagon?" the faun continued, a little concerned by the blank expression on their faces. "Or a wineskin?" he went on, quite worried now. "I'll drink from a wineskin, you know. Perhaps just a cork I could suck on?" he ventured desperately, completely unnerved by their continued wide-eyed silence. "Oh, dear! Oh, dear! Oh, Venus! Oh, Juno! Oh, Ceres!"

he finally moaned, giving up and sorrowfully stroking the nubby horns extending from his forehead.
"You don't have any wine, do you? Oh, by the seeds of
Proserpina's pomegranate, I should have known!" He
sat down on the bed beside them and hung his head
in his hands.

"Don't be sad, Silvio!" Miranda beamed at him.
"Mom and Dad keep wine in the kitchen."

"Do they?" said Silvio, lifting his head and bright-
ening. "Do they indeed? Well, that's welcome news.
That plucks Jupiter's beard. Why, we shall have a
party! And we can dance. Do you like to dance? Come,"
he said, "I'll show you." Before they could protest, he
pulled them onto their feet, setting Miranda on his
shoulders and taking Shireen by one hand and Jared
by the other and spinning them around, his hooves
skittering expertly.

When they were all out of breath, the faun dropped
them back onto the bed and sat down at their side.
"Now," he said, "you've had my name, little ones. And
Miranda has introduced herself. Time for you other
two to tell me who you are. Particularly you, my lad,"
he added, giving Jared a great sparkling wink. "I've
been waiting to meet you."

Jared grinned back at him. He'd been wrong. Silvio

wasn't pathetic. He was perfect. Who cared if he wasn't all into pride and dignity like Lorenzo il Piccolo? Or wise like Maldini? Or clean? Those hundreds of years of dancing in the woods in the painting at the museum had definitely taken their toll. The thick goaty fur covering Silvio's legs was coated in dust and tangled with grass and leaves. But what did that stuff matter when he was so much *fun*? And when they'd filled him in on everything that was happening, Silvio's eyes lit up.

"Why, I'm just the faun for you!" he announced, bounding off the bed and balling up his fists as if he was about to take on a crowd of invisible enemies. "There's nothing like a faun for getting you out of a tight spot. You say there's a pack of thieves out there? And they've been around for hundreds of years? And they've broken into the store of one of your friends? Well, if I can't knock them down, I'll challenge them to a drinking contest, and then by Orpheus's lyre, you'll see what I can do!"

He came to a sudden halt and tugged on his goatee, a sharper look in his eye, as if he was trying to remember something.

"You say the girls had jewels in their scarves? And the lad wore a turban?"

Jared nodded.

"By Jove! I think I saw them!"

"You did?" Shireen asked. "Where?"

"In the museum," Silvio asserted. "Yes, by Venus's bottom, the very ones. They're the ones who stole the relic. I saw the whole thing. You can see down the wing of the museum from my little spot. I noticed them come creeping in after midnight, two days ago. A boy and two girls. Bigger than you, except for the youngest girl. They had a shifty look, and I haven't seen anyone wearing clothes like that for centuries. In need of a good bath as well, all three of them! They seemed to be looking for something in a painting and stopped in front of that one of the monks on the bridge. The boy had a leather pouch, and he took out a pinch of some kind of powder and blew it on the painting. There was a burst of light, and the next thing I knew, he'd reached into the canvas and pulled out that bit of cross. They were just about to do the same to another painting when one of the night guards came round and they scurried off before they were seen. I didn't care a brass denarius about it at the time, but if you say they've done mischief to one of your friends, by Bacchus's vines, they'll have to answer to me!"

Shireen looked over at Jared. He had a sloppy-looking grin on his face. He was already imagining himself confronting the thieves, with Silvio at his side.

There was a sudden sharp noise coming from the skylight. Maldini was back, beckoning them to join him on the rooftop. "Come on! Hurry up! They've taken my signore! But I've found them! They're at the Accademia. Quick, up on the roof! The faun can lift you up. And bring that idiot lion. He might be of some use. Come on! Quick!"

Getting onto the roof wasn't the hardest part. It was getting down to the *calle* below that was tricky. Lorenzo il Piccolo had obeyed Shireen's command in haughty silence, loping out of his closet and then leaping up to the skylight with one fluid spring of his powerful haunches. The kids grabbed coats while Silvio pushed the skylight all the way open and easily hauled himself up. Then he reached back to pull Shireen, then Jared, then Miranda after him. But now that they were up on the roof, what where they supposed to do? The curved red tiles slanted down crazily to a sheer drop two floors deep. It was hard to even see the bottom. Thick banks of mist were floating through the air, obscuring the view.

Maldini and Lorenzo il Piccolo had forged ahead, leaping down from the gutter to the alleyway below.

Once on the pavement, Lorenzo il Piccolo looked up to see raw fear on Shireen's face as she slid downward on her belly and then angled around to lean over the gutter and judge the distance. "Fool of a cat," he rumbled to himself. Look at the danger the pet had lured his lady into! He was about to climb back up when Silvio had an idea.

After telling the children to stay put, Silvio climbed back up to the skylight, his hooves skidding and slipping for purchase on the tiles. He lowered himself into the bedroom and quickly reappeared, a piece of paper clutched in his hand. Then he slid back down to where the kids were squatting precariously on the ledge and handed it to Jared.

It was Miranda's drawing of the forest.

"Hold it up," Silvio told him.

"Why?" Jared frowned. He wasn't sure how this was supposed to help.

"It's too far for me to jump," Silvio explained. "But if I climb into the drawing, you can throw it down onto the *calle* and then I can climb out."

"Then what are we supposed to do?" Shireen broke in.

"Then you jump," Silvio answered, his white teeth flashing. "And I catch you."

Shireen raised her eyebrows. "You'll catch us?"

"Yes," Silvio assured her. "As sure as Ulysses's bow was strong, I will catch you."

Miranda wasn't buying it. She began to tremble, and edged as far from the side as possible.

"Miranda," Jared told her, touching her arm, "we can trust him. He'll catch us."

Shireen nodded in reluctant agreement. But Miranda was still shaking her head.

"Look, I'll hold you," Jared urged. "We'll jump together."

Before she could argue any more, he gave Silvio a thumbs-up and spread out the drawing. The faun climbed in, his body shrinking magically. Jared plucked up the drawing and threw it down onto the alleyway below. As soon as it had floated to the ground, Silvio stepped out and positioned himself beneath the gutter, his arms stretched out wide.

Maldini halted his pacing and trained his golden eyes up to the crouching children on the ledge. His whisking tail had gone still. High above, Shireen took a deep breath, crossed her fingers, whispered a quick prayer, and leaped.

Jared leaned over the side of the gutter, his heart pounding as his sister's body cut a dark track through the curling mist. What if Silvio missed her?

Then he breathed a huge sigh of relief. She was safe. The faun had caught her and set her on her feet. Okay, then. Time to do his part. He edged down the gutter toward Miranda.

She had one hand held out to keep him back. "*No! I can't do it! It's too far!*"

Jared knew there'd be no convincing her, so he ducked under her outstretched hand, wrapped his arms around her, and hurtled their bodies into space. He couldn't believe how fast they were falling, and clutched his arms more tightly around Miranda. The *calle* came rushing at them. Then Silvio had them in his arms and was putting them down, a broad smile on his face. *Awesome!* Jared thought. He looked up to see how far they'd plunged. *That should be on Xbox!* It was ten times better than any trick he'd ever pulled on a half pipe. He wanted to do it again. But he didn't have time to savor the rush of the jump. Maldini was already bolting down the *calle*, calling back over his shoulder, "Come on! Come on! Hurry up!"

It was a good thing it was foggy. The mist swallowed them up before anyone could get too close a look and wonder what they were doing chasing through the city with a cat, a stone lion, and an oversize faun. Before any of the stray wanderers they passed could stop to stare, they were gone, vanishing into the floating gray.

But it didn't hide them entirely.

Shireen heard a many-throated, curious growling echoing through the air as they ran through the narrow alleys and mist-shrouded squares. She'd left her ring on. She hadn't wanted to take the chance that something would happen to Lorenzo il Piccolo if she took it off as they dashed through the city. What if he turned back to stone in the middle of the street? But as she went bolting past them, the other lions of Venice sensed her presence and began stirring. "Little girrrl? Little girrl?" they called out in their stone and marble voices as she raced by. She turned to wave, but Maldini wasn't letting up, so she had to keep running, up over a bridge or around a corner where she could just make out the vanishing tip of the cat's tail. As she disappeared, the lions froze back into their ancient hardness, their slumbering thoughts troubled by a faint dream of a dark-haired girl dashing madly past them.

At last they were across the great wooden span of the Accademia bridge and at the very doors of the gallery, utterly winded.

"That's where I left them," Maldini purred as they

stood there panting. He pointed at the double doors of the museum. "They were headed inside."

"And who do you mean by 'they'?" Lorenzo il Piccolo growled, stalking up to Maldini, a dismissive curl on his lips. "We've done what you've asked. Now tell us who we are hunting, and why we are here."

Maldini bristled. But he could see the question echoed on the kids' faces, so he filled them in.

He'd hurried back to his signore's shop and found the plank nailed over the door. There was no getting in that way, so he'd leaped up onto a low wall adjoining the store and from there climbed to the rafters of the building. There was a gap between the beams and the roof, which he'd used a thousand times to go down to the fish market at dawn, when the boats were coming in to unload their catches. He had slipped through the narrow space into the shop. It was empty. He'd continued cautiously into the back room. It didn't look good. The table where his signore took his meals had been overturned. A glass-fronted bookcase had been thrown to the ground, its volumes strewn all across the floor. There'd been no sign of his master. The thieves must have taken him.

He'd nosed around through the scattered books and glass shards and picked up a strong, unfamiliar scent.

He'd followed the smell out the back door, then on through twists and turns until the trail came to an end at an abandoned boatyard. Maldini had sniffed the ground furiously, widening his nostrils to take in the faintest residue of smell. But the scent had disappeared at the edge of the cobbled stone as it dropped off into the canal. Which meant only one thing: the thief kids had taken a boat and were on the canal somewhere. Anywhere. There'd been nothing to do but wait and hope that they weren't done with their mischief. He'd padded up to the top of a pile of abandoned lumber to stand watch.

He didn't have to wait long. Before the church towers had tolled the next hour, he'd seen them silently row to the decaying slip of the boatyard, land, and climb out. Then he'd followed them all the way to the entry of the Accademia gallery, where he had seen them huddle, blow a puff of glowing powder from the pouch the boy held in his hands, and push open the doors of the museum.

"They're still inside?" Miranda asked, eyeing the heavy wooden doors uneasily. On closer inspection she could see that they were slightly ajar. The image of the snarling thieves crouching behind the window of the old man's store came flashing back.

"They were when I left to get you," Maldini replied. "We'll have to go in to find out for certain. Now come, we've delayed long enough." He darted forward, up the marble steps, and through the door.

10
A Flash in the Gallery

What do you say, my lady?" Lorenzo il Piccolo asked. His stone tail was swishing lazily, cutting a swath of shadow through the dim light falling from the iron-bracketed lantern illuminating the misty square. "Shall we follow him? Or have you had enough of being ordered around by this domestic animal? I can accompany you back to your quarters if you wish."

Shireen hesitated. Now that they'd followed Maldini all the way to the museum it was obvious what they needed to do, but she could see the look on Miranda's face. She *was* just nine. A pill. But a nine-year-old pill. And those thief kids had looked really fierce. "What do you think?" she asked Jared.

"We can take them," he replied. "We've got Silvio." He was rolling his shoulders, like a boxer getting ready for a fight, the way Silvio had done when he'd gone bounding around their bedroom with his fists all balled up.

"That you do!" the faun agreed. He lowered his voice to a whisper. "Come on, then. After me. But quiet, now. We'll want to surprise them. And take my word on it. By Diana's bow, if anyone tries to harm you, I'll give them such a thrashing they'll think Hercules himself had come back to life!"

Shireen couldn't help smiling. Fine, then, if he'd sworn by *Diana's bow* . . . She edged over to Miranda. "It's okay, we can trust Silvio and Lorenzo. They'll keep us safe. Plus," she swallowed hard, forcing the words out, "we've got Jared." She pointed over to where their brother was entering the doors at the faun's back.

"Jared?" Miranda looked up, surprised.

"Yeah." Shireen bit her lip. "I know he's a goof sometimes. Okay, lots of times. But he'll keep an eye on us."

Miranda took a deep breath and nodded. She clenched her fists in her coat pockets and headed to the door. Shireen made a mental note to herself:

Okay, Jared. You owe me. Big-time. Then she called to Lorenzo il Piccolo. It was time to go. The lion twitched his whiskers in disgust at the danger that fool of a cat was leading his lady into, but strode in at her side.

The museum opened into a small, dimly lit atrium with two curving staircases on either side. There was no sign of Maldini. Which way had he gone? Right or left? They stood there for a moment, unsure of which stairway to climb.

Lorenzo il Piccolo sighed and took the lead. Couldn't they detect the cat's scent? It was overwhelming. "This way," he purred to Shireen as he climbed the stairs to the right.

They reached the landing and saw the familiar line of galleries stretching out beyond them. The deserted halls were dark but not completely black. A few pale lights burned in glass sconces on the walls for the night guards on their rounds. But there was no sight of the guards. Or of Maldini. Lorenzo il Piccolo led them on, his tail twitching eagerly. Now that Shireen had commanded him into action, it didn't matter why they were there. He would show her the value of a lion. They moved farther into the museum, down one long hall and then another. The lion's mane had flared out and his sharp claws were extended as he stalked along, sniffing at the air.

The door of the room where the first relic had been taken from the Carpaccio painting loomed ahead. A line of police tape was stretched across it, sealing it off. Was that really just yesterday? Jared wondered. He stared into the cordoned-off gallery. It seemed like a month since they'd been there.

An explosion of light burst in on his thoughts.

It took a second to register what had happened. The burning flash came from the far end of the hall. Then there was a sharp whimpering animal cry and the sound of running feet and calling voices. By the time Jared had cleared the dazzle from his eyes, the hall had gone dark again and Lorenzo il Piccolo was bounding forward. Silvio cantered after him. Jared put his heels to the floor and took off to catch up, Miranda and Shireen trailing him. They'd barely gone forty paces when Silvio came to a sudden, skidding halt. Jared stumbled into his back. The faun was bending down, lifting a limp black mass from the marble floor.

From somewhere far down below they heard a door slamming hard, the sound of escaping footsteps, and a girl's voice calling out, "Run, Rashid, run!"

BAUCOM

With a quick glance to make sure no one was in the
square, they hurried out of the museum. Miranda
was carrying Maldini. A patch of fur on his back was
singed, but it could have been worse. The powder the
thief children had thrown at him had burst into flame
a foot or so above him. The shock of the explosion
had knocked him out for a few minutes, but he wasn't
burned too deeply. He'd be okay. Mainly he was angry
with himself, he'd sputtered to the others. If he'd been
a bit more patient, he could've spied on the thieves
without giving himself away. But as soon as he'd
spotted them huddled together in front of another
painting, he'd felt a surge of rage and leaped forward,
his claws extended, snarling, "Where is my signore?"
They'd heard his furious hiss, and before he could get
his claws on them, the boy had thrown that powder at
him. And now they had escaped.

"At least we learned something," Miranda said
encouragingly when Maldini had finished telling his
story. They were sitting on the wooden platform at
the base of the newsstand facing the museum. She'd
set Maldini in her lap and was softly stroking his fur,
careful to avoid the singed area.

"What is that?" the cat asked doubtfully.

"One of the thieves, the boy—he's definitely Rashid. We heard one of the girls say it," she explained, "while you were knocked out. Right, Shireen?"

"What? Yeah," Shireen confirmed, but she was distracted. She glanced around anxiously. Where was Lorenzo il Piccolo? They hadn't seen him since he'd taken off down the hall. She'd thought for sure that he'd be waiting for them outside the doors, or—and this thought had her very worried—that she'd find him farther out on the square, turned back into a statue. Every other lion her ring called into life froze again when she moved far enough away. She wasn't sure why it hadn't happened yet with Lorenzo il Piccolo, but what if it did?

"He is not like other lions anymore," Maldini said when she voiced her question. "Now that he has made his oath to you, he will remain as he is until you release him."

"Oh," Shireen answered, relieved. But still, where was he?

They waited for another half hour. But after a few late-night tourists, all bundled up in scarves and coats, had wandered through the misty square and stopped to give them a long curious look, Maldini decided they had to go. Lorenzo il Piccolo could find his own way back to the apartment. He must still be chasing Rashid and the two girls. Shireen objected, but Maldini was firm. They were pressing their luck. So they began the long walk back to the apartment, Shireen looking down every *calle* for a sign of the little lion.

They were just about home when Jared realized another problem. "Shireen," Jared said, pulling up as they entered the alleyway to their building. The fog had mostly cleared as a cold breeze had blown in, sweeping the floating city. A star-dusted winter sky shone above. "How are we going to get in? We don't have a key!"

"Do you still have Miranda's drawing?" Maldini asked, weaving his way between them.

"I think so," Jared answered. He reached into his coat pocket. "Yeah, it's here."

"Good," Maldini replied, and proceeded to tell them what to do.

"You mean we go *into* the drawing?" Shireen asked incredulously.

"Silvio will help you," Maldini assured her.

"But how can you be sure it will work for us?"

"It will work. Just take his hand."

Jared agreed first. He wasn't completely convinced, but he couldn't come up with a better idea. It wasn't like they could ring the doorbell and ask their parents to let them in.

He looked over at Shireen. "Let's try."

"But, Jared . . . even if we can get *in* the picture, what if we can't get back out again?"

"C'mon, we have to give it a try. What else can we do? And it worked for Silvio twice already."

Shireen took a deep breath, deciding. Finally she said, "Okay, let's try."

Jared spread the drawing out on the ground. Silvio, carrying Miranda, who'd fallen asleep, shifted her on his shoulder. "Cupid's arrow," he said with an encouraging grin as he stepped one hoof into the forest. "We'll have some sport in these woods. Shireen, take your brother's hand now, and Jared, you hold on to me."

Jared clasped Shireen's palm in one hand and took Silvio's with the other. They felt the faun gently pulling them and stepped forward. It was like they were walking through an electric curtain. A shimmering wall of force pressed against every surface of their bodies as Silvio led them through the plane of the drawing. They could sense themselves shrinking. Then they were absolutely small and warm and blinking, dazzled by the glint of the crayon sun in the paper-white sky above them. Jared rubbed his eyes and looked around. It had really happened! They were inside the drawing! All around them were waxy brown tree trunks topped with vague green swirls of color. The grass beneath their feet was springy and fresh. For all its crayon-drawn shapes, this was a real forest. He could climb those trees if he wanted to.

He stood there marveling. There was a vague sweet smell in the air, like crayon shavings. It was like he'd tumbled back to what all of life felt like when he was in nursery school. He'd forgotten how great that was.

Silvio had already ambled off in the direction of the thatched house. Jared and Shireen were about to follow when they felt everything shifting. The trees to either side of them bent inward. The paper sky creased and began to close in on them. It felt like they were being folded up.

They were. Maldini had taken the drawing in his mouth, doubling it between his sharp teeth. He leaped up, and they felt a sickening lurch as he made his way up to the skylight on the rooftop. They were on their way back into the apartment.

Lorenzo il Piccolo returned just after dawn the next morning, landing on the skylight with a pounce and slipping into the bedroom with an angry twist of his tail. The jolt of his stone paws on the foot of the bed woke Shireen. She smiled widely at the sight of him. But Lorenzo il Piccolo just gave her a stiff formal nod and curtly offered his report. The thief kids had escaped him, and he was in no spirit for banter. From the Accademia, he sourly indicated, he had followed them to the boatyard on the Fondamenta dei Mendicanti. He'd been about to leap onto the stern of the boat they were relaunching into the canal when they'd heard him coming and thrown some of that fiery powder at him. It couldn't burn his stone skin, but it blinded him momentarily. By the time he'd blinked the flash out of his eyes, their boat was too far down the night-blackened canal for him to follow.

The lion's failure to capture the thieves had been a serious blow to his pride. So Shireen held herself to one brief hug of his thick stone neck and let him withdraw sulkily to his closet, where he sat in glowering silence, brooding his revenge.

She shook the others awake. Jared sat up, kicked away his blanket, and swung himself out of bed. "Aren't you going to change?" Miranda asked him as she saw him cram the hanging tail of his shirt back inside his pants. They'd slept in their clothes after climbing out of the crayon forest drawing, too exhausted to bother putting on their pajamas.

"No," Jared answered.

"Not even your underwear?"

He shook his head.

"That's totally gross," Shireen said with a grimace. How could he stand it?

She grabbed fresh clothes for herself and her sister, and the two girls crept quietly into the hallway bathroom to get dressed. Miranda brought back a tube of first aid cream and called Maldini out from under the bed, where he was ever so delicately snoring. While Miranda gently rubbed the ointment on the cat's singed back, Jared rapped his fingers against the surface of the crayon forest to get Silvio's attention.

"Medusa's snakes!" the faun complained, wandering out of the thatched hut and rubbing his eyes. He crossed the foreground of the drawing. "Morning already?" he huffed as he came swelling into the room. "Don't you children ever do nothing? What's wrong with you?"

"Shh!" Miranda whispered. "Our parents are still sleeping. Don't wake them."

"Ah, yes." He put his fingers to his lips. "But where's that honest grape nectar you promised me? I'm not human, you know. I must have my tongue wet or my fur will lose its shine."

"*Lose* its shine?" Shireen asked incredulously. She was standing by the bedroom door, pressing her ear up against the wood. It was earlier than when Mom usually woke them, but someone had to be watching out. Just in case.

"Well, yes." Silvio's white teeth flashed in a grin. "You have a point." He tugged on his goatee and ran an apologetic hand over his goat legs, brushing off an ancient layer of dirt. "I'm delicate, you see. When I'm not watered, I wilt."

"If you can help us rescue my master from those thieves," Maldini purred grimly from his place in Miranda's lap, "I'm sure the children can attend to your thirst. I hear there is wine in the kitchen."

"Bacchus's grapes! You have a bargain!" Silvio boomed. He lowered his voice as he caught Shireen flashing a shushing look at him. "To be sure, to be sure," he whispered, "I'd help even without the prom-ise of wine. Not that the wine's not welcome. Don't mistake me: I'll accept the wine!"

"But how are we going to rescue your signore?" Miranda asked, her hand pausing hesitantly over the cat's back. "We don't know where he is."

"Then we will have to capture the thieves to find out," Maldini answered.

"Capture them?" Jared angled round from where he'd slumped back down on the corner of his bed, trying to hold back a massive yawn. What had they gotten—four, maybe five hours of sleep? "You want us to *capture* them?"

Maldini nodded.

Jared glanced over at Silvio. The faun bowed his arms together in front of his chest and flexed his pecs. "Nothing to it," Silvio boasted.

"Okay," Jared agreed, combing his fingers through his hair and grinning back at Silvio. "I'm game. Shireen? Miranda?"

Shireen gave him a look. "Yeah, I'm game. But this isn't some skateboard trick. It's going to take some *brains* to find them. Half of Venice is looking for the art thieves. How are *we* going to track them down?"

"Half of Venice does not have Rashid's tale in their living room," the cat purred sternly. His golden eyes had once again narrowed down to slits. "Let your father keep reading it to you. There is a clue for us in there. I am sure of it. Why else would it hold your names?"

Jared blinked. He'd almost forgotten that part. He still didn't get what it meant, or how it could be possible. But the cat was right. If they were going to track down Rashid and the girls, the story was the only clue they had.

11

"A Crusade?"

A crusade?" Miranda put a hand on her father's arm to stop him from reading further. "That monk who found Rashid in the doge's courtyard—he was in Venice to launch a *crusade*?"

"Mmmm," her father answered. His eyes were skimming across the next set of lines.

"Dad!" Shireen interrupted him, shoving down her blanket and leaning forward to get his attention.

"Yes?" He held a finger to the line of text he was translating.

"A crusade? What's that all about?"

Jared fought irritation at his sisters. Why, exactly, did they care about some old crusade?

Too late. Dad's eyes were lighting up. He was balanced on the edge of Miranda's mattress, the book in his lap, totally oblivious to the creatures lurking in the room all around him: the cat under the bed, the lion in the closet, the faun hiding in the thatched-roof cottage in the drawing on the wall. Jared sighed. It had been a quiet day. More lessons in the morning, then a really long field trip with their mother to the Arsenale, the shipyard where the fleets of the Venetian empire used to be built—which might have been interesting if half the old buildings hadn't been turned into art museums. Then the wait until supper was over and Dad had come into their bedroom to read. He'd finally been getting back into the story when Miranda and Shireen interrupted him with their pointless questions.

"The crusades?" he said, putting the book down. *Oh no,* Jared thought. *Here we go again. Professor mode.* Couldn't Dad have been a soccer coach? Or something else that was normal? But it was too late. He was starting to lecture. It was much worse here than in the States. At least at home their house was big enough so he and Shireen could just kind of wander off when he got going, as long as Miranda stayed in place. In this tiny apartment, they were just plain trapped.

"The crusades," his father was saying, "were terrible. They went on all through the Middle Ages. Everyone was fighting over Jerusalem because they thought it was the holiest city in the world. Muslim armies took control of it, then a pope or king from Europe would send men to try to take it because they thought it should be run by a Christian ruler. Richard the Lionheart—you know about him, from the story of Robin Hood? Prince John's brother? He was fighting in a crusade while Prince John was running things in England. And there were lots of Muslim heroes. Saladin? You've read about Saladin at school?" He squared his glasses on his nose.

"Uh, no," Jared and Shireen admitted, though Miranda had a look on her face like she'd done a voluntary book report on him.

Dad frowned. "Well, you should have."

"Ok, Dad," Shireen said before Miranda could butt in. "We'll Wikipedia him. But what about the monk in the story? Why was he in Venice trying to start one of those crusades? What did that have to do with Rashid?"

"Oh," he said. He started to describe the whole

setting of the tale. The story happened around the end of the twelfth century. The pope in Rome wanted to launch a new crusade because Saladin, the Muslim general, had just won control of Jerusalem and the pope wanted to conquer it back for the Catholic Church. But he wasn't strong enough to mount a crusade on his own. He needed soldiers from everywhere, including Venice, because back in those days Venice was really powerful. But the doge wasn't interested in sending his soldiers to fight for Jerusalem. Venice had gotten rich by trading. The doge didn't want to spend all the city's money fighting; so the pope sent a monk, Fra Bartolomeo, to convince the doge to join the fight. And what was strange was that all of that was real, their father mused. There really had been a Fra Bartolomeo in Venice, trying to persuade the doge to aid the pope.

But the book they were reading, he went on, was just a story. Rashid wasn't real. There wasn't a historian in the world who would believe he'd existed, and besides . . .

"Dad," Jared finally cut in. "Maybe you could just read it to us."

"Oh! Okay! Sorry, I got a little carried away." He smiled sheepishly. "I've lost my place. Where were we?"

"The monk, Fra Bartolomeo," Jared reminded him. "He made Rashid go with him after he found him with the, um, you know, the uh . . ." He couldn't say it. He wasn't sure he could get the words out of his mouth without giving the secret away.

"The treasures," Shireen jumped in, shaking her head at Jared. Could he be any more obvious? "Fra Bartolomeo kidnapped Rashid after he found him with the treasures in the doge's courtyard. But the story doesn't say where he took him. Only that a week passed and Signor Isaac and Rashid's uncle were going frantic looking for him, and then Fra Bartolomeo came back. Alone. He showed up at the doge's palace to try to convince him about the crusade. You were just starting to read that part, remember?"

"Great, yes, thanks," their father nodded. "You *are* listening!" He found his place, took another half minute to get the Latin straight, then started to read.

How can you refuse?" Fra Bartolomeo was glaring at the doge.

They were in the doge's audience chamber. The sky beyond the bank of windows was a deep purple black. Night had fallen over Venice. The doge was seated at the middle of the long table, his red-cloaked counselors flanking him, Maria and Francesca standing behind their guardian. Fra Bartolomeo had given them a dismissive look when he had been ushered into the room. The doge noticed. "If you have something to say, Maria and Francesca will hear it," he informed Fra Bartolomeo coldly. "I am Venice, and these girls are mine. Now speak."

The monk's dark eyes glittered angrily under his hood, but he collected himself and began. All the time he was speaking, Maria couldn't get the image out of her head: Fra Bartolomeo sweeping across the courtyard of the palace; the turbaned boy crouched over his book, a strange, almost ecstatic look on his face, his hands moving over the opened page, and then, as the monk called out to him, his palms filling with glowing treasures. She'd gasped and taken a step back up the stairs, clasping Francesca's wrist. Then Fra Bartolomeo was bending over Rashid, whispering something to him. And then they were gone, the monk pulling the boy after him through the gates of the palace, disappearing into the dark.

What did it all mean?

"War," Fra Bartolomeo was telling the doge firmly. "The Muslims have taken Jerusalem. They control all of the Holy Land. It is a sacrilege. It is an insult to all

Christians. That is our land. The land of *our* God. We must take it back from these infidels! How can you refuse, my lord? We are at war with the enemies of our faith. While you sit here, they are gathering their strength. Do you think that they will be content with this triumph? Do you not know that soon, very soon, they will launch their fleets from the Holy Land to take our cities from us? To destroy our churches? To destroy our faith? There is no avoiding this battle. God wills it. The pope demands it. If we do not bring the fight to Jerusalem, the infidels will assault us here, in our homes, in our cities."

The monk's voice rose. "Have they not told you what they have seen?" He was pointing an accusing finger at the two girls. Maria could feel the heat burning from his cowl-shadowed eyes. "Our enemies have already been here, in your own palace, armed with magic. You cannot avoid this fight, mighty Doge, it has already come to you. Our foes have sent their assassins here, to Venice. They will stop at nothing. They will attack us through the hands of a child. Have these girls not told you what they have seen? The time for waiting has passed. You must join the battle now!"

The doge glanced from left to right, taking in the looks of his counselors. Their expressions were grim.

"No," he pronounced. "This is not our war. And Maria and Francesca—leave them out of this. They have told me

what they saw. It was some trick of the light. It means nothing." He rose, his ermine-fringed robe sweeping behind him, his counselors scuffling out of their chairs to take their places beside him.

"A trick of the light?" Fra Bartolomeo's voice rose disbelievingly. "You believe that was a mere trick of the light? The boy was here! In your own palace. Armed with magic. Do you believe he was some mere bookseller's nephew? No, I tell you, it was a plot! His Muslim uncle and the Jew who came with him brought the boy here to kill you. They sought to strike you down, in your palace, so Venice would be without a leader—weak, ready to fall when the infidel fleets appear on the horizon. That boy is a magician. An assassin. He has brought this war to you!"

The doge looked back at Fra Bartolomeo. "So you say. But where is the proof? Bring me the proof of this magic and we will talk of this again. But until then, I wish to see no more of you."

He turned his back and glided from the room, his counselors flanking him.

Maria and Francesca were beginning to follow when the monk's voice caught them. His tone had shifted. The rage was gone. He was now pleading.

"You saw, daughters of Christ, I know you saw. Will you not help?"

"Help?" Francesca paused. She turned to the monk's imploring figure. "Help how?"

"Shh, Francesca," Maria took the younger girl's hand. "The doge has spoken. This is not our business. Come, come now." She led her from the audience chamber, the weight of the monk's eyes heavy on her back.

"Christendom," his voice called out against the closing door as Maria guided Francesca in the direction of the crowd of counselors scurrying at the doge's back. "You hold the fate of Christendom. The doge must send his troops to Jerusalem or Christendom will fall. We must take back Jerusalem."

The fate of Christendom? The words were running round and round in Maria's head an hour later. They were in their bedroom, in the doge's private suite of chambers. Francesca was already asleep, her chest rising and falling, her long golden hair fanned out over the pillow. But Maria couldn't rest. What had the monk meant? They held Christendom's fate? How? Why? Because of what they had seen the boy doing?

She felt uneasy. The doge, her guardian, had been so certain when they told him what had happened. "Your eyes deceived you," he'd insisted. "There are no magic books." Francesca had nodded mutely and Maria hadn't corrected him.

No one corrected the doge. But she knew otherwise. That wasn't moonlight in Rashid's hands. His palms had been filled with treasures. Treasures he'd pulled out of the book.

She closed her eyes and crossed herself. Was Fra Bartolomeo right?

"I still don't get it." Miranda was looking up at their father. He'd just closed the book and asked them to say their prayers. She reached out to tug on the edge of his shirt before he made it out the door. "What do Rashid's treasures have to do with the monk's crusade? It doesn't make any sense. Rashid's not even from Jerusalem. He's from Spain. They're in opposite directions. Why would the monk believe there's any connection?"

"When people are sure that they're right," their dad answered, "they can believe almost anything." He paused as if he was going to say something else, but then he just leaned down to give her another kiss. "It's just a story, sweetheart. Now go to sleep." He closed the door behind him.

"Does she believe him?" Miranda asked her brother and sister once the coast was clear. She sat up, frowning. "Maria? She can't believe Fra Bartolomeo, can she? It's so obvious that he can't be trusted. He kidnapped Rashid!"

"And Rashid kidnapped my signore," Maldini purred sternly as he crept out from under her bed. "So perhaps *he* is the bad one. And those girls. Have you thought of that?"

It was Jared's turn to frown. "Rashid and the girls? No way. There's got to be a reason why they took your master."

"And maybe there is a reason Fra Bartolomeo took Rashid," Maldini answered, his golden eyes flashing.

"You really believe that?" Jared asked.

Maldini paused. "No. I do not trust this monk. I do not trust anyone who wishes to start a war. But tell me, based on what has been happening here, in Venice, now, not from what that book says: What reason do we have to trust Rashid and his companions?"

"Just, well . . ."

"Well, what?" Maldini pressed.

"Well, just because," Jared answered lamely.

"Because you are sure you are right?" the cat responded sharply. "And so you believe. Even when the facts say something else?"

Jared looked to Shireeen for help. She shook her head. It was all too confusing.

"Enough of this," Maldini purred. "We will find no answers this way. There is only one fact that matters. Those thieves have taken my signore. We must find them. Then we can discover whom to believe. Jared," he finished curtly, "please call the faun."

Jared felt as though his brain would explode as he started tapping on the crayon drawing to get Silvio's attention. Rashid couldn't be bad. No matter how scary he and the two girls had looked in the old man's shop, there had to be a reason they were stealing things. But the cat's words bothered him. There was something about the way Maldini was talking and looking at him that he didn't get.

And then, as Silvio emerged from the cottage and began crossing the clearing to the surface of the drawing, he suddenly realized what it was. *It was his fault!* The very first night *he'd* held onto the die instead of putting it away somewhere safe, like he should have. *He'd* let it fall out of his hand and wake up the book too soon. *He'd* called Rashid and the others to life before that was supposed to happen. Maldini had been saying it all along. Right from the beginning things hadn't been going the way he'd expected. Rashid, Maria, and Francesca had come to life too soon. They'd started their robberies too soon. Even if there was a reason for what they were doing, they'd ended up kidnapping Maldini's signore. If it wasn't for him, for that stupid little mistake, for always wanting to do things his own way, the old man wouldn't be missing. The shopkeeper would have had a chance to explain everything, and they'd have been on their guard. They'd have been able to protect him with Silvio and Lorenzo il Piccolo. But they hadn't been there when he needed them. And now he was gone. It was Jared's fault, and Maldini knew it. The cat was just too polite to say it. Jared felt sick.

"Medusa's snakes! What's eating you, lad?" Silvio demanded as he came climbing out of the forest, a rakish grin on his face. His arms were full, a half-empty bottle of wine in one hand and a stack of books and postcards balanced in the crook of his other arm. Jared ignored him. The feeling at the pit of his stomach was getting sharper.

"Where'd you get that?" Shireen asked Silvio suspiciously, pointing at the bottle. "That's not a crayon bottle. That's real."

"From the kitchen." Silvio beamed and took a swig. "While you were gallivanting around Venice this afternoon."

"You stole my parents' wine?"

"Sampled. I merely sampled a bottle or two." He gestured vaguely back at the drawing that Miranda had carefully retaped to the wall, wiping his mouth with the back of his hand. A scattering of tiny glass bottles were littered at the foot of one of the trees. They were empty.

"How much did you drink?" Shireen cried out. "You think my parents won't notice all that wine missing?"

"A point, a point, you have a point." The faun smiled roguishly. He set down his load of books and postcards on Miranda's bed and tugged on his beard. "Aha!" he announced, spotting the red crayon on the floor. "Easily solved." He picked it up and carefully colored in the empty bottles in the drawing, then reached in to pluck them out. "Here." He handed the refilled bottles to Shireen. "Just slip those back into the kitchen when you get a chance. They'll never notice a thing."

"But it's *crayon*!" Shireen burst out.

"Wine ferments." Silvio shook his head mournfully. "Your father is a man of the world. He'll understand."

"I hope you've been saving your allowance, Jared," Shireen snapped at her brother, taking the bottles from Silvio in disgust. "You're going to need to buy some wine to feed your pet."

"Pet?" Silvio echoed. He drew himself up to his full height and expanded his chest. "Minerva's owl, I'm no pet. I am a faun of the ancient Roman line. Tell me," he added, raising an eyebrow. "Could a pet do this?" He puffed out his cheeks, swelled his throat up like a bullfrog, and let out a loud volley of burps.

"Silvio, you fool." Maldini twitched his whiskers as Miranda burst out laughing and Shireen fought back a grin. "Stop that nonsense. We have work to do." He pawed at the stack of books and loose pile of postcards on Miranda's bed. "Come, children, I need your help."

"What are those?" Miranda asked.

"Museum guides," the cat answered. "I had Silvio gather them from around the apartment while you were out this afternoon." He began sorting through the cards. "I take it he found these, too." The postcards all had images of paintings or statues on them.

"Mom collects them," Shireen explained. "But why do we need all this stuff?"

"We need another plan," Maldini told her. "My signore has been missing for a full day, and we can't just roam the city at random looking for him." He poked at a postcard. "The thieves always go after relics. So I have been thinking. Rather than waiting to catch up with them, we must find a way to get ahead of them."

"But how?" Jared asked, avoiding Maldini's eye.

"By knowing where they are going next," the cat responded matter-of-factly. "We must discover the location of every prized relic in Venice. And then we must be there first, waiting for them."

Jared thought quickly. There must be hundreds of relics in Venice! How were they going to guess the right one? But this was no time to argue with Maldini. Who was he to tell the cat they shouldn't try? So he chose a guidebook and started skimming it, as though he were convinced. Shireen and Miranda followed suit, and before long they were all working through the guides and postcard stack, trying to map out where Rashid and the two girls might be headed next.

A church bell tolled off in the distance, sending little echoes of sound rippling across the canal waters. As if it had rung for him, Lorenzo il Piccolo came stalking out of the closet. It was the first appearance he'd made since early that morning.

He strode over to Shireen. "My lady," he growled in his low gravelly voice. "Will you permit me to make a social call?"

"A social call?" She looked up from the book in her lap.

"Yes," Lorenzo il Piccolo affirmed. "I wish to visit my father."

"You have a father?" She looked at Lorenzo il Piccolo and tried to think. Did he mean a sculptor or stonecutter? How could a statue have a father?

"Yes," Lorenzo il Piccolo replied, a little ill-temperedly. "Don't we all? May I make the visit?"

"Um, yes," Shireen answered. "Of course." She had no idea what he was talking about. Judging from the looks on Jared and Miranda's faces, neither did they. Maldini, meanwhile, took the lion's request with utter annoyance.

"Fine time to abandon us," he said archly.

"I will never abandon my lady," Lorenzo il Piccolo answered pointedly. "As for you, cat, I owe you nothing."

He was off before Maldini could respond, springing up to the jamb of the skylight and wriggling through onto the roof outside. "Call me if you have need," he said, turning briefly back to hold Shireen's gaze, "and I will come."

She knew she could trust him. If he said he'd be back, he'd be back. So she set aside the mystery of this visit to his "father," waved off the questioning looks the others were giving her, and returned to the guide-book, resisting the impulse to climb up onto the bed under the skylight to see if she could get one last look at him. He'd be back. She knew he'd be back.

12
Proof!

Another day had passed. They hadn't made any progress with Maldini's plan. There were just too many guidebooks to look through to have any guess of where the thieves were going to turn up next. They were stuck in the bedroom again. Night was falling over the skylight. Silvio had hidden himself inside the thatched cottage in the crayon drawing. Maldini was under the bed. Lorenzo il Piccolo hadn't come back. A gloom was sinking over all of them. And it didn't get any better when their father came in, settled himself on the corner of Jared's bed, opened the book, and began to read.

The door creaked open. Rashid sat up, startled by the noise, and looked around. Where was he? Had it all been a bad dream? No. He was where he had been last night, where he'd been for almost a week: in the cramped cell on the island where the monk had taken him. He hadn't been dreaming. He was still the monk's prisoner.

Fra Bartolomeo was standing in the doorway, still draped in his black robes, studying him. One of the guards was hulking at the monk's side, a long sword dangling from his belt, a loaf of bread and a pitcher of water in his hands. The monk gestured the guard into the cell. "Feed the boy."

Rashid eyed the food suspiciously. He was aching with hunger and thirst, but he'd finally figured it out. It must have started that first night at the doge's palace. Everything had happened so quickly. One second he'd been staring up at the severe figure looming over him in the courtyard, then the monk had clasped a hand over his mouth and hauled him through the palace gates to the nearest dock, waving his squad of guards to follow. They'd taken him to a boat anchored in the lagoon and locked him in a cabin. He'd heard the slap of sails unfurling and felt the slow rocking motion under his feet as the ship set out onto open water. "Uncle Mounir!" he'd shouted. "Uncle Mounir! Help me!" But no help came.

After that everything was a blur. Sometime during the night a guard had entered the cabin and pushed a plate of food in Rashid's face. "Eat!" he'd commanded. Rashid had shaken his head. He didn't trust himself to say anything. He wasn't going to let them hear him crying again. He'd barely had time to wipe the tracks of tears off his cheeks. But the guard wouldn't let him refuse. He'd held the point of his sword to Rashid's throat and forced him to swallow the cold, greasy stew. The next thing Rashid knew, it was morning and they were marching him off the boat, half-dragging his dull, woozy body across a harbor and up a hill to a gray cluster of stone buildings overlooking the wooded slopes of a small island. They must have crossed quite far out into the sea, he realized. There was no sight of land beyond the island's shore. But there were other monks there, dressed in robes just like the ones cloaking Fra Bartolomeo. One of them, a heavy, red-faced man with closely shaven hair who seemed to be in charge, had given Rashid a curious look and started to question Fra Bartolomeo. But Fra Bartolomeo had waved the portly friar off dismissively, flashing a letter with a red wax seal in his face. He'd snapped something about the pope before ordering his troop of guards to steer Rashid to a long line of empty whitewashed cells. They'd thrown him inside one of the cramped cubes and bolted the door.

Later that day Rashid had been vaguely aware of Fra Bartolomeo coming in to stare at him, but he'd been too bleary to do anything except gaze back. He couldn't figure out why he felt so dull minded. "Watch him!" the monk had ordered the guards. "I must return to Venice to speak with the doge. I will be back within the week." And then it was day after day of lying there listlessly as the rectangle of light from the barred window above his straw pallet crept across the cell floor before fading into dusk. One evening Rashid had finally figured it out: They must be feeding him something that made him so groggy and weak. He had turned his back on the bowl of watery pasta and beans the guard had shoved through the cell door and crawled back to the pallet.

Now it was morning. He could hear a sparrow singing through the barred window. The sun was throwing its light into the cell, indifferent to his fate. And Fra Bartolomeo was back, eyeing him curiously. "Ah," he whispered, gesturing at the uneaten bowl of food, a net of flies buzzing over it. "Clever *ragazzo*."

He broke a loaf in half, tore off a mouthful, and dipped it in the pitcher of water. Rashid watched him swallow. "Come, boy," Fra Bartolomeo said. "Eat. The food is good. I need your mind sharp today." He held out the loaf.

Rashid started to refuse. But what was the use? The

guard was already stepping forward menacingly, a hand on the hilt of his sword. Rashid took the bread from the monk's hand. "Good boy." Fra Bartolomeo smiled thinly down at him. "It seems you are capable of listening to reason." He reached into a pocket of his robe and held out the treasures Rashid had pulled from Ala ad-Din's cave: the rings, the die, the bag of powder. "So, tell me, what were you planning that night in the courtyard? It seems the doge is not convinced of the evil you can do. We will have to show him how these things work. Then perhaps he will understand the danger you have brought into his house. Those Venetians. All they care about is trade. They would do business with anyone. They care nothing for the purity of the Church. But I will teach them. They will learn the danger that you and your kind pose! Show me," he continued, setting aside the rings and holding out the powder-filled pouch. "What can this do?"

Rashid stared at it vacantly.

"Guard!" the monk commanded.

The soldier came over and forced Rashid's hand into the bag. Rashid pulled out a palmful of the dust and let it fall.

A golden flash of light burst through the cell. The monk and soldier drew back, alarmed. But nothing more happened. The powder drifted to the floor and extinguished itself—all except a few grains, which lay there pulsing like unexploded seeds of light.

The monk thrust his own hand into the pouch, sifting through the dust. He threw a twist into the air. Nothing happened. He tried again with the same lack of result. "Now why is that, boy?" He glared at Rashid. "Why will it not work for me? What devil's power do you possess?"

Rashid shook his head helplessly. His fingers tingled, but he had no idea how he had made the powder explode.

They made him reach into the pouch again and again. Each time, the monk studied him carefully as the dust fell from his fingers and exploded into light, searching to see if Rashid was muttering some secret words or spell over it, demanding that he explain what was happening. But there was nothing to see or to tell. Rashid had no idea how he was making the powder flash. Eventually the monk gave up. He tucked the leather pouch back in the pocket of his robes, and then the guard was forcing one of the rings onto Rashid's finger, jamming it over his knuckle. It flared with light and again the guard stepped back, pulling in his breath with a sharp hiss and crossing himself.

But it wasn't the light that held Rashid's attention. A sweet singsong voice was calling out to him. "Boy! Boy! What are they doing to you? Do you need help?"

He looked around, startled. The voice was coming from

a little brown-feathered sparrow sitting on the window ledge of the cell.

"Fly!" Rashid shouted out desperately. "Quick, fly to Venice! Find my uncle, at the house of Signor Isaac. Tell him that I am being kept prisoner. Tell him to come!" But instead of flying out of the window, the bird darted into the room and landed on Rashid's shoulder, a curious gleam in its pomegranate-seed eyes.

"You speak sparrow?" it chirped happily.

Before Rashid could respond, Fra Bartolomeo reached out and trapped the bird's soft head between his thumb and index finger, and with one violent flick of his wrist, snapped its neck.

"No games!" he spat out, dropping the broken body onto the floor. "Have you not seen? There is no one here to help you." He pulled Rashid's hand closer to get a better look at the shining ring. "So, this is another thing you can enchant. What were you planning to do with this? Make the birds of the air your infidel spies? How does it work, boy? Tell me how it works. You will tell me the secret of this black art!"

Rashid collapsed to his knees beside the dead bird, shaking his head in despair.

Fra Bartolomeo jerked him back onto his feet. "Tell me!" he shouted. He caught hold of the silver chain hanging around Rashid's neck and was twisting it in a knot. Rashid could feel the metal biting into his skin.

"You will tell me your plan," the monk raged as the chain twisted tighter and tighter, cutting off Rashid's breath. "You will teach me how your magic works. And then we will see who will win this war!" Then his eyes widened. He was looking through Rashid, staring into an invisible place. "I will do it!" he exulted. "I will do it! I will lead the conquest!"

Rashid's fingers were scrabbling at the chain, trying to break it before it completely cut off his air supply. Red lights were flashing in front of his eyes. "Enough," the monk spat, letting go of the silver links and pushing Rashid away. He staggered back, sucking in deep gulps of air.

The monk wiped his hands against his robe as if he'd been touching something filthy. "That is enough. For now. But you will tell me, boy. You *will* tell me." He spun on his heel and strode from the cell.

Rashid woke with a start. Someone was squatting over him, shaking him by the shoulder. Night had fallen. A blazing torch had been placed in a bracket on the wall, casting flickering shadows. He sat up and pushed himself hard against the wall of the cell, his fingers reflexively touching the bruise on his neck.

"Do not worry, boy," Fra Bartolomeo whispered. The dancing shimmer of torchlight outlined the monk's robed body; it looked like a giant bat had flown into the cell and was hovering over him, looking for a vein to pierce. "I will not harm you. As long as you are obedient."

"How long have you been here?" Rashid asked, trying to keep his body from trembling. Somehow the thought of Fra Bartolomeo crouching over him while he slept, watching him, was worse than anything that had happened earlier. He darted his hand up to feel the weight of the pen hanging from the chain around his neck and then quickly pulled it away. The pen was still there. The monk hadn't taken that away from him yet. It couldn't do him any good. But it was his—the last link to his uncle and his real life. The life he used to have.

"Long enough," Fra Bartolomeo said with a tight smile. "Long enough to learn something. Can you smell it?" He extended his hand. Something was balanced in his palm. Rashid couldn't make it out in the swaying light.

"Smell?" he asked uncertainly.

"Yes, my boy, smell," Fra Bartolomeo whispered. He held his hand closer to show Rashid what he was holding. The dead sparrow was nestled in his palm. "Do you not smell it?"

"No," Rashid stammered, utterly confused. He was sliding his back along the wall, trying to get away.

"Why not?" Fra Bartolomeo's smile grew tighter. "It has been dead for most of a day. Why has corruption not set in? Why is there no stench? You should smell something. Here!" He flicked his wrist. The twisted mass of feathers and claws flew at Rashid. He caught it instinctively. "Look at it," Fra Bartolomeo demanded. "Look at it!"

Rashid reluctantly dropped his gaze. The bird's brown head was nestled against the tips of his fingers, bent at a terrible angle from its body. The black, seed-round eyes stared up at him sadly. Little specks of gold glinted from the feathers of its wings. But the monk was right. The body wasn't stiff and cold like it should have been. It was warm. The muscles beneath the feathers were still supple. And he didn't smell anything.

"Ahh, you see it too," Fra Bartolomeo breathed. "It is not dead. Nor is it alive. But it is not dead. Something is holding it back."

"What?" Rashid asked with a shiver.

"I think you know," the monk answered.

Rashid's eyes returned to the broken creature in his hand. What had happened to it? And then he noticed. Those golden specks on the feathers—he'd seen them before. The image came rushing back. The golden powder exploding in the air, then falling to the floor. The golden seeds lying there, still gently throbbing. He looked down to the floor. There they were. Right where the bird had fallen, Rashid could make out a faint scattering of the golden granules. That's what was sparkling in its feathers. Some of the powder must have gotten onto the sparrow's wings.

"Now, boy," the monk whispered, "bring it all the way back."

He pressed Rashid's free hand into the pouch, forcing him to take hold of a thick pinch of the powder and sprinkle it over the feathered corpse. There was a burning flash, and the next moment the sparrow was twitching in Rashid's hand, brushing its fluttering wings against his palm. Fra Bartolomeo stared at the revived sparrow in victorious wonder. He ran his fingers gently down its ruffled throat feathers, feeling the pulse of breath, then squeezed tight and choked the life out of it again. Rashid watched in horror as he tossed the bird to the floor and hurried from the cell, leaving the guard behind to stand watch. Minutes later he was back, carrying an ornate silver box. He opened it and took out what looked like an ancient yellowing human bone. A finger.

"Now this one," he commanded, setting the bone on the floor.

Rashid drew back in disgust.

"Do it!" The guard's sword was already halfway out of his scabbard. Rashid felt a wave of nausea run through his body. But what choice did he have?

He took another pinch of powder and threw. The golden dust rained down, and the finger was alive. It had reclothed itself with skin and was twitching on the stone floor, as if it had just been hacked off an invisible hand.

"Oh, yes!" The monk bent over to seize hold of the quivering finger. "Oh, yes!" He gazed at it in rapture for a long, sickening minute before turning back on Rashid. Then his eyes went distant again. "I knew. Oh, yes, I knew. I knew I had found you for a reason. I knew that God had given you to me. You have mastered a dark power. Now I will take it and use it for our cause. With your rings and your golden powder, who will resist me? I will lead the army to Jerusalem. Our enemies will tremble when they see that I have taken their magic from them! They will quail when they see that I can bring the very dead themselves to life! Yes! Yes! Now we can do it! Now we can bring this war to an end! Now we can reclaim the Holy Land!" His voice rang out with exaltation. "Now we will win! The doge asked for proof? Here is his proof. And more, far more. Proof and power. He cannot deny me now. *No one* can resist me now! I will do it! I will raise the dead to battle. I will win this war!"

13
The Third Side of the Die!

Their father had closed the book there, giving it a hard stare, as if he wasn't sure that he should keep going. "Kids, isn't this a bit creepy for you?" he'd finally asked. "Maybe we should pick out something else for tomorrow night." They'd shaken their heads and assured him the book was okay.

But now that he was gone, there was no point pretending. For a long time no one said anything. The image of Fra Bartolomeo scooping up the twitching finger and crowing in triumph was too raw. This didn't feel like an adventure anymore. It was more like opening a closet door and finding yourself sucked inside a horror movie.

Finally Maldini came from under the bed and called Silvio out of the forest drawing. "Come," he purred, pawing again at the guidebooks, "we must get to work."

But Jared couldn't make himself join in. The sick feeling wasn't a feeling anymore. It was a cancer. What had he done? What had he woken up? His mind was racing. He couldn't figure it all out. But some things were getting clearer. That bone Fra Bartolomeo had made Rashid bring to life—it was a relic. It had to be. And now Rashid and the girls were out there stealing more. You didn't have to be a genius to guess why. The monk had come back to life too. They were stealing those things for him. But why? Why were they working for Fra Bartolomeo? And what was the monk planning to do with the relics? He tried to remember everything that had been stolen: a foot, an arm bone, part of the cross. . . . What else had Dad read to them from the paper? What was Fra Bartolomeo up to? He was going to bring all those things back to life?

And where was Maldini's signore? Where had they taken *him*?

Jared let his head fall back on his pillow. He couldn't make himself think about it anymore.

Everyone else was hard at work. Only Lorenzo il Piccolo was missing. He still hadn't come back from his visit to his "father." Every now and then Shireen glanced up uneasily at the skylight, but there was no sign of him yet. Jared forced himself to his feet and got a wad of the postcards. He started thumbing through them listlessly, trying to concentrate on the endless paintings of Mary and Joseph and Jesus, and the thousand and one saints Mom had taught them about that he'd never paid attention to.

What is the point? he was thinking a quarter of an hour later as he turned over the twentieth postcard of Saint Mark and ran his eyes dully over the next image. It was hopeless. They were never going to guess where Rashid and the girls were going next. There were too many churches and museums and relics in Venice. He looked over to try to catch Shireen's attention, but she ignored him. He couldn't blame her. If he hadn't gone rifling through the bag of treasures in the old man's shop, they'd never have been in this mess in the first place. He'd opened that closet door, and pulled his sisters along behind him. And now the old shopkeeper had been yanked through it too.

He closed his eyes and took a deep breath. He'd gotten them into this trouble. It was up to him to find the way out. But what could he possibly do?

He decided that the one thing he had to concentrate on was Maldini's signore. If it wasn't for him, Maldini's signore wouldn't be gone. He had to get Fra Bartolomeo out of his head. If they could just find the old man and bring him back to his shop, then it could all be over. The rest of it wasn't his responsibility. It had all happened a long time ago. If they could just track down Maldini's signore, then everything would be okay. But how? The question kept running through his thoughts, but his mind drew nothing but blanks.

Unless . . . Jared's heart suddenly leaped. He jammed his hand under his pillow and pulled his die out of its hiding place. There it was, staring him in the face. Why hadn't he thought of it before? He started speed-flipping through another stack of postcards. A minute later he'd found it. It was a match, a perfect match.

"Um, hey," he called out. "I think I found something."

"What?" Maldini purred.

He held the card up for them to see. It showed one of Carpaccio's paintings: *Saint George and the Dragon*. Their mom had taken them to see the original their first week in Venice, at the lodge house of the Scuola di San Giorgio degli Schiavoni. The knight was clad in gleaming black armor, charging a dragon astride a coal-black horse. The tip of his lance had pierced the dragon's scaly beak. A trampled scattering of human bones lay all around the horse's hooves and the dragon's taloned feet. The dragon was rearing up, the coiled mass of its tail lashing the ground behind it, its blue and green and gold wings extended wide. Its eyes were full of hate.

"Ulysses's dog! That's a fierce-looking creature!" Silvio muttered.

"Doubtless," Maldini responded dryly. He'd leaped up onto Jared's bed to get a better look. "It's a dragon. They are a fierce breed." He went quiet as he studied the postcard. After a moment he cocked his head up at Jared. "How will this help us?"

"We're never going to guess where they're going next," Jared explained slowly, unconsciously shifting his weight from one foot to another, as if finding his balance on his skateboard. "There are too many relics. And even if we do find the thieves, they could always get away on their boat."

"So?" Shireen said impatiently.

"So . . . if we could be up in the air, we could see

where they were headed," Jared answered.

"How are we going to do that?" Miranda asked.

He held out the wooden cube. "There's a dragon on my die, remember? I think . . . I *think* all I've got to do is roll it and bring the dragon in the card to life. Then we can ride on its back. We can follow their boat. Maybe that will take us to Maldini's signore."

"You want to call a *dragon* out of the postcard?" Shireen demanded, dumbfounded. "A *dragon*?"

"Um, yes," Jared answered.

"Are you nuts?" She lit into him. "Did you get a good look at it? Did you see all the dead people? It'll kill us!"

"No, it won't," Maldini interrupted. He was studying the postcard with a slow thoughtful look. "At least I don't think it will. That's not the way the die works. If Jared summons the dragon, I think it will have to obey him. Silvio, what do you say? When Jared first brought you to life, could you have done anything to hurt him?"

"First brought me to life! First brought me to life?" Silvio flared at Maldini. "I'll tell you what, Mr. Cat—you've never lived until you've been a faun in a forest, a flask of wine in your hand, a buxom wench dancing alongside you!" he added to the others, his natural good temper swiftly reasserting itself. "Helen's lips, I'll teach you about life before all this is done, just you see! But to your point, to your point"—he turned back to the cat—"no, I don't believe I could have done the lad any harm, even if I had wanted to, sweet fellow that he is." He rubbed Jared's hair. "I daresay the dragon will be quite safe. Docile as a lamb. And if not, he'll have Silvio the faun to reckon with!"

"Well, then, let the reckoning begin!" a low voice growled. It was Lorenzo il Piccolo, rumbling at them from the skylight, back from wherever he'd been on his visit to his "father." "Do you not catch that scent? The thieves have returned, and they are close. Enough of this talk. Let's be on our way!

"Shireen," he growled in an afterthought, "my noble father sends you his greetings. Now come!"

They were back on the roof. Silvio balanced on the shadowy edge of the stone gutter, holding out the postcard of *Saint George and the Dragon*. Twenty feet down the rooftop from him, Miranda, Maldini, and Lorenzo il Piccolo waited as Jared got ready to roll the die into his cupped palm. In the distance a church bell rang the hour. It was eleven o'clock. Time to get on with it. Jared stole one last look at the postcard. From this distance, he couldn't make out the dragon against the enfolding blanket of night, but he knew it was there, snarling in pain at the lance jutting through its open mouth. He closed his eyes, breathed a quick prayer, and tumbled the die.

Nothing happened.

The cube had turned to the image of the troubador. Jared took a deep breath and rolled it again.

The shining engraving of the book rolled face up.

"Hurry up!" Lorenzo il Piccolo urged.

Jared rolled it a third time. The die turned over in his hand, trembled on its edge, then flipped over.

A bitter howl of pain and rage split the sky and echoed across the rooftop as the third side of the die burst into light. Half a second later Jared heard a leathery flapping of wings and then a scuffling of sharp claws across stony ground. He peered across the rooftop to the postcard in Silvio's hands. There was another set of noises: a high whinnying groan of agony and a muttered oath. What was going on? He darted across the gutter to Silvio. In an instant, he could make out what had happened. The die had woken the dragon a fraction of a moment before its spell had animated Saint George and his horse. While the knight was still frozen, the dragon had snapped the shaft of the lance buried in its mouth, hurled itself across the rocky ground separating it from the saint and his charger, and lashed out one razor-sharp claw, savaging the squealing horse's flank. It was about to sink its fangs into Saint George's neck!

Jared grabbed the postcard and shook it fiercely.

The dragon froze mid-lunge and turned its massive head. Saint George feverishly reined in his wounded, rearing horse and looked about, equally astonished. The dragon blinked its scaly eyelids. It had spotted Jared. Saint George had seen him too. For a moment the knight and the dragon both froze inside the postcard, and then, before Saint George could stop it, the dragon wheeled its long-tailed body around and advanced menacingly on the foreground of the picture.

Jared dropped the card and scurried back just in time. The dragon had broken the plane and hauled itself out onto the roof. Its muscles rippled down the length of its twenty-foot body. It began to advance across the tiles, yellow eyes trained on him. Jared spun around. Shireen and Miranda were backing up to the far corner of the guttered ledge, terrified looks on their faces. Maldini and Lorenzo il Piccolo were holding their ground on the slanting tiles. But what did that matter? Suddenly everything was very clear. Shireen had been right. This wasn't a game. A cat and a dog-sized lion didn't have a chance against the creature he'd woken up. He'd risked his sisters' lives. If he didn't get charge of the dragon now, they were all dead.

He braced his foot against the gutter and turned back around to confront the approaching beast. "Stop!" he shouted. "I command you!" To Jared's utter amazement, the dragon stopped. But it didn't look happy.

"Who are you?" it rasped. Its voice made Jared feel as though a piece of sandpaper was being dragged across his brain. Its long tongue roved uneasily around the broken shaft still piercing the roof of its mouth.

"I am your master," Jared answered, in a voice that didn't sound the least bit masterful to his own ears. He could feel his whole body quaking. He barely knew what he was saying. The words were coming out before he had time to think.

"My master, you say?" the dragon slurred angrily. A bloodstained drop of saliva spilled from the corner of its mouth onto the tiles of the roof. "I have no master! I am my own master; no one masters me!" Its scaly eyelids blinked slowly.

Get off the roof! Jared's mind was yelling at him. But again he heard himself speaking: "I am your master as long as I have this." He held up the glowing die. It shone like a piece of starlight in his hand.

"That!" the dragon sneered. Another viscous drop of blood fell from its mouth. "You put your trust in that? Let me tell you something, boy: I will swallow that bauble in an instant. Then I will feast on you!"

"Try it, then!" came another voice. Jared turned in surprise. It was Maldini, stalking down the gutter to his side. "Devour the boy or acknowledge his power over you. But do it now. We're in a hurry."

"Maldini!" Miranda shouted.

"Now, dragon! Do it now!" Maldini insisted.

Jared saw the muscles in the dragon's shoulders bunching. Its claws probed for a foothold on the curved tiles as it prepared to spring. On the far side of the roof, Silvio shook out of his trance, seized hold of the spiked tip of the dragon's tail, and pulled with all his strength. "Forget the boy," he shouted as he tugged, a fighting grin on his face. "First you have a faun to deal with. By Bacchus's grapes, you shan't touch that lad until you've dealt with me!"

The dragon laughed, flicked its massive tail, and

sent Silvio sprawling across the angled slope of the roof. He lay there stunned, barely able to stop himself from sliding down the veering tiles, over the edge, and onto the alleyway below.

With a low roar, Lorenzo il Piccolo went on the attack, hurling himself onto the dragon's throat. Again the scaly beast was too quick. With one quick snap of its neck, it sent Lorenzo il Piccolo flying. The lion landed with a crash, a line of red tiles shattering underneath him. Now there was nothing barring the dragon's path but Jared and Maldini. But the cat didn't appear frightened. "Do it," he calmly repeated, pressing forward and twitching his whiskers. "Show us who is master."

The dragon laughed mockingly and prepared to leap at Jared. *That's it,* Jared thought as he felt his body going completely numb. *It's all over.* But this time the dragon's great rear quarters remained curled under its haunches. Its eager, hungry claws remained trapped in the tiles of the roof.

It couldn't move.

"Do it!" Maldini said again. "Show us who is master."

Still the dragon couldn't budge.

"Now do you see?" Maldini asked. "You cannot do it. There is a greater power at work here than you command. You cannot hurt them. Now acknowledge them. Who is this boy?"

The look on the dragon's face changed. With a long, slow, yellow-eyed blink, its rage turned into confusion, then to bitter acceptance. "Very well," it finally grumbled, only half coherently. Blood was now pouring from its mouth. "He is my master."

"Good," Maldini replied, "and don't forget it. Now, we must be on our way. Silvio! Lion! Over here."

Silvio and Lorenzo il Piccolo picked themselves up and scrambled over to the children, casting wary looks at the dragon. But Jared wasn't ready to leave things like this. He was still trembling with shock at what had just happened. He couldn't believe they were all still alive. But it wasn't right. Beating the dragon this way wasn't right.

"Maldini," he whispered, edging toward him, "I don't know what I was saying. I don't want to be the dragon's master. He needs to help us because he wants to, not because he has to. I want it to be like how it is with Silvio."

"A dragon is not a faun," Maldini hissed. "You cannot make friends with it."

"Maybe not," Jared answered. "But I want to try."

"We don't have time for this!"

"Maybe not." Jared looked the cat in the eye. "But I can't ask him to take us anywhere if we don't try."

Maldini went very still. Jared could see the muscles of his throat tightening, his tail frisking back and forth furiously.

"Very well, then," the cat finally purred. "What do you propose?"

Jared stared over at the sullen dragon. How could he make friends with that? But it was what he had to do. He knew it. He had to try.

"Silvio," he called to the faun.

"Yes?"

"I need some things from inside."

Jared quickly explained what he wanted, and in a moment the faun was climbing back up through the skylight. It took a few minutes. Jared could sense the cat's growing impatience. Lorenzo il Piccolo paced the rooftop's edge. He hadn't forgotten the powder Rashid had thrown at him. And after the dragon had tossed him across the rooftop, his dignity was more wounded than ever. He wasn't going to let the turbaned boy and those girls escape him a second time. "The thieves' scent is fading!" he growled. "They will get away."

"Quiet, Lorenzo," Shireen told him. She glanced

over at Jared worriedly. "I think Jared knows what he's doing."

Finally Silvio was back, carrying a large bath towel and a huge bottle of aspirin. Jared took the supplies from his hands. He indicated for Silvio to follow him, then started down the gutter to where the dragon crouched, staring sulkily at them.

"Dragon," he began, awed by the blood pooling on the tiles under the beast, "we need your help. But first we want to help you. Only, you have to promise to be good." *Well, that couldn't have sounded dorkier,* Jared berated himself.

"*Good?*" the dragon sneered thickly. Another spurt of blood from his mouth splattered on the roof. "What is good? I am not good! I am a prisoner."

"No, you're not," Jared answered. He forced himself to stand closer to the dragon's gaping jaws and look him directly in the eyes. The creature stared balefully back but didn't reply. Jared took that as all the promise he was going to get. "Silvio," he instructed, "get over there, behind his head. When I tell you, pull the lance out."

Silvio was about to protest, but the determined look in Jared's eyes silenced him.

"Okay, dragon," Jared continued. "This will hurt

at first, but then you'll feel better. I promise. Take these." He opened the bottle, and before the dragon could stop him, he'd reached into his open mouth and poured twenty or thirty aspirin down his throat. The dragon spluttered, but swallowed.

"Now, Silvio!" Jared commanded. "Pull!"

With one mighty wrench Silvio yanked the lance out. The dragon howled, gripped by pain. Tears splashed from his yellow eyes. But he was hardy. And the source of his agony was gone. For the first time since Carpaccio painted Saint George's lance piercing him five hundred years ago, he could close his mouth. His jaws snapped shut and he gave Jared an almost grateful look. Jared hurriedly wrapped the towel around the wound to

stanch the flow of blood. He knotted it firmly under the dragon's jaw. "Breathe through your nostrils," he told him. "All right, then!" He turned to his astonished sisters as he swung his leg over the dragon's back. "Let's go!"

14
Over the Lagoon

They were in the air, seated on the dragon's back, flying through the dark Venetian sky. Jared was straddling the dragon's neck, shouting directions. Shireen was behind him, her hands clenched around her brother's waist. The great stroke of the soaring creature's wings beat inches from her back. Silvio came next, holding Miranda tightly in his lap. Lorenzo il Piccolo was behind them, growling instructions for Shireen to pass on to Jared: "That way! That way! Follow the scent!" Maldini was at the very rear, a fighting look in his golden eyes. Hundreds of feet below, the city spread itself out for their inspection.

From this glorious, terrifying height, Venice looked like a map of itself: the miniature squares, the bell towers rising into the night sky, the maze of alleyways, the black ribbons of canals threading through the floating city. The cold air rushing past their faces stung their cheeks. The thudding beat of the dragon's wings echoed in their ears. As the floating city spun by beneath them, Jared felt his heart pounding harder and harder. He'd never been so frightened, or so happy.

But as they flew on, peering down intently for any sign of Rashid and the girls, he felt the first exhilaration start to fade. He'd taken too long with the dragon on the rooftop. The little boat wasn't anywhere to be seen. The night breeze had blown the scent away. Lorenzo il Piccolo had stopped calling out directions as the last trace vanished into the winter air. They were left to guessing, wheeling around in wider and wider circles.

They might not have spotted the thieves, but their soaring passage through the night air wasn't going unnoticed. As the patchwork of *calles*, *campos*, and canals passed beneath them, Shireen heard an occasional burst of puzzled growling. Her ring's glowing spark was calling out to the city's dozing lions, though never long enough to set them in pursuit of her. Before too long, though, other sounds began to fill the air: rustling and fluttering. The great flap of the dragon's wings had woken the fat-breasted pigeons sleeping on the roofs of Venice's bell towers and campaniles.

Within minutes, hundreds of them were speeding alongside the dragon, just feet from the rise and dip of his wings. "Who are you? Who are you?" they were cooing. Their eyes went wide as they realized how huge the dragon was and took in the sight of the cat, lion, faun, and three kids perched on its back. "What are you doing?"

"Hello, pigeons!" Miranda called out. She waved at the flanking escort of birds, the ring on her finger growing brighter and brighter as they zoomed close.

Then she recognized one of them. It was Daniela, the young pigeon who'd steered them through the mist to the old man's shop. She veered in and landed on Miranda's outstretched hand.

"Buona notte!" she said. "What is this bird you're flying on? *Mamma mia!* The wings on him! Is he from Rome?" she chirped excitedly. "Everything's bigger and better there. I've always wanted to go. It's so boring in Venice. Maybe he could take me!"

"He's not a bird!" Miranda responded, delighted to

see Daniela again. "He's a dragon."

"Ooh, I've heard about those," Daniela cooed appreciatively. She gave the dragon another long look. "But what are you doing on his back?"

"Looking for thieves," Miranda answered. She gestured at the city whizzing by beneath them.

"Is it fun?" Daniela asked. Then she thought of a better question. "Do your parents know?"

"No," Miranda said, looking around nervously. "It's a secret."

"Well, that's the thing for me," Daniela responded. "Not to mention that dragon of yours! You'll introduce me, won't you? When we find the thieves for you. Tell me what to look for!"

"Sure." Miranda grinned happily. Jared wasn't the only one who could help! Daniela listened attentively as Miranda described Rashid, Maria, and Francesca. Then she whirled away, delaying her return to her flanking companion birds just long enough to wing right past the dragon's great spiked head and catch his eye flirtatiously. Then she was off, passing the description of their quarry to the other pigeons and dispersing them far and wide before disappearing into the night.

And still the dragon, with his riders, flew. The

minutes were ticking by and there was no sight of the thieves. Jared's heart was sinking, and the same thought kept hammering away at him: He'd taken too long getting the dragon into the air.

Down below, the bells started to ring the half hour. It was eleven thirty. He called out to Shireen. "See anything?"

"No, not a thing!"

Jared frowned, bent over the beast's neck, and directed him higher. The dragon's wings dipped heavily and they soared up. Venice seemed to shrink as their sight line lengthened. But still there was no sign.

"Where to, boy?" the dragon rasped through his bandaged snout.

"I don't know," Jared confessed.

The dragon blinked at him. "Some master," he snarled.

Jared looked back over his shoulder. They were all watching him. Shireen, Miranda, Silvio, Lorenzo il Piccolo, Maldini. He was the only one who could guide the scaly beast. He looked anxiously to Shireen. "Which way?"

She started to shake her head in exasperation. He'd done it again. Only this time he'd saddled them with a dragon. A dragon! Her annoyance grew. Why didn't he ever *think* before rushing into things? But then the image of him standing there on the roof, ordering the creature to obey him when it had come lumbering at them, came crowding into her thoughts. And she knew what she had to say.

"The number one boat," she shouted back.

"What?"

"The number one boat, not the eighty-two. We just keep going. It'll be okay."

"What?" he asked again. What was she talking about?

"Getting on the number one boat instead of the eighty-two, way back when this all started. That wasn't a mistake. We were meant to be late. So the English bookstore would be closed and we'd wind up in the old man's shop. He and Maldini had been waiting for us, remember? Our names are in the book. You don't have to work it all out. This was supposed to happen. Just keep going."

"Where?"

"Wherever you say. You'll get us there."

"But I don't know where we're going!"

"Yes, you do, Jared. You do."

"You really believe that?"

"Yes." She nodded. "I do."

Jared swallowed and started to say something. The die, he needed to tell her what he'd figured out about rolling the book side of the die too soon. If she was going to trust him, she needed to know about that too. But Shireen shook him off. "C'mon, Jared. You called the dragon to life. You mastered it. We'll follow you. You just can't ever tell anyone that I said that. Ever! Okay?"

"Okay." He grinned back, putting his doubts away. He could tell her about the die later. She trusted him. That was the big thing. This was no time to mess that up. He was turning to veer the dragon off in a new direction when out of the corner of his eye he saw a grey speck come wheeling in.

"We've found them!" It was Daniela. "On their boat, making their way into the lagoon. Quick, this way."

Jared shouted the news to the dragon, who swung around to follow the darting pigeon. She was heading north, out over the wide stretch of water between Venice and its walled cemetery island. Then she veered off to the east, leading them farther out above the lagoon. Even this late at night there were boats plying the waters: great lumbering vaporettos hugging the perimeter of the city, and smaller, speedier vessels—water taxis, ambulance boats, and police launches, their cabin lights winking yellow or blue. But as Daniela guided them still farther out, the bobbing lights fell away. They'd left the main city of Venice far behind.

Then, in the gloom below, Jared saw a tiny flash of sparkling light. It had burst out of nowhere and extinguished itself almost immediately. But as the dust-speckled glow reflected off the inky water, he had time to make out a rowboat. Two small figures were pulling at its oars, while a third was kneeling in its prow.

Shireen had seen them too. "There they are!" she cried.

Lorenzo il Piccolo confirmed her verdict. His nostrils were flared wide, sifting the night's smells.

"Yes," he growled, "yes, my lady, I have their scent! Quick now, on them! They shall soon see what comes of making a fool of a lion!"

"Dive," Jared instructed the dragon. "There, up ahead!"

The dragon spread his wings, caught the current, ducked his snout, and they were speeding forward and down, down, down, until they were skimming the surface of the water, the guiding convoy of pigeons outpaced and forgotten, the dark wavelets of the lagoon snatching at their speeding feet, their zooming progress devouring the space between them and the slow-moving boat ahead.

"No!" Maldini suddenly called from the dragon's tail. "Wait! Shireen, tell Jared the dragon must climb. We can't catch them yet."

"Why not?" she called back over her shoulder.

"My signore is not with them! We must see where they have taken him."

"He's right," Miranda yelled over the rush of wind. "Tell Jared."

Jared didn't want to do it. The sheer joy of this soaring flight across the surface of the lagoon, the knowledge that in less than a minute they would be on the kidnappers in their boat, the knowledge that he'd done it, that he'd taken charge of the dragon, that he could command it to snatch them up in his claws was so pure, so intense, that Jared almost couldn't stand giving it up. But this wasn't about him. And he knew that, too. So he leaned forward and shouted, "Up! Up!"

The dragon turned his neck and narrowed his eyes. Did the boy truly intend to call him off? Wasn't it enough that he had made him his servant? But the towel-bandage tied around his snout made it hard for him to grunt more than one or two words, and Jared's look was insistent. *Up,* he had commanded. So, with a dismissive snort, the dragon did as instructed. He dipped and flapped his wings and raised his scaly body high into the night sky to join the circling company of pigeons.

Below them the boat shrank to miniature and then dissolved into the murky hollow of the night. But now Lorenzo il Piccolo had the scent, and wherever the boat steered, they followed it.

In the far distance behind them, the bells of Venice were tolling midnight.

The little rowboat came to shore on an island on the far outskirts of the lagoon. Jared had seen the flash of light burst over the dark waters and then tumble its glistening sparks into the waves three more times as they spied from the dragon's back. Rashid had been using his powder to navigate the darkness of the lagoon. Now, as the boat scraped in against the pebbly shore, Rashid sprinkled the powder on a piece of driftwood. The makeshift torch leaped into flame, and he led Maria and Francesca across the shore to a stone walkway that ran to the collapsed outer wall of some long-neglected settlement. The one Jared guessed

must be Maria had a sack of some sort slung over her shoulder.

Jared took a calming breath as the circling flight of the dragon brought the sight of Rashid and the girls directly into view. He'd seen them all before, crouching behind the window of the old man's store, but this felt different. And the questions—impossible questions—were crowding in. Could this really be the same boy Fra Bartolomeo had been tormenting in his cell centuries ago? Was that really Rashid, alive and prowling around Venice eight hundred years later? He knew it couldn't—shouldn't—be true. And yet, how could a stone lion come to life, a faun and a dragon spring out of paintings, a cat talk? If all that could be real, why not Rashid? And if this *was* him, and those were the two girls from the doge's palace, how far off could the monk be?

Jared pushed his hair back from the fringe of his cap and made himself shake all those problems off. *Come on*, he told himself, the wind stinging his eyes. *Remember: the number one boat.* Shireen was right. That hadn't been a mistake. He just had to keep going, even if he couldn't see the end of it yet. It couldn't be that different from having the edge of his board hanging out in space at the top of a half-pipe when he didn't know what trick he was going to pull and all the kids at the skate park were watching. He just had to lift his heel, kick the board, and take off. There was no time to wonder if he could nail it. He'd hit the trick or bust a rib trying. He leaned over the dragon's neck and pointed out a landing spot on the island's shore.

Glad to be on the ground again, everyone slid off the dragon's back just as Daniela came swooping down from the sky. Landing at Miranda's feet, she flashed her glittering eyes and chirped, "So, the introduction?"

Miranda bent down and let the pigeon climb up on her wrist. "Mr. Dragon," she said, holding the bird up to the dragon's glowering eye. "Can I introduce you? This is Daniela."

The dragon took in the little bird, who had fanned out her pearl-gray tail feathers and was gazing at him with wide, admiring eyes, like he was a movie star. "Tell him to come see me when your adventure's done," she whispered to Miranda. "He can find me at the Chiesa di San Giorgio dei Greci. I'd like him to meet my parents!" With that, and a rolling coo at the thought of how her dull, sleepy-eyed pigeon mother and father would respond if the dragon actually came calling on her, she flapped her wings and was off.

Miranda watched her disappear into the night sky, leading the flight of pigeons who'd accompanied her back to the center of Venice. Then she turned to the crumbling wall fronting the beach. There was a gap where an entry door must have once stood. The stone walkway led through the opening to a darkened court-yard surrounded by a cluster of ancient buildings. She looked over at Jared and Shireen, stuffed her hands in her pockets, and followed them as they headed for the gap in the wall.

15
A Long-Awaited Meeting

They were standing in the walled courtyard. Just ahead, Shireen could make out the remains of a stone well. Flanking the yard on either side were two long, low buildings squatting grimly in the faint moonlight. Beyond the well stood a much taller building made of red brick. It looked like a church. Broken shards of marble clung to its facade. Two wooden doors hung off their hinges at the entrance to the building, a black mouth giving onto a desolate interior. Shireen looked at the shadowed doorway warily. Did they have to go in there?

"What is this place?" she whispered.

"A church," Maldini answered. He picked his way forward. "There were once many of these built on the islands all throughout the lagoon."

Shireen and the others crept after him. Hearing no command from Jared, the dragon waited at the far end of the courtyard, his wings tucked round his steaming body. Lorenzo il Piccolo made straight for the door. "In there, my lady. I can smell them."

Maldini flicked his tail. "The lion is right: They are inside the church. I have their scent too. Silvio," he continued, "you go first. Shireen, keep Miranda safe at the back."

"What about the dragon?" Jared asked.

Maldini glanced at the sullen beast. "Leave him here," he answered. "He's too big to fit inside. Come."

Jared looked at the dragon regretfully. Maldini was probably right. Still, he'd feel a lot better if the dragon were with them—no one would mess with a dragon! But the others were already at the door, so he hurried forward to catch up.

As they entered the church, Silvio tugged Jared's knit cap and grinned encouragement. "Never fear, my lad, Silvio the faun is here. Those thieves shall learn a thing or two tonight."

"Hush!" Maldini whispered. "They'll hear us."

Silvio made an elaborate gesture of putting his finger to his lips, and tippy-hoofed forward.

It was even darker in the church than in the courtyard. If it wasn't for the light of the rings on Miranda and Shireen's fingers and Jared's gleaming die, they wouldn't have been able to see a thing. As they crossed the marble floor, they picked up sounds from somewhere ahead—a low echo of voices. They were coming from above. At the very rear of the church, behind a shattered altar, Jared could see a dim flicker of light outlining a narrow stairwell. The swaying light was falling down the steps—Rashid's driftwood torch! They must have gone that way, up the tower!

Lorenzo il Piccolo was already at the stairs. Crouching low on his paws, his stone mane bristling, he silently mounted the first step. Maldini went next, then Silvio, ducking his head through the low opening. Jared, Shireen, and Miranda followed. As Jared started up, he glanced back to check on Miranda. She had an intent look on her face, her eyebrows fiercely pinched together. She gave him a quick thumbs-up and kept climbing the spiraling staircase, one step behind Shireen.

They mounted one level, the narrow walls of the

stairwell pressing in on them. The sounds drifting down from above became sharper.

One more level, then another, then another still, and now they were just one cramped, twisting rise of the stairs from the top. They could make out the voices clearly now. Rashid and his companions were arguing.

"We have enough, I tell you," one of the girls was saying. "We must go back now. Fra Bartolomeo is waiting, and you know him, he is not patient. He will start to hurt the others."

"No!" Rashid answered angrily. "Not without the die and the rings, or we will never escape him. We should never have let the merchant take them. They are our only chance. There must be some way we can find them. Something we haven't thought of yet."

"They are *lost*, Rashid," came the words of the other girl. "The old man gave them away—he told us so! We will never find them. We must discover another way."

"And you *believed* him?" Rashid demanded. "How can you? Whoever has them, you can sense them. We have *all* sensed them! They are here, in Venice!"

Jared, Shireen, and Miranda froze on the cramped landing, staring at one another. The rings and the die! So that was what the thieves had been after in the Ghetto! Miranda gave a loud gasp.

"Shh!" Shireen whispered hurriedly.

But it was too late.

Rashid reacted instantly. "Someone is coming!"

Lorenzo il Piccolo was the first to respond. He was off in a flash, bounding up the final flight of steps. Maldini and Silvio followed hard on his heels. Jared was just one stair behind, brushing aside the sudden burst of fear. Shireen and Miranda hung back for a second before realizing that just hiding in the dark would be pointless. As their footsteps pounded up the stairs, Lorenzo il Piccolo's fighting roar sounded down the stairwell, followed by shouts of panic. There was a mingled hubbub of scuffling and blows, and then Silvio's oath: "By the vat! By the bottle! By the sacred grape! Calm yourself or I shall trample the wine out of you! Stop that now! Stop kicking!"

Shireen climbed the last stair, turned the corner, and stepped into a round room. The fighting was already more or less over. To her right she could see Silvio. He had grabbed the two girls under their shoulders and had one dangling at the end of each arm. They were wriggling and squirming and kicking at his goaty shins. Rashid was lying on the far side of the room, flat on his back, his torch on the floor. Lorenzo il Piccolo was crouched on his rib cage, ignoring the blows Rashid was raining on his stone body, taunting his fallen enemy. "Is that all you can do? No magic powder to throw at me this time!" Jared was bending over the lion, trying to call him off Rashid's chest. Beyond Rashid was a gaping hole in the brick wall at least six feet wide, stretching all the way to the ceiling. The Venetian night hung like a dark, twinkling curtain behind it.

Maldini alone felt no triumph. He had taken in at a glance that his signore wasn't in the room—just the three thieves, a half-filled sack, and a few partially eaten loaves of bread.

"Where have you taken him?" he spat. "Where have you taken my signore?"

Maria and Francesca finally quit struggling. Silvio was too strong. Jared signaled to the faun to put them down and they sank to the stone floor, drawing their knees up beneath their robes, pressing their trembling backs against the curve of the wall, and looking about in disbelief. The cold night air was flowing freely into the chamber and they pulled their brown capes more tightly round their shoulders. Francesca, her eyes wide with shock, reached her hand out to Maria, who took it and began to stroke it gently.

Jared picked up Rashid's torch, lodged it in a metal wall bracket, and asked Silvio to get Lorenzo il Piccolo off of Rashid.

Silvio gave his captives a warning glance to stay put, hoofed across the room, and hauled Rashid from under the lion and onto his feet.

"That boy is my prisoner," Lorenzo il Piccolo protested. He turned to Shireen to plead his case. "My lady!"

That was all the chance Rashid needed. He looked around wildly, scooped up the pouch of powder from where it had fallen when Lorenzo il Piccolo had flattened him, and made a scrambling dash for the stairwell. Silvio caught him just in time.

"No, you don't, my boy." The faun grabbed Rashid's shoulder and spun him around.

"Let me go!" Rashid howled. His turban had fallen off, and his thick hair fell over his startlingly green eyes. "Let me go!" A flicker caught on the silver chain fastened around his neck.

"Where is he?" Maldini hissed over Rashid's shouts of protest. He was stalking back and forth across the room, scrutinizing each of the three captives in turn. "Where is my signore?"

Maria took in the astonishing cat and his insistent demands, then the mystifying spectacle of the towering faun and the sulky lion. She crossed herself, closed her eyes, and breathed a prayer. A strange calm seemed to come over her. When she opened her eyes, she said to the cat, "It was you, that night at the museum? You were the one following us? You and your companions?"

"Answer my question," Maldini purred grimly. "Where is my signore?"

"Do you mean the old man? The one from the shop? Is that your signore?"

"Yes," Maldini answered. "Where is he?"

"I'm sorry," Maria replied, her face softening. "He is not here. We took him to Fra Bartolomeo. We had no choice. The old man came upon us when we were in the store. If we had let him go, he would have had us imprisoned, and then we could not have returned to the island."

"And what of that?" Maldini growled. "You are thieves! Why should you be allowed to escape? Is your freedom so much more important than the life of my master?"

"No," Francesca interjected, her gray eyes pleading. "You do not understand!" Her voice was trembling. "We are not concerned for ourselves. Our freedom was lost long ago. We must protect the others."

"What others?" Maldini demanded.

"The children on the island," Francesca explained, choking back a sob. "The monk is holding them—scores of them—hostage! If we do not return with what he has commanded us to steal for him, he will harm them!"

"What do you mean?" Shireen's voice hitched in alarm. She turned back to Maria. "What children?"

Maria started to reply, but Rashid cut her off. "Maria! Tell them nothing. Look at her hand. That girl has your ring! And that one," he continued, pointing at Miranda. "She has Francesca's. And you!" he said, rounding angrily on Jared. "Let me guess. No, I know it. You have my die!"

"It's not your die," Jared retorted, startled by the rage in Rashid's voice. "It's mine."

"No, it is not! It is mine! Now return it!"

"Careful, boy," Silvio warned, tightening his grip on Rashid's shoulder. "Behave yourself."

But it was Maria who silenced him. "No, Rashid," she said. "I do not care. They can keep them. Those things have been nothing but ruin for us. Let them have them. It was a mistake to try to find them again." Rashid was about to protest once more, but she added a more soothing tone to her voice. "Have faith, Rashid, have faith. God is here too. Your God and mine, by whatever name we call Him."

Maria tipped her face toward Shireen's. "What is your name?" she asked her, pushing herself up from Francesca's side. Behind the grime, Shireen could trace out the line of Maria's face through the uneven torchlight. She wasn't pretty, Shireen thought, but somewhere in her dark hair and dark eyes she had something stronger than prettiness. She had what Venice boasted of. She had serenity.

"Shireen." She hesitated briefly before asking, "And you're Maria?"

Maria nodded, then continued her line of questioning. "Do you know what this is?" She lifted a cross hanging from a golden chain around her neck.

It was Shireen's turn to nod.

"Do you acknowledge it?" Maria asked.

Shireen paused for a minute. Maria met her gaze, and she nodded awkwardly. "Yes, I do."

"And your brother and sister?"

Shireen nodded again.

"And the others?" Maria asked, casting a doubtful glance at the lion, faun, and cat.

"I serve my saint, my city, the Virgin, and my lady," Lorenzo il Piccolo growled. "They acknowledge that cross, so that cross is mine," he added with finality.

"And if they left it?" Maria asked the lion, looking deep into his unblinking stone eyes. "If they traded it for another banner, then who would you follow?"

The lion didn't answer, but his eyes were puzzled. The question had never occurred to him. Maria held his gaze a minute longer. It seemed as if she were weighing him. "And you, Signor Cat?" she asked, turning away from Lorenzo il Piccolo.

"I serve my signore," Maldini snapped back. "That cross is not mine. Much evil has been done in its name."

"And much good."

"Not always," he purred angrily.

Maria took this in but didn't respond. She merely returned Maldini's challenging look with one of her own. "And you, goat-man?" she asked at last, turning to where Silvio was still restraining Rashid by the broken wall. "Do you follow my Lord?"

"I follow the grape, little girl," Silvio responded. "And I am no goat. I am a faun. As to that thing around your neck, it means nothing to me. But if this boy and his sisters admit your Lord," he added, gesturing at Jared, "then I will honor him too. So long, that is, as he would drain a glass of wine with me."

"He would," Maria said, "and forever take your thirst away besides."

Silvio raised a skeptical eyebrow at this. Take his thirst away? Then what good was life?

Francesca, meanwhile, had had a chance to calm down while Maria was speaking. She was studying the scene in the room with less frightened eyes. Miranda had caught her attention. They resembled each other, she realized. Instinctively, Francesca reached out her hand and beckoned for Miranda to sit down beside her.

Maria took this in. "Very well," she said. "You have answered my questions. Now we will answer yours."

"Yes, you will," Maldini snapped, "but do it briefly, and then tell us where we might find my signore."

"You intend to go after him?" Maria asked, surprised.

"Of course," the cat responded curtly. "Wherever my signore is being held, we will go there to free him."

"You can't!" Rashid broke in. He struggled against Silvio's restraining arm. "Fra Bartolomeo has powers you do not know. You cannot simply go to him. He will destroy you, and the children he has imprisoned there. You do not know who you are dealing with!"

"Calm yourself, my lad," Silvio said, pressing

Rashid back. "We know about this monk of yours. But, by Bellona, he does not know about us!"

"What do you mean?" Rashid asked, his voice laced with suspicion.

"There's a book," Jared answered. He stepped closer. Despite the hostility in Rashid's face, Jared was determined to meet his look. They had to get Rashid, Maria, and Francesca to trust them, or they'd never let them know where to find Maldini's signore. "We already know that Fra Bartolomeo kidnapped you," he explained. "How he took you away from your uncle and you haven't been home since. I'm sorry," he added lamely, seeing Rashid's face turn from anger to ash. He was blinking rapidly, as if he'd just seen something terrible. His right hand was up against his chest, nervously fingering the pen looped to his silver necklace.

"A book?" Francesca's voice lifted at this new mystery. "You read about Rashid in a book?"

"And about you and Maria, too," Miranda blurted out. "You're all in it! And what's so weird is, so are we. We just haven't gotten to that part yet." Suddenly her eyes lit up. "Or maybe we have. Maybe this is it! Shireen! Jared! Maybe this is it!"

Shireen squatted beside her. "What do you mean?"

Miranda answered slowly, as if she was still just getting it clear in her head. "We're in the book; we know that. We saw our names. But, you know, we could never figure out how. Except, I guess, that our stories cross, or we end up in Rashid and Maria and Francesca's story sometime. And . . . I think that's . . . now."

"This?" Shireen gaped. "Now? This is where we show up in the book?"

Miranda nodded. "I think so."

Shireen felt a shiver run through her, felt that first shock of seeing their names mixed in among all the handwritten Latin words coming back to her. If Miranda was right, if this was where they were going to appear on that page, then it was like everything they were doing had been scripted in advance—like it had all already happened, like somebody was moving them around, watching them. She knew this was exactly what she'd told Jared: that it wasn't all a mistake, that what they were doing was supposed to happen. But somehow what felt comforting then now felt nonsensical, and even sinister. She glanced around nervously, as if half-expecting to see someone hiding in the shadows, spying on them, controlling them. But all she saw were Rashid, Maria, and Francesca staring back at her, as confused as she was. *Get a grip,* she told herself, edging closer to Lorenzo il Piccolo.

Jared, taking in Rashid, Maria, and Francesca's incomprehending looks, began to explain from the beginning, from wandering into the old man's store and finding the treasures, through to this very evening of taming the dragon, riding on its back, and arriving at the island. When he was done they all looked at one another uneasily. Jared couldn't help noticing how the three others were staring at their jeans and sneakers, the Tony Hawk watch on his wrist, Shireen's puffy North Face coat. He wondered if his sisters felt as awkward and weird as he did, like they were in a medieval history museum and three of the costumed figures from one of the dioramas had stepped through the exhibition glass and were giving them a serious looking over. Except it wasn't really like that. These weren't dressed-up mannequins. These were kids, just like them. Just, well, from eight centuries ago!

Maria finally broke the silence. "There is something hidden from us. Something we cannot fathom. But I do not think it is an accident that we have met. We must have faith. It will become clear."

Maldini flicked his tail impatiently. "Why don't you make it clearer right now?"

"Very well," she replied, her voice surprisingly calm. "You wish to know about the children Fra Bartolomeo is holding, and how we all came to be together, serving the monk, thieving for him? How he stole our lives from us?"

"We wish to know where to find Maldini's signore, and what we will confront when we get there," Lorenzo il Piccolo rumbled. "Not your life story."

Maria met the lion's fixed gaze. "You are right," she said quietly. "What is my life to you? What does it matter who I was before? That past is no more." She paused one more time, and for a moment her eyes went distant, as if remembering some version of herself she no longer had access to, someone completely lost. Then she shook her head as if banishing that memory, and began.

16
A Vision

I t was like every other day. We went to Mass, Francesca
and I, at the Basilica of San Marco. I loved it there—
the priest swinging his brazier, the incense drifting
through the air, the acolytes singing . . ." Maria's voice
went quiet for a second and her eyes closed, as if she
were back there, in the cool dark vault of the enormous
church. When she started up again, looking back into
that incredibly distant time and still, somehow, finding herself inside it, it almost felt like they'd all gone
back there, with her and Francesca, as they rejoined
the company of palace guards waiting for them at the
church doors and followed them to the southern edge

of the piazza. The doge's palace, with its walls of pink-ribboned marble, was rising above their shoulders as they mounted a bridge spanning a canal. "And that was it," Maria said, her voice trembling. "That's when it began."

The pavement ahead was blocked. A murmuring crowd had gathered outside the palace gates, filling the strip of space between the doge's residence and the green waters of the lagoon. In the center stood a man on a wooden platform, preaching to the crowd. A cowl was drawn over his head, obscuring his face. But from their vantage on the top of the bridge, Maria knew who it was. There was no mistaking the taut energy stiffening his long, cloaked body.

"Let me show you," Fra Bartolomeo's voice was calling out. "Let me show you what we have to fear!" His hooded gaze was sweeping over the mass of upturned faces. He was holding a small leather pouch. He untied its strings and reached inside. When he withdrew his fingers, they were filled with a sparkling powder.

"Here, child, you!" he commanded, singling out a young boy in ragged tights and a frayed cotton shirt. A cut of crudely barbered hair framed his blue-eyed face.

The boy stepped forward uncertainly.

The monk took hold of one of his hands and poured the glowing powder into his palm. "What is your name?" Fra Bartolomeo asked.

"Marcello, father," the boy answered, unable to take his eyes from the golden heap of dust in his hand.

"Very well, Marcello." The monk pointed toward the soldiers standing guard at the palace gates. "Throw it!" he commanded.

The boy hesitated.

"Throw it!" the monk repeated. "In the name of the pope, Marcello, throw it!"

Marcello smiled. He knew that name. He stepped forward and released the dust.

The powder burst into flame and the guards fell to the ground, stunned. Behind them the doors of the palace had swung loose on their iron hinges.

"Do you see?" Fra Bartolomeo opened his arms to the shocked crowd. "Where do you think this magic powder came from? I seized it from a Muslim boy, here in Venice, in the very courtyard of the doge's palace! I have taken him into custody. But there are more like him. Scores. Hundreds. Waiting to creep into the city when we are not watching. Armed with magic to weaken us before the infidel armies invade. The Muslims have taken Jerusalem. They will not stop there. They are pledged to attack every city in Christendom. This is the proof! We cannot let that happen. We must take the fight to them. We must destroy them on their own lands, or they will destroy us. *Now* do you understand the danger we face?" He let the question hang in the air. The crowd had gone still. "Do you not see our peril? Do you not see what must be done? Venice trembles on the edge of destruction. Do you not see? I have pleaded with your doge for his assistance. I have begged him to protect you. I have urged him to take the war to the infidels before they bring it to us. But he has refused."

Maria and Francesca's guards were trying to press closer to the girls, but they kept getting separated as more and more people packed onto the canal bridge to see what was happening. The guards started pushing people out of the way, but that only made things worse. The crowd was shouting at them to let them see what the monk was going on about. Fra Bartolomeo turned to study the commotion on the bridge. A smile played across his face. "Do not fear," he continued, as if he was speaking just to Maria and Francesca, as if he'd been waiting for them. Had he been? Maria's pulse raced. Did he know this was the hour they always returned to the palace from Mass? She pushed the thought aside and returned her attention to what he was saying. His voice had become softer, almost gentle, but it was still carrying across the gathering crowd. "I know what we must do. I have seen. I have had a vision. Help has been sent. God has sent someone to deliver us from the danger at our doorsteps and in our courtyards. I have seen them. They are here, among us. When the mighty will not serve, God chooses the weak to lead the way. I have seen who he has chosen. I have seen who will lead Venice in this fight. I have seen them. Those girls! There!"

Maria felt all the blood running out of her cheeks. Francesca gasped and tried to force her way back to the guards. But it was too late. There were too many people in the way. And now the monk's outstretched finger was pointing directly at them. The whole crowd—on the bridge, stretched out along the pavement outside the palace gates—had swung round to stare, whispering and muttering. Before the straining guards could shoulder their way back to them, Maria and Francesca felt hands on their backs, shoving them down the steps into the heart of the throng.

"Be gentle, my friends!" Fra Bartolomeo called out. "Be gentle with our daughters. They are our defenders. Be gentle with them. Open the way."

His words had an instant effect. Within moments a path had opened through the crush of packed bodies, sealing behind them to cut off the guards, but clear enough to bring them into the presence of the monk without harm. He descended from his platform and strode up to them, his hand plunging into the pocket of his robe and then lifting high for all the crowd to see. This time he was clutching two golden rings. A tremor ran the length of Maria's body. She'd seen those gleaming bands before. She drew back in fear, but the fence of bodies encircling her and Francesca was too tight. In an instant the monk had their hands in his. He was slipping the cold metal around their fingers. And then the golden bands were blazing with light, and all around them circling flights of sparrows and pigeons were winging in on Francesca, their eyes and their feathery warblings directed toward her: "Child, oh child, who are you?"

But no one was paying any attention to the birds. Their voices had been drowned out by a rumbling volley of low-throated roars. Maria sought the source. A line of winged lions had shaken loose from the recessed embrasures on the palace walls and were flexing their muscles, unfurling their bronze and marble wings, leaping into the air, and calling out to her, "Little girrrllll? Little girllll, what do you want from us?"

"Do you see?" the monk's voice soared out triumphantly as he turned his smoldering eyes back on the terrified crowd. "Do you see? We are not alone. Help has been sent. The birds of the city are with us. The lions of Venice are with us. Do you not see? Our time has come. Venice will lead the crusade!"

"What do you want?" the doge demanded. Hours had passed. They were inside the palace now, in the doge's audience chamber. He had gathered all the members of the Signoria, his council of advisors, curtly ordering them to seat themselves at the long table while he interrogated the monk. Maria and Francesca were standing behind the doge, numb with shock and fear and nervously touching the golden rings gleaming on their fingers. The powder-filled pouch lay on the table within reach of the doge's hand.

"*Want*, my lord?" Fra Bartolomeo answered quietly. He stood alone in the center of the room. "I want nothing. I want what God wants. I want what the pope commands. I want to save your city."

The doge pressed a finger against his lips. "So you say. And from whom are you offering to save us?"

"We have discussed this before." The monk sighed.

"The enemies of our faith are endless. We must take the battle to them. Or, as you have seen, they will bring it to us."

The doge threw his eyes to the ceiling. "*What* enemies? You mean that *boy*? The bookseller's nephew?"

"Yes, my lord. That devil in child's guise. Surely now you can no longer deny what I have told you? He came here, into the very seat of your power, armed with magic! You asked for proof. I have given you proof." He gestured at the pouch on the table and pointed at the glowing rings on the girls' hands. The folds of his robe loosened as he turned, and for just a moment Maria thought she saw something dangling from a twist of leather tied about his neck, something yellow and wrinkled. It seemed to be twitching, like a wriggling length of eel, cut off at the tip. But before she could make out what it was, he'd quickly tucked it back under his collar. Francesca choked back a barely controlled sob.

"Come, my girl, do not be afraid." The doge rose from his chair and touched Francesca gently on the cheek. "I will allow no harm to come to you. Now show me that ring, and yours, too, Maria."

He held their hands for a minute, examining the images engraved on the rings' crowns. "These are what you saw?" he asked them in a low voice. "That night in the courtyard, you saw the boy conjure these from the book?"

"Yes, my lord," Maria answered. Francesca nodded in silent agreement.

"Then you were right. It was no trick of the light. I was mistaken." He returned to his seat and studied the monk again. "So. The boy worked magic. What does that have to do with my wards?"

"They must lead the crusade, my lord."

"To Jerusalem?"

"To Jerusalem. As I have said before, the Muslims have taken the city. We must reclaim it for Christendom. That is where the battle must be. If we do not, then, as you have seen, our foes will send their assassins to you."

"You wish *these girls* to lead a crusade to Jerusalem?" the doge asked disbelievingly.

"I do not wish it. I have *seen* it. I have had a vision. They have been chosen."

Maria's heart was pounding. His words mystified her. How could he have had a vision of her and Francesca leading a crusade?

But Fra Bartolomeo seemed so certain.

"No," the doge sternly pronounced. His lean body

had stiffened under his red robes. His jaw was tight.

"No, my lord? No? You think you can still say no?"

"I will say what I wish."

"You will defy God?"

"You are not God."

"He has spoken to me."

"In a *vision*?" the doge demanded skeptically.

"Yes, and today, in a miracle. You think you can deny it? You think you can refuse?" Fra Bartolomeo snapped back. He crossed swiftly over to the shuttered windows of the council chamber and threw them open.

A roar of sound came crashing into the room. The throng of people filling the length of paved stone between the walls of the palace and the lagoon had doubled, even tripled. Maria could hear her name rising up in the air, and Francesca's, too. At the sight of the monk silhouetted against the windows, the clamor grew. "Crusade! Crusade!" The guards were struggling to hold back the frenzied mob.

Fra Bartolomeo swung back around on the doge. "The people of your city know the truth of my words. The birds know. The lions know. They have seen what I have seen. Yet you still think you can say no? You have no choice!"

The doge held Fra Bartolomeo's look, his lips tightly compressed, the line of his jaw taut. Maria could tell that he was struggling to hold back his rage. But he couldn't ignore the sights and sounds outside: the shouting mass, the circling birds, the soaring flights of lions darkening the air above the lagoon. The people of his city were in panic. At any moment, if he didn't do something, the crowd could come bursting through the line of soldiers drawn up to defend the shattered palace gates, demanding his protection, or, if he refused to give it . . .

Just as he began to give Fra Bartolomeo an answer, Consigliere Dominiato, the leader of the Signoria, hurried over and whispered something in his ear.

The doge nodded silently as Dominiato explained himself, glancing up briefly once or twice to take in the two girls. Finally he waved the advisor back to his seat. "Very well," he informed the monk. "We will call a muster. You will have your army."

"Not an army, my lord," Fra Bartolomeo corrected him. "That is not what I have seen."

The doge tightened his lips again. "*What* have you seen?"

"These two girls, as I have said, and with them, a host of children, in a great fleet at sea, sailing to the

Holy Land to sweep Jerusalem clean of assassins and enemies of the Church, to win the city once and for all."

"You are planning a crusade of *children*?" The doge pushed back furiously from the table, rising to his feet.

"I am not planning it," the monk answered with otherworldly conviction. "God wills it."

"You're insane! Guards!" The doge barked orders to the soldiers at the door. "Take this madman away!"

Before the guards could seize him, Fra Bartolomeo fixed his eyes on the girls. "Do you believe? Maria, Francesca, do you believe?" Maria shifted back uncomfortably, but he wouldn't let her escape his unflinching look. "I have asked for your help before. Do you not remember? Do you *now* believe?"

In a voice so soft it was barely heard came the answer. "Yes." The word escaped Maria's lips before she was even aware of having formed the thought. "Yes, I believe."

"Maria!" the doge exclaimed.

"My lord, please." She took his hand and turned her face up to him, imploring. "God wills it. Surely God wills it. I do not understand it either. But look, Fra Bartolomeo is right." She pointed out the window to the lions, who had caught her name from the frenzied crowd below and were growling it as they gyred past the palace windows. "Marrriaaa! Marrriaaaa!" She swallowed and made herself go on. Because all at once, she knew. It had come to her with absolute certainty. What was happening was real. Impossible, but real. What else could explain flying lions? Talking birds? Glowing rings? None of them was a magician's sleight of hand. Fra Bartolomeo wasn't a fraud, and he wasn't crazy. Something was happening. There was something they were supposed to do. The doge couldn't wish it away, no matter how much he wanted to protect her and Francesca. She did believe.

"Do you not see, my lord? God has planned this. He put us here, in your house, for this day. When the sisters of the convent brought us here to sing for you years ago, and you had pity on us and took us in to be your wards. Surely that was God's purpose! Surely that is why he moved your heart. To make room for this day! Do you not believe?" She loosened her hand from his grasp and held her glowing ring up again, as if offering proof for the words she couldn't find any better way to express.

"Francesca?" The doge inclined his head toward the younger girl. His voice was catching.

Francesca reached for the hand Maria had just let

go of. "My lord, Maria is right. How can we doubt it?"

"But how will you fight? How can children fight?" The doge bent over them, seizing them furiously by the shoulders. There was an ache in his eyes deeper than anything Maria had ever seen. "You will be slaughtered. What weapons can you carry? I can't allow it!"

"The lions will defend them, great doge," Fra Bartolomeo interrupted. "They will need no other weapons. I have seen this too. They will need nothing else. . . ." The monk paused, and when he continued, he was almost whispering. "Nothing but the weapons of our faith." He reached under the collar of his robe and pulled out the wrinkled, quivering cut of flesh tied to the leather thong around his neck.

The doge pulled back in horror. "What in Hell's fire is that?"

"It is not from the inferno, my lord. It is a relic. The bone of a saint."

"That . . . is not . . . a bone." The doge drew his wards away from the monk.

"No, not any longer," Fra Bartolomeo agreed. His eyes were glowing. "Life has returned to it. And with life, power. You will see, my lord. Arm these girls and those who follow them with the relics of our faith and you will see. Empty every treasure house in the city. Arm your children with the relics of all our saints and you will see. With the lions of Venice flying above them and the saints of Christendom, restored to life, going before them, they will cross the waters to the Holy Land and march unharmed to Jerusalem. Nothing will stop them. The flag of Venice will fly in the city of King David. Your name will live forever, and the Holy Land will be ours once again!"

The doors of the council chamber opened and the members of the Signoria filed out, the doge at their head. He motioned for Maria and Francesca to follow him. Fra Bartolomeo fell into step at their side.

They descended the stairway to the palace courtyard and continued through an arched portico to the gates, still hanging loose on their powder-shattered hinges. At the sight of the doge, the chanting, singing crowd stretching up and down the *fondamenta* fell into an expectant silence. Maria could see thousands of faces turned toward her and Francesca. People were turning to one another, pointing at them, whispering their names.

"People of Venice," the doge called out, beckoning Francesca and Maria to him and grimly resting his hands on their shoulders. "I have tested the monk. Our path is clear." He paused for a moment, bracing himself, then triumphantly raised his hands to the night sky. "God has favored our city! These girls have been summoned! They will lead a crusade to the Holy Land. The children of Venice will form their army. Do not be afraid. Fra Bartolomeo has seen it in a vision. Their victory is assured. Only our children have the innocence and the purity to win this battle against the evil of our foes. God has chosen them to win this battle for Christendom.

"Do not be afraid," he repeated as his words began to sink in. "We will not be with them, but we will not send them alone. The relics of our saints will go with them to protect them." He pointed to the flying pride. "The lions of Venice will fight at their side. No harm will come to them. The monk has seen everything. They will sweep into Jerusalem like a mighty river. And when they return, the name of Venice will ring throughout the world. Their fame will live forever.

"Parents, prepare your children. One Sabbath hence, Maria and Francesca will lead them to free Jerusalem!"

᠅ ᠅ ᠅

The ships were drawn up at the anchoring quays of the *fondamenta*, line after line of sail-draped vessels with the red-and-gold pinions of Venice flying from their topmasts. Children from across the city—hundreds of them—crowded their decks, shouting their good-byes to their parents, promising to come sailing back, victorious, before spring turned to summer. But they weren't ready to lift anchor yet. There was one more ceremony to complete. A crowd of five thousand Venetians was drawn up in front of the ships, standing shoulder to shoulder on the bridges and filling the silver-tipped gondolas rocking and bobbing on the lagoon. The only person missing was Fra Bartolomeo. He had departed five days earlier, telling the doge that he had to report to the pope in Rome and would then sail from the port at Rimini and meet the children en route. But Maria wasn't thinking about him. Her eyes were on the doge. He was in his full robes of scarlet velvet trimmed with the fur of a white fox. He had held her and Francesca back while all the other children boarded the ships, telling them to wait with him at the foot of the gangplank leading up to the deck of the lead vessel. Now he turned and beckoned to the priest of the Basilica of San Marco. The priest walked forward, a young novitiate trailing him. He was holding an ornate golden box in his hands. When he had drawn level with the doge, he blessed it and lifted it up for the crowd to see, then placed it in the ruler's hands.

"These are the relics of Saint Anastasia, Saint Theodore, and Saint Stephen," the doge called out. "They will go with our children as Fra Bartolemeo has asked, to guard them on their way." He turned to the novitiate, placed the reliquary box in his hand, and gestured him to board the ship. Before he could proceed up the plank, the priest touched the novitiate's elbow, holding him back just long enough to exchange glances with the doge, as if seeking reassurance. The doge nodded and the priest released the novitiate's arm. Clutching the golden box reverently in his hands, he joined the cheering children on deck.

And then it was time. The doge called the two girls to him and gravely returned their golden rings. He had been keeping them safe in his possession. As the metal slid over their fingers, the light blazed and the air filled again with lions and birds, and the assembled multitude sent up its thundering shout. The doge pulled Maria and Francesca in to his chest and held them fiercely tight. "Do not fear, my girls," he was whispering, "do not fear. I will allow no harm to come to you."

Maria felt warm tears sliding down her cheeks as she held his embrace. She didn't know how to tell him that they were out of his protection now, that as soon as they boarded the ship and drew anchor there was nothing more he could do to defend them. They were in God's hands, and the monk's. But Francesca found words for it. She bent down to kiss the doge's ring and then looked up at him. "We are not afraid." She smiled. "We believe. It is destined.

"Come," she said, taking Maria's hand and leading her up the sloping plank to the ship. "It is time."

A score of trumpets blasted from the top battlements of the palace. The captain drew the railing closed. His crew winched in the anchor. The sails flapped, caught the wind, and billowed tight, and the line of ships eased off from the quay. The flotilla of gondolas trailed after them as far as the mouth of the lagoon before turning back to Venice, leaving behind a carpet of flowers the gondoliers had lofted into the air, floating in the wake of the receding ships and the shouting, laughing, waving children shrinking to nothing on the horizon.

17
The Island

And then?" Shireen asked. Maria had fallen silent and a look of a pain had come across her face as she sat in the high tower, her tale dwindling on her lips.

"And then," Maria said at last, favoring Shireen with a grim smile, "we were betrayed."

"Betrayed?" Shireen echoed. "How?"

"By the doge," Rashid said, his voice harsh with anger.

"No!" Maria protested. "It was the council. I am sure of it. The doge would never have done it on his own!"

Rashid tightened his lips but said nothing further.

"What are you talking about?" Miranda asked. "What happened?"

Maria hesitated.

"On the first night," Francesca spoke up, "the captain of the fleet ordered the sails of all the ships drawn up. He said he was waiting until morning before voyaging farther. He told us to sleep, but Maria and I couldn't. We were on the deck, watching the lions flying above us. My birds had remained behind, in Venice. But the lions had followed the ships across the sea. It was still hard to believe, but there they were, filling the sky." She paused for a moment, recalling the amazing sight, and then continued. "After a little while, we noticed something else. The captain was standing on the bridge, looking back over the water the way we had come, as if he was waiting for something. And then we saw it too."

"Saw what?" Jared asked.

"A second fleet of ships from Venice, filled with soldiers, following us."

"To help you on the crusade?"

"No," Maria shook her head. "To force us to come home." She raised one eyebrow. "To force *some* of us. The soldiers drew alongside our vessels, crossed over on gangplanks, and went deck to deck, picking from a list, ordering the children they named onto their ships."

"You too?" Shireen whispered.

"Yes," Maria answered somberly, her jaw tautening to keep back a tremble.

"But you didn't go?"

"No, we refused."

"Why?"

"We had promised the monk," she answered, almost helplessly. "And also, when the soldiers were done, we realized that all the noble and wealthy children of Venice had gone with them. As well as the novitiate from San Marco, with the golden box of relics. How could we abandon the ones who were left? We who were also orphans before the doge took us into his palace?"

"But at least you had the lions, right?" Miranda asked. "They were still with you?"

Maria shook her head. "That's what made it even more terrible. The soldiers had a decree, signed by the doge, with his seal on it. They read it to the lions. 'I am Venice,' it said. 'I order you home.' They obeyed." Her voice had gone flat, as if she was trying not to hear the words she was speaking.

"The lions left you?" Lorenzo il Piccolo rumbled, stalking across the ruined tower room. "The lions of Venice?"

"The doge commanded it." Francesca smiled sadly at him. "We did not blame them."

"Well, yes, of course," he growled. "If the doge decreed it. But still . . . Ma Donna, they were your protectors, as I am Shireen's! How could the doge have commanded this? How could he order them to dishonor themselves so?" He flashed a look at Shireen as if to assure her that he would never, ever, abandon her in such a way.

"The decree was written before the soldiers caught up with us," Maria answered quietly. "I am sure the doge expected us to obey his order to come home. He thought we would be returning to Venice also. With the lions. He never would have commanded them to leave us if he had known what we would do. He never would have allowed the council to convince him. I am sure of it."

"But that means they'd decided it didn't matter if the poor kids were all alone, without the lions to protect them, or any relics to take to Fra Bartolomeo!" Miranda exclaimed. "They only cared about the rich kids. It was all an act, right from the start. When the doge sent you off on the crusade, he and Dominiato were planning all along to bring you back and leave the poor kids to their fate!"

Rashid was nodding grimly, but Maria and Francesca said nothing. There were tears in the younger girl's eyes, and for the first time Maria couldn't meet their questioning looks.

They were all silent for a while. But time was passing. They couldn't stay there all night. So Jared finally pushed the story on.

"What happened next?" he asked.

Maria took a deep breath and forced herself to continue. "When dawn broke, we drew the ships alongside one another and took a count. Over half of us were gone. Without Marcello, the tanner's son—remember the one Fra Bartolomeo picked to throw the powder at the palace gates?—I do not know if we would have had the courage to go on. If it hadn't been for him, we might have turned back after all."

"Why?" Miranda asked. "What did he do?"

"He performed a miracle," Maria answered, half-smiling at the memory—though there was something bitter in the smile, something she was keeping back.

"A miracle?" Jared echoed.

"Yes, a miracle," Maria confirmed. "Or, at least,

that's what we thought. I had noticed him earlier, when we'd first set sail. There was a basket of salted fish on the deck, for the voyage. Whenever Marcello thought no one was looking he'd sneak one of the fish out, stick his hand in his pocket, and then rub something on it, something sparkling. Then he'd grin and laugh and throw the fish overboard. I couldn't understand why. The second or third time I saw him do it, I almost thought the fish had started wriggling in his hand before he threw it back into the sea. But that wasn't possible. The fish were dead."

"The powder!" Jared broke in. "He was using the powder!"

"Yes," Maria agreed. "He must have kept a little bit from the dust Fra Bartolomeo gave him at the palace gates. But I didn't make the connection then. I didn't yet know everything the powder could do." She broke off, her eyes darkening.

"So that morning, on the ship," Miranda prompted her, "he did it again? He brought one of the fish to life? That was the miracle?"

"Yes," Maria answered. "Only this

time he showed it to us all. When we saw the fish squirming and flopping in his hand, when we saw that it had been brought back to life, we believed again. God was with us. He had sent a sign. We should continue."

So the ships had sailed on, all that day, through the night, and into the next morning. At last, toward midafternoon of the third day, a low, wooded island came into sight on the eastern horizon and the ships began to steer toward it.

"Captain?" Francesca asked, wiping a fleck of sea spray from her face as she leaned over the rail. All around her, clusters of children were napping on the deck, wrapped under their cloaks for warmth. Off to one side of the ship, a gang of boys had drawn a tight circle around a sailor who was teaching them knot-tying. Another mixed group of girls and boys, led by Marcello, had climbed halfway up the rigging of the mainmast and were defying the orders of the chief mate to climb down. Maria was settled by the fo'c'sle, one of the youngest of the little crusaders sitting cross-legged in front of her while Maria braided her long auburn hair. "Is that the Holy Land?" Francesca continued her question to the captain. "So soon? I thought we would not be there for many more days."

"No," the captain answered her, studying the island as it grew in size before their approaching vessel. "This is the monk's island; his monastery is here. This is where we are to meet him. We will rest for a few days and draw fresh provisions for the ships before we go on."

As they anchored in the small harbor and disembarked from the ships, Francesca and Maria saw Fra Bartolomeo waiting for them on the dock. He was not alone. The harbor was filled with sleek, narrow-prowed ships. Tanned, weather-beaten men with knives in their belts and swords hanging at their sides were lounging on their decks. At the sight of the scores of children eagerly disembarking from their ships, the men wandered over to the rails of their vessels and studied them greedily. One of them called across the harbor water to Fra Bartolomeo in a language that Maria and Francesca didn't understand. The monk's lips twisted in a half smile at the man's words, and beneath the covering cloak of his hood he gave an almost imperceptible nod of his head, but he offered no other reply.

"Merchants," he said to Francesca, noting the girl's uncertain look. "Bringing supplies to the island. They must travel well-armed," he added, seeing her eyes drawn to the men's daggers and swords. "There are pirates on the seas in these dark days. Come now, the monastery is ahead."

But here again was a surprise. As Fra Bartolomeo led the shouting line of children up a steep path from the harbor and through the grim gates of a gray-stoned tower, there were no monks to be seen. Instead they noted half a dozen guards in heavy chain mail who tipped their spears to Fra Bartolomeo as he passed. They entered a stone courtyard filled with more rough-looking men, some in breeches and satin waistcoats, some wearing jerkins of cured leather and sporting billowing capes, all with long swords or short cutting blades hanging from their waists. They were shouting and haggling with one another, exchanging pouches of gold, precious stones, jewel-encrusted plates and goblets, bolts of silk. The children's calling voices died down. Francesca and Maria felt their hearts clutching with dread. But Fra Bartolomeo gave no sign that anything was wrong. He led the uncertain company of children through the mass of men. Maria and Francesca felt the men's eyes coolly judging them as they passed.

They went through a low doorway, flanked by a

trio of guards, and into a long whitewashed hallway. All along the length of the hall, doors opened into small sleeping chambers, each furnished with a pair of straw-filled pallets and a wooden table holding a bowl of fruit and a pitcher of water. Farther down the hall, one chamber's door was closed, a thick wooden beam latching it in place. But there was no time to ask what was behind that door. As they passed along the long corridor, Fra Bartolomeo sent three or four children into each open room, instructing them to eat and then to rest.

When all the children were settled, he guided Francesca and Maria through a series of winding passages to a smaller courtyard. A guard stood at the base of a steep twisting stairwell that led to Fra Bartolomeo's own quarters. These were composed of two rooms: a sleeping chamber like the cells the children were given, and a study lined with overcrowded bookshelves. Against one wall stood a curious cabinet. It had dozens of ivory-handled drawers, each no more than three inches high. A number of drawers were slid open. They were lined with crushed purple velvet and notched with rows of half-cylindrical grooves. Within a few of the hollows they could make out fragments of wood, cuts of hair, and even, here and there, what looked like wrinkled slices of skin.

Fra Bartolomeo saw Maria and Francesca eyeing the cabinet and hurriedly drew a curtain across the entrance to his study. Then he pointed to a pitcher of water and bowl of fruit on the ledge of a windowsill and guided them toward it. "Eat, drink, rest. We have a long journey ahead of us."

Francesca took a bunch of red grapes from the bowl. But Maria hesitated, a set of questions hanging on her lips. Where were Fra Bartolomeo's brother monks? Why did the buildings need such heavy guarding? What were those other men doing here? And suddenly, another thought came to her. A terrible thought. The very first time she'd seen Fra Bartolomeo, he'd been stooping over the bookseller's nephew in the moonlit courtyard. The monk had taken him away, marched him out of the courtyard behind a company of soldiers dressed exactly like the ones guarding the island. The boy, Rashid— where was he? What had Fra Bartolomeo done with him? Even if Rashid had been planning something sinister, he was just a boy. A tide of doubt came rushing in, shaking her. They'd launched a crusade because of the boy? Because of Rashid and his magic book?

But something in the glint of Fra Bartolomeo's cowled eyes kept her silent. Standing before him, Maria remembered that she was still just thirteen years old, and a long way from home.

She swallowed her questions and picked a plum from the bowl of fruit, avoiding the monk's gaze. She bit the fruit and felt the sugar of its juice on her tongue. She took another bite. All at once a great weariness overtook her. Francesca had already curled up on one of the pallets. Her eyes were closed, her breathing deep; the grapes slipped half-finished from her hands. Maria managed one last bite and then she couldn't keep her eyes open any longer. She sank down onto the pallet and slept.

When Maria awoke a long time later, the room was lit only by the dripping candle on the desk in Fra Bartolomeo's study. The dividing curtain was drawn back and she could see the monk bent over the desk, a tumble of oddments spread across its surface, a feathered writing quill in his hand, a diagram or sketch of some sort unfolded before him.

"Ah," said Fra Bartolomeo, turning in his chair as he heard her stir. "You have woken. Good, it is about time."

Maria sat up and looked about. Francesca was still asleep. "What time is it?" she asked, yawning and rising to walk over to Fra Bartolomeo at his desk.

"Late," he answered. He paused for a moment and then added, a curious pleasure lifting his voice, "And yet my time has not begun."

"What do you mean?" Maria responded, hesitating at the entrance to his study.

"Do you truly want to know?" he replied, turning his face directly to her. There was something malevolent beneath the shaded fringe of his cowl, something vain and cold and mocking. Something terrible she'd never seen before. She almost stumbled back.

Then something else struck her. Her ring! She glanced down at her hand. Her ring! Her ring was missing. She darted a look over at Francesca and saw that hers, too, was gone. The monk must have slipped them off their fingers while they were sleeping.

"Who are you?" she stammered, fear filling her. "Why are we here? What do you want with us?" Her voice was cracking but she forced herself to continue. "Did you really have a vision?"

Fra Bartolomeo laughed, a low, sneering laugh that cut the air like a blade of ice. "Oh yes, Maria, I have had a vision."

"Of Jerusalem? Of the crusade?" she asked, desperate for him to confirm this.

Again that cruel laugh escaped his throat.

"You are a foolish girl!" he hissed. "Did you really think I would let you march to Jerusalem and risk losing what is mine to possess? What is mine to command! Did you think that *that* is what I have seen? You leading the crusade? *You?* When *I* am here? Now tell me," he continued, a raging look in his eye. "What have you brought me? Where are the relics I was promised?"

18

"You Swear It?"

But you didn't have any relics!" Jared exclaimed.

"No," Maria said slowly. "The Venetian soldiers had taken everything back with them. We had nothing to give him."

"What did he do when he found out?" Shireen asked gently.

In the high tower room, so far distant from Fra Bartolomeo's lair but with the echo of his sneering voice still in her ear, Maria looked beyond the shattered wall to the moon that shone over the rippling waters of the lagoon. Shireen and Miranda leaned toward her.

"He sold Marcello," Maria finally answered, pressing her fingernails into the palms of her hand. "He made Marcello stand on a table in the courtyard while the men bid for him. He made us all come and watch."

"The little boy? With the fish?! Fra Bartolomeo *sold* him?" Miranda's face went white. "Why? What would they want with him?"

"Who do you think they were?" Rashid answered grimly. "Pirates! Fra Bartolomeo had gone seeking them when he said he was going to Rome to inform the pope of the crusade. After he'd sent all the other monks away from the island. He had no desire to follow commands any longer. He wanted all the glory for himself. So he used that letter he had from the pope to order them to leave, and then he went seeking the pirates. They weren't hard to find. The seas are full of them. They will do anything for money. The monk was sending them relic-hunting for him. But they will trade in anything. Fra Bartolomeo sold the boy cheap. They could sell him again as a slave for far more. Easily. At any port in the Mediterranean."

"You never saw him again?" Shireen turned to Maria, her heart thudding in her chest.

Francesca, her eyes full of tears, answered for her. "No . . . and we don't know how we can ever find him."

"And then?" Shireen asked quickly, seeing the ache in Maria's face and trying to hurry her past the memory.

"He threatened to sell all the others into slavery. All the children who had followed us, if Maria and I did not serve him." Francesca's voice was shaking.

"Serve him?" Maldini asked quietly. "How?"

"By *stealing* for him," Maria broke in, spitting the word out in shame. "By stealing the relics we had failed to bring him, stealing whatever the pirates couldn't bring him." She paused again, and then made herself go on. "After the auction was finished, Fra Bartolomeo had all the other children taken back to their rooms and locked them in. Then he led Francesca and me to another room. The one behind the barred door. When he swung it open, Rashid was inside. 'Meet your new companion,' he told us. 'You have not brought me what I commanded, so now you will get what I need. Rashid will accompany you. He will tell you how to use these things.' He reached into the pocket of his robe and threw our rings, the die, and the powder bag at our feet. 'Since *they* will not work for me, *you* will.'"

"And you did it?" Shireen asked.

Maria shook her head resignedly. "He returned the next day and told us we must go with Rashid and steal one relic for each one the doge had promised. At first we refused." Shireen could scarcely bear the hurt she saw in Maria's eyes as she continued the story. "He laughed as if we were playing an amusing joke, then had the guards lead the other children into the castle square again. He sold another child to the pirates. A girl."

"After that," she concluded grimly, "we did as he said. We had no choice. If we did not obey, he would have sold them all into slavery. So we went everywhere he sent us. A church in Rome, a palazzo in Siena, the duke's treasure house in Milan—wherever he had heard there might be some saint's bones or apostle's hair or a piece of the cross."

"But if Fra Bartolomeo gave you the rings, and the die, and the powder . . ." Shireen spoke slowly, not sure that she should ask this question. "Why didn't you use those things against him?"

Rashid stared at her. "Have you ever been really afraid? So afraid that that is all there is? Nothing but you and your fear? Fear waiting for you when you wake up, and when you go to sleep, and when you dream?"

"No," Shireen admitted, kicking herself for having asked.

Rashid shrugged, as if there was nothing more to say.

Jared eyed him cautiously. He was remembering that first moment in the museum, when Silvio had woken up in the painting and started walking toward him. And he'd bolted. Rashid was right. Who were they to judge? Would he have done any different if Fra Bartolomeo had kidnapped him?

"Tell us, then," Maldini commanded. "This exploding powder of yours—tell us how it works. Perhaps now that we are here we can use it to better effect."

"It doesn't just explode," Rashid informed them, his green eyes flashing. "If you know how to handle it." There was a note of pride in his voice, as if, in the midst of all his fear and misery, this was something he could hold on to. Something that was just his. Mastering the golden dust. "I can make it do anything. I can explode it. I can open a door or reach through a painting. I can blow three grains from the palm of my hand and part the air. How do you think we sail our boat when Maria and Francesca are too tired to row? I can make the powder do anything. Ask the lion!"

Lorenzo il Piccolo narrowed his eyes, his claws tensing.

"And the die?" Jared asked, jumping in before things turned bad. "Did you use that, too?"

"I did," Rashid answered.

"How did it help?"

"Have you tried it?" Rashid challenged him. "Have you seen what it can do?"

"Yes," Jared answered. He couldn't stop himself from grinning as he nodded toward Silvio. Rashid wasn't the only one who could handle the magic.

Rashid's eyes widened. "I'd forgotten about that side," he admitted.

"It never lit up for you?"

"No," he answered. "Only the one with the map on it."

"The map side?" Jared asked curiously. "I've never rolled the map side."

"Well, I have," Rashid boasted. He paused for a second. "Can I hold it?"

Jared hesitated and then held the die out to Rashid. "You have to give it back. It's mine now."

"If you know how to use it."

"I do know how to use it!"

Shireen was staring at them. She caught Maria doing the same. They traded glances. In the middle of everything that was going on, this is what they were arguing about? Who could roll the die better?

"Maybe you both know how to use it," Shireen suggested. "How about that?"

Jared and Rashid swung round on her.

"Maybe you should just keep out of this, okay?" Jared grumbled.

"You too," Rashid said to Maria as she started to say something.

Maria gave him a long look.

"Fine! I'll give it back," Rashid told Jared, less angrily. "Just let me hold it."

Jared swallowed hard and dropped the die in Rashid's hand.

"You see," Rashid explained, still half proudly, pointing at the surface of the die with the tiny parchment cut into it. "If you roll this side in front of the right map, the parchment unscrolls, and then whatever you want the most, it shows up on the map so you can find it."

"And what did you want the most?" Maldini asked. "When you rolled it?"

Rashid ducked his head. "To satisfy Fra Bartolomeo," he admitted, the brief burst of pleasure fading from his face.

"By finding the relics he needed? When you rolled the die, it showed where they were located?"

Rashid nodded, frowning.

"And you used the rings?" Maldini purred, turning

to Francesca and Maria. "To help steal what he wanted? You used the rings to find help in each city the map sent you to?"

"It was the only way we could protect the other children; we could think of no other way," Maria said, pleading for their understanding.

"Couldn't you have gone back to Venice?' Miranda asked. "The doge must have been frantic, worrying about you. Why didn't you go back and ask him to rescue the others?"

Maria shook her head sorrowfully. "No, Miranda. That was not possible. We knew the doge was looking for us. Everywhere we went we saw his soldiers pressing through the crowds, asking if anyone had seen us. And at sea, too, more than once we saw his vessels, flying Venice's banner, searching for us. But we avoided them. We had to. He abandoned the poor children once already! If we had sought his protection, how could we know that he would not abandon the poor children again? How could we know that once we were safe he would not surrender them to their fate, to Fra Bartolomeo and his plans?"

"But what *is* he planning?" Jared burst in, that sick feeling coming back. "What does he want with all those things—all those relics? If he's not trying to gather an army, even a children's army, like he told the doge, with the relics to protect them, then what is he up to?"

"I don't know," Rashid answered. "None of us do." He looked around to Maria and Francesca for confirmation. "Just that . . ."

"Just that what?" Shireen pressed.

"Just that he's putting them together somehow," Rashid answered. "He has a diagram in his study that he's following, and he's piecing all the relics together, bone by bone. He thinks they can help him win the crusade on his own somehow. I think it's almost finished." Rashid gave a shiver. "The thing he's putting together, it's almost done."

"It is sacrilege," Francesca whispered.

Shireen had a question she couldn't stop herself from asking. "So, I get why you and Maria couldn't quit while Fra Bartolomeo had the other kids prisoner. But, Rashid," she went on carefully, trying to justify her question, "Fra Bartolomeo kept sending you away from the island, right? To steal for him. But his crusade, it was against your own . . . um . . . people. Why did *you* keep going back to the island?"

"Because it was *my fault!*" Rashid slammed his hands on the stone floor. "Marcello? And that other girl Fra Bartolomeo sold? It was *all* my fault. If I'd never opened my uncle's book. If I hadn't let myself go down into the treasure cave. If I'd just told my uncle what had happened. If I hadn't stolen the book. If I'd just given it back to him instead of trying to get away without being caught!" Angry tears began streaming down his cheeks. He grabbed a brick from the floor and hurled it through the hole into the night.

"If I hadn't done any of those things, then none of this would have happened. I'd never have gone down to the doge's courtyard to try to get back into the magic cavern. I'd never have found the rings and the powder and the die. Fra Bartolomeo never would have seized them from me. He'd never have taken me away. Maria and Francesca never would have led the other children on a crusade. If I just hadn't taken Uncle Mounir's book, if I just hadn't read it, none of this would ever have happened. It's all my fault!"

No, it's not! Jared wanted to shout out. *No, it's not! You were just being curious.* But then the feeling that had been eating away at him came back, and the memories of the die rolling on the floor of their bedroom with the etching of the book glowing, the black-furred cat glaring at him when they realized what he'd woken up, what he'd made happen, how he'd messed everything up, all because he'd been too lazy to put his die away— and all of a sudden he knew exactly how Rashid felt.

"You must put that aside," Maldini purred quietly up at Rashid, though just for a second Jared thought the cat had turned his head around at him too. "What is done is done. Now we must fix it."

"Fix it?!" Rashid burst out. "How?"

"We will find a way," Maldini answered calmly. "But now, quickly, finish your tale. How is it that you are here, now?"

"We met the merchant," Francesca spoke up.

"The who?" Miranda asked, a memory of something Maldini had told them vaguely coming back to her.

"I do not know his name. None of us do. He was from Venice, but he had spent all his life exploring. He had found his way to the island from the empire of the Great Khan with goods to sell—a bone of the Buddha, he called it—but Fra Bartolomeo was not interested. The merchant was about to leave, together with all the other traders and pirates. The monk was sending them all away. He said he had no more need for them, now that he had us. But early in the morning of the day that they were leaving, the merchant bribed one of the guards and came to see us in our cell. He offered us an exchange." Francesca rubbed a finger against the rough front of the stone wall. "He wanted our rings and the die. And in return he offered us escape. Not a true escape. Not freedom from the island or a return home. But an escape, at least, from the sin of our thieving, and relief for the children who had followed us—release from the fear and hunger of their lives in the prison cells."

"What do you mean?" Jared asked. "What kind of escape?"

"Sleep," Francesca replied, her eyes distant at the memory. "Hidden in a powder that we could mix with our water, and that he would find a way to slip into the water of all the other children and the well of the island. A charmed sleep from which Fra Bartolomeo could not awaken us. A sleep that would claim him, too, and all his guards."

"And?" Miranda asked, although she already knew the answer. She'd remembered now: the merchant pushing through the door of Signor Isaac's shop with the rings and die in his hand, telling him they were from Rashid, his friend's nephew, challenging the old book merchant to risk his shop on the roll of the die. So *that's* how their treasures had ended up in the old man's store!

"We agreed," Rashid answered bitterly. "Much good it did us."

"What do you mean?" Miranda asked.

"Look at us!" he pointed angrily at the girls and himself. "Has anything changed? Have we done anything except to make it worse? The merchant came. We gave him our treasures. He gave us the powder. We mixed it into our water. . . ." He paused.

"And you fell asleep?"

"Yes."

"And then?"

"And then," he answered, "three days ago, we woke up."

"Just like that?" Miranda asked.

"Yes, just like that. But look at you." Rashid's voice caught as he gestured at Miranda, Shireen, and Jared hopelessly, his eyes again taking in their Levi's, their American footgear, everything strange and new about them. "Look out there!" He pointed through the crumbled gap in the tower wall, where Venice gave off an electric glow and the crawling pilot lights of late-night boats cut across the lagoon. His face was streaming tears again. *"Look what has happened! Everything is different. The world has changed. . . . I don't understand. . . . We are lost. . . . I will never see my uncle again. . . . We will never go home. . . ."*

"You will," Maldini purred firmly. "You will. As soon as we have freed my signore, we will find a way. You will go home."

Jared looked at the cat. Really? How?

But Maldini was already hurrying on to the next thing. "Tell us, though. What about the other children?"

"They woke up too," Maria answered. "We could hear them in their cells, calling for water and food."

"And Fra Bartolomeo awoke the same day?"

"Yes, and all his guards. He has no idea what happened."

"What do you mean?" Jared pressed.

"He does not know," Francesca answered. "He thinks no more than one night has passed while we were dreaming. He has not left the island since we all awoke. He does not know that the world has changed."

"You mean he thinks it's still . . . *then?*" Jared

demanded incredulously, struggling for the right words. "He doesn't know that it's now?"

"He thinks that now is . . . then," Francesca replied.

"And why wouldn't he?" Rashid broke in, the anger swelling his voice. "Nothing has changed on the island! The children are still captives. Fra Bartolomeo's desires are as they ever were. And we are once again his thieves. He sent us out again the very next day!"

"But something *has* changed on the island," Maldini interrupted gravely.

"What?" Rashid demanded.

"You have taken my signore to Fra Bartolomeo. The monk will have had time to question him while you have been away again. He must know by now that the world has altered, that time has passed."

Rashid swallowed, taking this in. "And you still think you can help us?

"Yes," Maldini purred. "We can help. We must try. Even if we did not want to, it has been written."

"What are you saying?" Rashid's green eyes widened. A touch of moonlight blinked off the silver chain hanging round his neck.

"It is in the book. I am sure of it. I do not know how it happens. My signore did not tell me everything. But about this he was clear: Your story is in the book. Everything. From beginning to end. And Jared and Shireen and Miranda, they are in it too. Miranda was right. We were destined to meet tonight. Here. It has already been written, and so has everything else. We must go to the monk's island and seek a way to help. I am sure of it. Now, will you stop resisting and tell us how to find the way?"

"But, Maldini!" Jared couldn't keep the thought to himself any longer. "How can you be so sure? You said it yourself: Things aren't happening the way they're supposed to! Not the way you expected! Your signore didn't know he was going to get taken to Fra Bartolomeo's island. I messed it all up! How do you or Miranda know for sure that the book says this is how we're supposed to meet? How do you know we're still supposed to go to the island?"

"What do you mean?" Rashid swung round on Jared. "What do you mean that you messed it all up?"

"I think . . . well, I guess I'm pretty sure . . ." Jared took a deep breath. "I let the die roll to the side with the book on it too soon. I didn't mean to. It was an accident. But it was my fault. And so you and Maria and Francesca—you all woke up too soon. And then you took Maldini's signore, before he could explain everything to us. Maybe Maldini's signore did read that we were going to go to the island to try to rescue everyone. But not like this."

Shireen was staring at Jared. Of course that would explain why things weren't going the way Maldini had expected.

"I'm sorry," he muttered. "I wanted to let you know earlier, when the dragon was flying us. But I . . ." his voice trailed off.

"What?" Shireen asked, trying to take this all in. Why on earth hadn't he told them earlier? She started to voice her exasperation. No one else in the family ever had the courage to let him know how much of an idiot he'd been. That was always left up to her. But he was looking so guilty that she didn't have the heart.

"I wanted to prove that you could trust me."

"We do." Miranda spoke up before Shireen could respond. "Right, Shireen? Remember, on the roof, when the dragon wanted to eat us? We didn't know what was going to happen—no one did, not even Maldini—and Jared kept us safe. Right?"

Now Shireen's temper did flare up. Did Miranda always have to jump in with the right answer? And why, of everything, did she have to remind her of that? Wasn't it enough that she was some kind of child prodigy? Was she a mind reader too? The image of Jared standing on the roof, die in hand, holding the creature back, had made Shireen put her faith in him once already. Now Miranda was telling Shireen she had to do it again? But then she took a deep breath. Even if Miranda should have waited to speak up, she was right. And besides, this wasn't about her sister. This wasn't even about Jared. It was about what they needed to do next.

"It's okay, Jared," she assured him. "C'mon. It wasn't like you did it on purpose. The die just fell out of your hand while you were sleeping. It could have happened to anyone."

Jared could hardly believe what he was hearing.

"Okay, Maldini." Shireen turned to the cat before things got awkward. Even when she really felt it, it wasn't like she and Jared had a whole lot of practice in how to be nice to each other. "What are we supposed to do now?"

"We go to the island," Maldini purred determinedly.

"You still wish to help us?" Rashid asked, astonished. "Even if what Jared says is true?"

"Yes," Maldini affirmed. "We must. What choice do we have? What else can we do?"

Rashid held himself silent for a long time, trying to make sure he understood everything clearly. Beyond the gaping hole in the tower wall the first trace of dawn was beginning to light the horizon. Rashid spied the gleam and turned to the cat. "Which way is east?" he asked.

Maldini leaped up onto the stone lintel at the edge of the collapsed wall. He leaned out and studied the sky. "That way," he pointed.

Rashid bent over the cloth sack they had seen Maria carrying from the little rowboat into the ruined tower and pulled out a water flagon.

"Have you drunk from it?" he asked Maria and Francesca. "Since we last refilled it?"

They shook their heads no.

He cupped his palm, filled it with water, and quickly washed his face, hands, and arms, then slipped off his shoes and washed his feet. When he was done, he retrieved his turban from where it had fallen, carefully unfolded its lengths of cloth, laid the fabric on the floor, knelt, and stretched his hands out in front of him.

Miranda leaned toward Francesca. "What's he doing?"

"Praying," Francesca answered.

"Like that?" Miranda asked. She half-reached her arms out in front of her in imitation of Rashid, as if she was trying to feel what it would be like to pray that way.

"Yes," Maria chimed in. "It is our brother's way."

"Your brother?" Miranda asked, confused.

"Is this your sister?" Maria responded quietly, pointing to Shireen.

"Yes," Miranda answered, unsure what that had to do with her question. "Of course."

"Shireen," Maria continued, this time pointing at Miranda, "what do you say? Do you agree? Is Miranda your sister?"

"Yes," Shireen replied, just as uncertain as Miranda what this had to do with anything.

"And Jared is your brother?"

"Yes," Shireen repeated, her impatience rising. She glanced over at Jared to see if he was making any more sense out of this than she could, but his eyes were on Rashid, studying him intently as he prayed, as if there was something he was supposed to be learning.

"In the same way?" Maria pressed.

No, Shireen almost answered. Of course not. No matter how much trouble he got them into, no matter how thickheaded he was, Jared was her real brother. Miranda was, well . . . Then she saw Miranda peering intently at her, already starting to bite her lip as if she knew what was coming. "Yeah," she nodded, meeting

Miranda's asking look. "She's my sister. In the same way."

"And Rashid is our brother," Maria responded. "In exactly the same way."

Rashid was picking himself up and brushing the ancient mortar dust from the cloth of his turban, which he began to refold. Maria still had her eyes fixed on Shireen. What was she trying to tell her?

"Well?" Maldini purred impatiently, pacing in front of Rashid. They needed to wrap this up now before the day fully broke and the floating city woke up.

"You will help us?" Rashid asked as he set his turban carefully back on his head. "You will try to rescue the children? Not just the old man from the store?"

"Yes," Jared broke in before Maldini could speak. He didn't know how they were going to pull it off. But the cat was right. What choice did they have? He'd messed everything up. Now it was time to put it right. Even if this wasn't what was written in the book, it was what they had to do. He glanced over at Maldini before turning back to Rashid. "Yes, we will. That's exactly what we're going to do. We're going to bring everyone home. The kids, Maldini's signore, all of them. Everyone goes free."

"You swear to it?" Rashid insisted.

"Pan's flute, boy!" Silvio burst out. He put a hand on each of Rashid's shoulders and looked him squarely in the eye. "Who do you think we are? You think this lad's word can't be trusted? You think we'll betray you? Not as long as wine is wine and a faun is a faun. Swear to it? Aye, I'll swear to it. By Helen's lips, by Juno's shoulders, by Venus's—"

"Silvio!" Shireen cut him off.

But Rashid was grinning. Just for a second. "Jared, you agree?"

"Yep." Jared grinned back. "I promise. I swear to it. Shireen? Miranda?" he turned to his sisters. "You agree?"

They nodded their heads firmly.

"Very well," Rashid said. "We have an agreement. We save everyone."

"Good." Maldini nodded. "Now we must go. Rashid, Maria, Francesca, be waiting for us tomorrow night in your boat. When you see us in the sky, on Jared's dragon, set sail for Fra Bartolomeo's island. We will follow you."

"*Dragon?*" the three asked in unison.

19
The One Good Thing

The next night they were mounted on the dragon's back again, straddling his spine as his wings beat, throwing eddying currents of winter air over their shivering bodies. They were wheeling through the chill air, the star-crowded night above them, the silver track of the moon on the waves below. But this time they were flying over deeper waters. The dragon's powerful wings had carried them south, over the Adriatic Sea itself. Far below them the little boat carrying Francesca, Maria, and Rashid scudded over the ocean waves as Rashid blew puff after puff of magic powder into its stretched canvas. He paused only to throw the occasional glance skyward to ensure that the dragon and its half dozen riders were keeping pace on this midnight dash to Fra Bartolomeo's island.

Miranda could see nothing but a smudge of gray shadow where Venice had been, and against the smudge a set of dark flying pinpricks. Loyal pigeons! she thought. Somewhere back there was her apartment, and inside it her parents, sleeping, with no idea that she was gone. She pressed herself against the faun, wondering if she would ever sleep in her warm bed again, or hear her mom's voice calling her to breakfast. From his perch on the dragon's tail, Maldini saw her troubled look and nimbly made his way down the dragon's spine. He settled himself in front of her and nuzzled her gloved hands.

"Don't be afraid, Miranda," he purred, holding her blue eyes in his calm gaze. "I'll get you home." Miranda gave a small, brave nod and looked back to Venice one last time. It made her happy to think that the pigeons might be following them—maybe Daniela! But she knew even they would have to drop off before too long; it was much too long a flight for them, this far out over the sea. Sighing, she turned her face forward to what lay ahead.

The day following their meeting with Maria, Francesca, and Rashid had been a long one, dull and anxious all at once. After making their vow, they'd returned to the roof of the apartment just before Venice shook itself out of slumber, utterly exhausted. It was a good thing the fog had rolled back in, masking their flight from any early risers. They had had just enough strength to send the dragon back into his postcard until they needed him again and then to crawl through the skylight before tumbling into bed and immediate sleep.

Luckily it was Saturday. Dad had let them sleep in and had been happy enough to let them fritter the late morning and afternoon away while their mother, still feeling ill, rested, and he got caught up on grading student essays. He hadn't seemed to notice how sluggish they were, or the nervous glances they kept shooting one another whenever they thought about what they had to do that night. But finally the day had ended. Mom had gotten up, still in her pajamas, long enough to have supper with them and then Dad had sent them off to bed. On Maldini's advice they had curled up after lights-out for a brief sleep before the night's adventure began. As soon as all the humans were asleep, the cat had sent Silvio creeping through the darkened apartment to collect the things they would need. Lorenzo il Piccolo, as usual, had refused to take instructions from the cat, and with Shireen's permission he had let himself out through the skylight when they had lain down—he said he wanted to go pay his respects to his "father" again.

When everything was gathered and Lorenzo il Piccolo had returned, Maldini had woken them, directed Jared to take the backpack he'd had Silvio fill, and they'd scrambled back onto the roof, where Jared once more summoned the dragon from the postcard. There was still nothing friendly about him. He'd glowered at the children and managed to trip Silvio with his tail as the faun was trying to climb onto his back. But the wound in his snout was getting better, and when Jared had stripped off the old towel-bandage and replaced it with a fresh one, he hadn't jerked his head away or hissed.

"Where to tonight, master?" he'd grumbled, though less bitterly than the night before, as Jared mounted his long, scaly neck. Jared had adjusted the straps of the blue backpack Maldini and Silvio had prepared for him—there didn't seem to be much in it, just the book the old man had given them, a postcard, and a key—and once the others had climbed up, he told the dragon to fly back out to where they'd left Maria, Rashid, and Francesca.

And now here they were, miles and miles out to sea, speeding southward over the Adriatic. As they left the city, the growling of the city's lions, unsettled by Shireen's ring, was replaced by the sound of Jared and Maldini shouting out the details of a rescue plan as the cold air whistled past them. Eventually they all fell into silence, and the beat of the dragon's wings in their ears took on a regular, pounding monotony. Miranda's head drooped, her eyelids slowly blinked shut, and she fell into a sound sleep in Silvio's arms.

"How much farther?" Shireen whispered to Jared, her hands clutching his waist.

Jared shrugged. Who could tell? Making their promise the night before had seemed obvious. What else could they have done? But now that they were winging through the dark, with the monk's island somewhere up ahead of them, the seriousness of what they were doing was sinking in. This wasn't a story their dad was reading to them anymore. This was real. Fra Bartolomeo was real. The danger was real. But he'd made his promise and he'd asked his sisters to agree. It was going to be up to him to make sure they could all keep it.

He leaned lower over the dragon, stroking its scaled neck, feeling the power in its body, and urged it on. And farther they flew. And farther still. Until, at last, out on the moonlit water ahead of them they could make out a swirling curtain of white mist, and then they were surging through the cold vapor cloud. Down below, they could see a blacker mass against the darkness of the sea—the boat beneath them was slowing and beginning to tack, shifting its course eastward in search of the harbor.

"Miranda," Shireen said, giving her sister a slight shake. "Wake up; it's Fra Bartolomeo's island. We're there."

Now came the hard part. Jared instructed the dragon to swoop low until they hovered a few feet above the boat. He told Maria, Rashid, and Francesca to land and explained Maldini's plan to them. Then he steered the dragon back high into the sky, out of sight of any night guards, ordering him to fly them to the shore where the little skiff was already headed. As soon as the beast's feet hit the sandy ground of the island, they all scrambled off. Minutes later the boat pulled in to the beach. Rashid secured it with a small anchor, and then he and the two girls waded through the surf to join the others.

Maldini had done a quick tour of the cove and now he was back, shaking sand from his paws. "We are alone. Rashid, quick, give Jared some of your powder." Rashid frowned but did as the cat commanded, pouring a small sprinkle into Jared's palm. Jared reached into the pocket of his coat and very carefully dropped the golden dust in.

"Good," Maldini purred. "Now, Jared, the postcard."

Jared pulled the postcard out of his backpack and laid it on the sand while Maldini headed over to the dragon and gave him his directions. The creature raised one horny eyebrow.

"Master?" he snarled at Jared.

"Do as Maldini says."

"As you command," he replied, but snorted in annoyance.

"Now, Maria," Maldini purred next. "You know what to do?"

"I do," she answered. "I drop the card in the courtyard."

"Very well," Maldini nodded. "Silvio, Lorenzo, dragon, you come with us."

Jared turned to Shireen and Miranda. "Ready?"

"Ready," Miranda affirmed. She reached out to give

the tips of Francesca's fingers a quick squeeze, then scooped up Maldini.

Shireen paused. She was looking Maria over. Scanning her night-shadowed face as she stood waiting at the edge of the surf foaming onto the beach.

"You lost your parents, right? Before the doge took you and Francesca in."

"Yes," Maria answered simply.

"What happened to them?"

"I don't know." Her voice was softer than a whisper.

"Neither do we." Shireen said. "I mean, we've got a mom and dad. But before them, there was someone else for me and Jared. We know a little bit, just not everything. You knew that, right? You knew we were adopted?"

"I guessed it," Maria answered.

"So we're the same. You and me and Jared. And Francesca too. We're the same."

"And Rashid and Miranda?" Maria asked.

"Yes." Shireen nodded. "Them too. We're all the same. Just in different ways. That's what you were saying earlier, right? When Rashid was praying and you wanted to know about Miranda, if she was my sister just like Jared's my brother? That's what you were saying. We're all the same, just in different ways?"

"Yes," Maria answered quietly. "It is what I have learned. The one good thing from all of this."

"And you're not going to forget that? When we go into the postcard, you're not going to forget?"

"No," Maria promised softly. She met Shireen's eyes. "I won't forget."

"Don't," Shireen answered. Suddenly she was smiling. "We're counting on you." She turned to Jared. "Okay. I'm ready." She took his hand and followed him into the postcard.

Jared wiped a bit of sweat off his forehead. It was daytime inside the dragon's postcard. Late afternoon, probably, judging from the sharp angle of sunlight illuminating a far-off fortified city with flags and banners flapping from its turreted walls. There was no sign of Saint George or his wounded horse. The knight must have retreated to the city after the dragon had come crawling out of the card that first time. Miranda was off to one side, still holding Maldini. Silvio was next to them. Lorenzo il Piccolo had taken his post alongside Shireen. She was surveying the barren, rocky landscape where the dragon and Saint George had been fighting their duel.

"Now *this* is gross!" she said with a wince. A litter

of bones and half-eaten body parts from the dragon's victims were scattered all around them.

She wasn't the only one who'd noticed the grisly remains. The dragon was sniffing at a length of thigh bone. He'd clearly had enough of the towel wrapped around his snout, because just then he'd snapped his jaws open, ripped the towel away, and made ready to crunch down on the bone.

"Hey! Cut that out!" Jared snapped.

The dragon eyed him resentfully. "You intend to starve me?"

"Just leave that alone, okay?"

The dragon swished his thick tail angrily. "Some master you are, boy!" he snarled. But he left the bone alone. Then there was a sudden jolt and Jared lost his balance. It felt like the stony ground had come rushing up at them. He looked around, startled, as the others picked themselves up and tried to catch their footing. Then it happened again. Jared lurched to the right, and as he pinwheeled his arms to regain his balance, he remembered what was happening. Maria must have picked up the card and tucked it away as promised. She and Rashid and Francesca were heading back to their boat. He couldn't see outside the world of the postcard, but he could hear the lapping of waves against the boat's wooden sides as they steered it into the deeper waters and around the end of the island. Fifteen minutes later there was a bump as the boat came up against the harbor wall, followed by the sound of a man's rough voice coming from nearby.

"Back at last, you brats. About time. He's been waiting for you."

20
Decide Now!

Rashid, Maria, and Francesca climbed out of the boat, shouldered the sacks containing the relics they'd brought back, and followed the watchman to the walled building on the hill. Except for their little boat and the ship that had first carried them to the island, the harbor behind them was empty. The inner courtyard of the monk's keep was equally, utterly still. The only spark of light came from a line of lead-paned windows on the top floor of the tower. Maria peered at the golden rectangle with dread. It was Fra Bartolomeo's study. He was up there, waiting for them. Francesca took Maria's hand and slowed her pace, while Rashid kept up with the guard.

"The card!" Francesca whispered.

Maria's heart jumped. She'd almost forgotten! She quickly reached under the fold of her dress, slipped the postcard free, and dropped it on the courtyard floor. She glanced down to see where it had fallen. The night was so dark that she couldn't make it out. Francesca smiled weakly at her and they followed the guard through the door leading onto the prison hall. All was quiet within. The captive children were slumbering in their cells.

They crossed through the door at the end of the hall, pushing deeper into the keep, passing the archway leading down to the underground dungeon. Was that where the monk was holding the old man? Maria wondered. But there was no chance to investigate. The guard kept them moving all the way to Fra Bartolomeo's tower and then they were there, shoved right into the study itself. Fra Bartolomeo was sitting at his desk by the relic cabinet, his arms folded across his chest, his face hidden by the cowl of his robe, awaiting their entry.

It took Maria a second, but then she registered it. The monk wasn't alone. Someone was with him. A brown-haired boy was seated beside him at the desk, reading. He looked up from the thin leather-bound book spread open on the desktop, shaking a trance-like daze out of his eyes and pushing a rough-cut lock of hair from his forehead.

"Marcello!" she burst out.

"Look," he said in a clear, happy voice, ignoring her exclamation and the incomprehending looks Rashid and Francesca were giving him. He held out his hand to Fra Bartolomeo. He was clutching a glass ball. A swaying smoky-blue flame lit it from within. "I found something else." He rolled the ball round on his palm for a moment, eyeing it curiously, and then set it down. The blue light flickered and went out. All around the dulled glass sphere, the desk was littered with more treasures: crowns inset with red and green jewels, silver necklaces, embossed rings, little vials filled with colored liquids.

"Marcello?" Maria stammered again. "How did you get here? Fra Bartolomeo sold you!"

"He bought me back," Marcello smiled, finally acknowledging her. "The same day. Didn't you know? He is so kind. I have been living with him here ever since." He pointed vaguely to the floor of rooms below. "It has been our secret. He has taught me to read. And look, he has given me this magic story. It is almost as good as the powder." He turned to the monk. "Shall I go back in?" he said, pointing at the volume. "Do you want more?"

"No, Marcello," Fra Bartolomeo answered, his voice creamy and smooth. "Not now. There is something else we need to do first. Guard," he continued, turning back to the soldier. "Take the bags these thieves have brought me, and the leather pouch that infidel boy carries. He won't need that anymore. Give it to Marcello. It belongs to him now."

"My uncle's book!" Rashid stared at the bound, hand-copied text spread out in front of Marcello. "*One Thousand and One Nights*! The Tale of Ala ad-Din!" He'd almost forgotten about the book, almost forgotten that it had been in his hands too, on that night so long ago, in the courtyard of the doge's palace, almost forgotten that Fra Bartlomeo had taken that from him before taking everything else. And now he'd given it to Marcello. "Give it back!" He lunged at the younger boy. "It's not yours!" But it was hopeless. The guard stepped in his path, bunching Rashid's collar in one strong fist and forcing the leather pouch from his grasp with the other. He tossed it to Marcello, who immediately untied it, a hungry look on his face.

"Infidel!" the monk's voice rose in crowing rage. He'd crossed the floor and was towering over Rashid. "Devil spawn! Did you really think I couldn't do without you? That I needed *you*? A *Muslim*?" His voice was dripping with disdain. "Did you think I could not find another child to serve me? And when you brought me that Jew . . ." Now the monk swung on Maria and Francesca. "What did you believe? That I would not know that the world beyond this island has changed? That I would just sit here, waiting for you to forge your plots?" He took them all into one sweeping, mocking gaze. His look of triumph sucked all the air out of their lungs. "Now show me what they have brought and take them away," he commanded the guard. "Marcello and I have work to do. We must prepare for our other guests."

Out in the courtyard, Maldini was sniffing the air, searching for his signore's scent. They'd waited for nearly twenty minutes to make sure the coast was clear and then they'd all followed Silvio out of the postcard Maria had dropped in the square. Everyone except the dragon. Jared had told him to wait inside the card. What they needed now was stealth; they couldn't have the dragon blundering around, raising the alarm. Once they'd found everyone and set them free, Jared figured he could call the dragon out of the card to help with the last stage of their plan.

"This way!" Maldini's purring voice was calling out now. "I have the scent." His whiskers were twitching with excitement as he started toward an iron-studded wooden door at the far side of the courtyard.

Half a second later he was bounding back toward them. "Someone's coming," he whispered. "Hide!"

They scattered, pushing back into the deep gloom pooled against the walls. The wooden door opened and the harbor guard emerged. His steps echoed across the courtyard as he trudged back toward the entrance gate, resting his spear on his shoulder. *Don't look around! Don't look around!* Jared sent silent mental messages.

The guard was halfway to the gate when it happened. His right foot went shooting out from under him and he fell to the ground. "Son of a Florentine!" he cursed as he picked himself up, peering into the darkness at his feet, groping blindly with his hand to find what had made him slip. "What is this?" he muttered, picking something up.

Miranda sucked in her breath. "The postcard!"

"Silvio! Lorenzo!" Maldini hissed. "On him!"

The guard spun around in Maldini's direction, dropping the card. It was a mistake. Before the guard could level his spear, Lorenzo il Piccolo sprang into the air, his stone head extended like a battering ram. A second later he crashed into the back of the guard's skull. The guard staggered, buckled, and fell to the ground, unconscious.

"Trials of Hercules!" Silvio nodded admiringly at Lorenzo il Piccolo as he trotted over to inspect the prostrate man. "That's a useful trick."

Lorenzo il Piccolo didn't acknowledge the praise. He was climbing onto the fallen body, his claws jutting from the ends of his paws, jaws open wide.

"Lorenzo!" Shireen whispered sharply. "Stop! What are you thinking?"

Lorenzo il Piccolo rolled his muscled shoulders. "He is an enemy. He must be dealt with."

She shook her head, horrified. "Not that way!"

"Then what shall I do with him, my lady?" he demanded archly. "I am pledged to protect you. I cannot leave him here. If he is found while we are inside, there will be ten or twenty others coming for us."

"Take him over there," Maldini said. He pointed toward the far side of the enclosure, where the night was thickest. Shireen nodded her agreement.

Lorenzo il Piccolo curled his whiskered lip back in irritation but did as instructed. He sank his teeth into the man's cloak and, with a great straining of his rear limbs, dragged him off into the well of shadows in the corner of the courtyard. "As *my lady* commanded me," he told Maldini curtly, rejoining the others.

Silvio gave him a great wink. "Don't worry, brother lion. We shall have some sport before the night is ended." He held out the spear the guard had dropped. "What do you say, my lad?" he asked, turning to Jared. He twirled the spear in his hand. "Shall we go make a name for ourselves?"

Maldini snapped at him. "A quiet name! Or should we leave you here to search the guard's body for a flask of wine?"

"By Jupiter, if there's a flask on the guard, then there's a barrel in the keep," Silvio answered merrily. "Barrel upon barrel! What are we wasting time here for? That monk has no idea what is about to hit him."

Maldini shook his head in exasperation. "There will be no hitting! And no spearing. Unless I say so. This is not a game, you simpleton of a faun! Lives are at stake." He stole forward, his tail switching in frustration. "Now follow me. Quietly!"

Jared, grinning amiably at Silvio's hurt look,

clapped him on the shoulder and led the way behind the disappearing cat through the wooden door. A long line of barred cell doors stretched out ahead of them.

"That was your *uncle's* book?" Francesca was whispering anxiously to Rashid. They were back in their whitewashed cell. The harbor guard had shut them in and barred the door before heading back to his post at the water's edge. "The monk gave Marcello your uncle's book and now he can go into it too? Into the magic cavern? Did he ever try to make you do it?"

"Yes," Rashid answered grimly. "When he first kidnapped me. But I could not make it work. I was too afraid to read the way you must read to enter the book. But what does that matter, now that he has Marcello, now that he has the powder, too!"

"What does it mean?" Her voice quavered.

"It means that we have very little time," Rashid responded. He stalked over to the door and began pounding on it. "Where are they? *Where are they?*"

Francesca covered her eyes to block out the doubts that were rising in the room.

"They'll come," Maria assured her with a hand on her back. "Jared and the others will come. Any moment now. They will be here."

"So what?" Rashid glared at her, his voice choking. "Does that matter anymore? Didn't you hear what Fra Bartolomeo said? He doesn't need us anymore. He's got Marcello. And he knows."

"Knows what?" Francesca trembled.

"That they're coming. That they're here." He pounded again at the door, this time so fiercely his palm ached. He knew it. He knew it with an utter, terrible certainty. Hadn't they heard what Fra Bartolomeo had said? *We must prepare for our guests.* The monk had found out. Somehow, he knew that Jared and the rest were coming.

It was a trap. And he'd led them all into it.

He should never have agreed with the cat's demands. He should never have let Jared and his sisters follow them to the island. It was his fault. Again. How many other lives was he going to ruin? They should have found another way. But it was too late. The monk knew what was happening. And now he had them all trapped.

Jared followed Maldini into the hall and looked anxiously about. There was no one there. Just a long row of barred doors, dimly lit by torches on the walls, and near the far end, coming from behind one of the doors, the sound of arguing voices. The cat was already bolting down the hall, calling out desperately, "Signore? Signore? Where are you?"

Jared's relief at hearing familiar voices was mixed with fear that Maldini's shouts would give them away. "It's all right, we're here," he whispered. Then he instructed the faun. "Silvio, open the door."

Silvio lifted the bar and Maria, Rashid, and Francesca came running out.

"Hurry!" Rashid said, darting his eyes around. "He could be here any minute. Faun," he rushed on, pointing to the courtyard entrance, "guard that door! There is a back way to the courtyard from the tower. He may be coming from that side. Lion, quick, take the door on the other end!"

"Rashid? What's wrong?" Miranda asked. He looked frantic.

"He knows! The monk knows you are here! *Hurry!*"

"He knows?" Maldini hissed. "What do you mean, he knows? Did you tell him?"

"Maldini! How could you say that?" Maria burst out. "We told him nothing. We don't know how he found out. But Rashid is right, we must hurry! He has been waiting for you. He's planning something. Please, please! Do as Rashid says."

Jared could feel his heart sinking. Fra Bartolomeo knew they were there? He was waiting for them?

"Well, lad, what do you say?" Silvio asked him.

"Do what they say," he answered, forcing his thoughts back on track. "We're all in this together. Rashid knows the layout of this place better than we do. If Fra Bartolomeo's on his way, we have to get ready. He's not going to take us without a fight."

"Well said, lad!" Silvio gave Jared's shoulder a quick squeeze and moved for the door.

Lorenzo il Piccolo looked over to Shireen, and she waved to him to take his post at the other door.

Then, as if they'd each had the exact same thought, all of them began to run from cell to cell, lifting open the door bars, waking the captive children, and urging them into the corridor. Within minutes the hallway was crowded with children blinking in confusion. But one person was missing.

"My signore!" Maldini exclaimed, stalking up and down the hall, peering into every cell to make sure that they hadn't somehow overlooked him. "Where is he?"

Jared's pulse was racing. Time was running out. If Rashid was right, then whatever Fra Bartolomeo was preparing, it couldn't be long before he made his way down from the tower. And no matter how hard Maria and Francesca were trying to calm them, some of the children were growing hysterical at the sight of a great faun at one end of the hall, a living stone lion at the other, and a talking cat in between. The hubbub was rising. Even if Fra Bartolomeo wasn't already on his way, it could only be a matter of time before they woke the guards sleeping in their night quarters. They couldn't stay where they were much longer.

Shireen and Miranda were looking at Jared desperately, waiting for him to tell them what to do next. Rashid had joined Silvio at the door to the courtyard and had pried it gingerly open. He peeked outside and then called out, "Jared, the courtyard's empty. Come, this is our chance. We need to go now!"

From the opposite end of the hall, Maldini gave a yowl and jumped at the door leading deeper into the keep. "Come, Jared," he growled. "My signore is through here! I have the scent again." His tail began switching furiously. "What are we waiting for? Come, we must rescue him! This way!"

Jared looked from one end of the hall to the other, feeling utterly paralyzed. *Give me a minute!* he wanted to shout. *Just give me a minute!* But they didn't have a minute. He needed to decide now. What was he supposed to do? There were scores of kids in the hall. The door was open. The courtyard was empty. The path was clear. Shouldn't they just get themselves and all the kids out of there, while they still could, before Fra Bartolomeo found them?

There was no more time to think about it. There didn't need to be. Something his mom had once said came flashing back to him. *When you're not sure what to do, do the right thing.* And it was obvious what that was.

"Rashid!" he called out. "Remember what we said. We're not leaving until we've got everyone. That was our promise, remember?" Rashid was nodding in agreement. "It's going to take both of us!" Jared continued. "But we can do it. Okay? We can do it."

"*Insha'Allah!*" Rashid shouted back, a calm smile lifting his lips. "*Insha'Allah.*"

21
Breaking the Locks

They were splitting up. When you couldn't choose one, you had to choose both. And there were two of them, so they had a chance. Jared rushed over to Maria. "Maldini's got his signore's scent, past that door. What's back there?"

"The dungeon," she whispered. "But, Jared, that is the route to Fra Bartolomeo's tower. If you go back in, I do not know if you will come out."

"You just take care of my sisters, okay?" He turned away from Maria before she had the chance to respond. "Shireen, Miranda? You guys help Maria and Francesca get the children back to the beach.

Rashid will go with you. I'll catch up along with Silvio and Maldini and Lorenzo il Piccolo once we've freed the old man."

He tightened the straps of his backpack and called to Silvio, "Okay, faun! It's time to make your name."

Shireen stood staring numbly at Jared as the faun came trotting up. Her lip was trembling. "Jared—" she started to say.

He cut her off. "The number one vaporetto. Remember what you told me?" And then he was off, Silvio, Maldini, and Lorenzo il Piccolo at his side, calling back over his shoulder to Rashid, "Take them to the beach! Just get them to the beach!"

Shireen watched him go, then reluctantly turned back to the hall full of children. They were gathered together in little clumps, their eyes wide and staring, whispering to each other. Maria and Francesca were moving up and down the corridor answering their questions, trying to calm them, trying to get them ready for their dash through the courtyard door, when Rashid said it was time. "C'mon, Miranda," Shireen said to her sister. "We need to help."

"Okay, okay," Miranda responded, giving one last look at the door closing behind Maldini's racing paws. She hurried over to join Shireen, who had taken the hand of the youngest of a cluster of girls in dirty, thin dresses who seemed frozen in place, unable to get over the shock of seeing the lion, faun, and cat.

"Thanks, sis," Shireen whispered to her as she kept gently stroking the little girl's hand. "I don't think they speak English. Just give them a hug or something. They're completely terrified. We can ask Maria or Francesca to translate so they'll know what to do."

Miranda nodded and turned to the nearest girl. She looked like she was about ten. A galaxy of freckles chased itself across her round face. *"Come ti . . . chiami?"* Miranda asked uncertainly, trying to remember if that was how Mom had taught them to ask someone's name in Italian. *"Mi chiamo Miranda."* She tried to concentrate on the girl's answer, completely forgetting that as long as she had on her ring, understanding different speech wasn't a problem for her or anyone nearby. Her mind was still on Maldini and the others. What were they going to run into back there?

Jared, Silvio, and Lorenzo il Piccolo followed Maldini's nose through twists and turns until they finally pulled up at a forbidding stone archway. There was still no sign of the monk. "There, he is there." Maldini sniffed excitedly toward the dark stairwell. "We must go down there."

"Me, too, Mr. Cat?" Lorenzo il Piccolo growled. He'd kept his silence as Jared had rushed them along at Maldini's heels, but now he couldn't restrain himself. "You require my assistance?"

Maldini studied the lion who had given him so much grief the past few days. He hated to give him the satisfaction, but more important—much more important—was saving his signore's life. "I need your help."

"*You* need *my* help?" the lion replied.

"Yes," Maldini repeated.

"The help of a *lion* of Venice?"

"Yes," Maldini said again, struggling to keep the exasperation out of his voice. "Will you give it?"

"My lady has empowered *you*," Lorenzo il Piccolo said to Jared, rolling his mane with vain delight. "You have heard the pet. What do you say?"

"Do as he asks," Jared answered firmly. "Whatever he asks."

"As you command, my liege," the lion replied. "So, cat," he added, turning his back on Maldini and striding over to the forbidding stairwell leading down into the dungeon. "Shall we?"

Silvio and Jared exchanged looks. "Pluto's river,

you two," Silvio pleaded. "Enough of this squabbling. Let's go make ourselves famous."

Jared tried to force a smile. A dungeon? Was he really about to go down into a *dungeon*? He took a half pace forward when he heard a noise. The distinct sound of panting breath and running feet was bearing down on them.

"Silvio!" he warned.

The faun whipped around, his features hardening, spear at the ready.

But it wasn't Fra Bartolomeo who hurtled around the corner—it was Miranda, sweat beading her forehead. Shireen was right behind her.

"I couldn't stop her," Shireen panted before Jared could say a word. "As soon as we finally got all the kids settled down and heading out to the courtyard, she just took off after you."

"Maldini!" Miranda cried, ducking past Jared to the cat, her golden ring gleaming. "You can't go down there without me! What if something happens to you?"

Jared was shaking his head in disbelief. Did she understand how dangerous this was?

"Shireen!" he growled.

"What did you want me to do? Let her run off

on her own?" Shireen shot back. "And besides, why shouldn't we be here with you? Just because you're the oldest doesn't mean you're any braver than us."

He swallowed an angry reply. There was no time for an argument. "Okay, fine," he spat. "Just stick behind us, and don't get yourselves hurt!" He turned back to Silvio, his voice pitching higher than he wanted. "All right, let's go."

The stairs beyond the dungeon archway descended into gloom. As they curled down the steps, not a soul was in sight. The whole keep felt eerily silent, as if it had been emptied out. At the bottom they pushed through a heavy wooden door, and the dim reaches of the dungeon spread out in front of them: block after block of thick, iron-barred cells, like cages at a zoo, barely lit by the occasional torch. Jared peered about uncertainly, trying to spot the old man, to no avail. Maldini wasn't hesitating, though. He was trotting down the lanes between the cells, furiously sniffing the air. And then he spotted something: a lone figure slumped on the floor of the center cage. With staccato yowls, Maldini launched himself at a gap in the square-framed iron grille. A moment later he was beside the motionless body, gently nudging the man's chest with his nose, purring anxiously, "Signore? Signore?"

"Is that him?" Miranda asked. She clutched the crisscrossed bars, pushing her face against one of the square openings. Could it be the old man from the shop? It was hard to tell. Thick chains were wrapped around his ankles. His arms were pinned behind his back with another loop of shackles. His head hung forward, and a cloth gag had been jammed in his mouth and tied around the back of his head.

"Signore?" Maldini mewed again. He'd stepped delicately onto the man's chest and was now nuzzling his cheeks. They heard a muffled groan, and the man raised his head ever so slightly from the ground. He pulled feebly against the chains around his wrists.

Shireen caught Jared's arm. "Rashid's powder! That he gave you! Hurry, use it to open the cell door!"

Rashid's powder? Jared's mind went completely blank for a moment. Then he remembered: It was in his pocket. He scanned the bars and quickly located a heavy rectangular box with a keyhole in it. He waved the others back and threw a pinch of golden dust onto the lock. There was a flash and the door creaked open.

"Lorenzo," Shireen whispered. "Guard the bottom of the steps. If someone comes, you've got to stop them."

"As you command, my lady." Lorenzo il Piccolo loped menacingly down the alley between the blocks of cages, swinging his maned head from side to side. Miranda had already slipped into the cell through the opened door and was crouched next to the groaning prisoner; Jared and Silvio were right beside her.

Shireen checked the alley between the cell blocks to make sure they were alone. There was still no sign of any guards. "Signore, it is me, Maldini," the cat was purring. He'd jumped aside as the man struggled to sit up. "Oh, Signore! Oh, my signore!" Maldini burst out as the man's eyes blinked open. "We'll get you out of here!" He beckoned the faun. "Silvio, help! Can you get the gag off?"

Silvio took hold of the coarse cloth and ripped it apart.

Maldini's signore's cheeks were badly bruised, his lower lip had been split open, and from the way he was dragging huge lungfuls of breath into his mouth, it looked like the gag had brought him close to suffocating. But it was him. There was no doubt. The sharp blue eyes. The deep wrinkle-lines on his weathered face. The white beard.

Jared was ready with another pinch of powder in his hand. There was a dazzling glow, and the chains fell away from the shopkeeper's ankles and wrists.

"Maldini!" the old man gasped, reaching out to stroke the cat's head. He looked around with great difficulty. "Where are my glasses?"

"I do not know, my signore." Maldini looked achingly up at him. His whiskers were quivering. "But come now, come with us. We must take you home. We will find you another pair. But we must hurry, Signore."

The old man was stroking the soft spot between Maldini's perked ears with a shaking hand. Suddenly he noticed the others in the room. "Jared? Miranda? Shireen?" he asked hesitantly. "*Ragazzi*, it is you?" Then he turned unsurely to Silvio, his blue eyes shining delightedly. "And the faun? You are Caius Marcus Silvanus?"

"That I am, by Jove," Silvio confirmed. But his face darkened as he inspected the damage on the old shopkeeper's face. "Vulcan's forge! What has that monk done to you?"

Maldini's signore blinked again, the wonder draining from his face. He looked around desperately. "Where is the lion?" The words were passing his bearded lips with painful effort. "We need him. It is in the book. We cannot escape without him."

Shireen felt the mad hammering of her heart. "He's down there," she stammered, pointing to the distant stairwell. "I sent him off to guard us. Was that wrong?"

"No, no," the old man reassured her, "so long as he is here. And the others? Rashid, Maria, Francesca, and all the other children? You have freed them? They are safe?"

"Rashid and the girls are taking them to the beach," Jared told him. "We've got to join them. We don't have much time. Can you walk? Silvio, help him up. We've got to get going."

"Wait!" the shopkeeper cried out, his voice trembling. He held his hand out, keeping Silvio from lifting him to his feet. "*Ragazzi*, forgive me. There is something I could not tell you. Fra Bartolomeo . . ." He was looking urgently up and down the line of cells spreading out all around them, as if expecting the monk to appear at any minute. "He knows. He knows you are here. Forgive me," he hurried on, his voice breaking. "Forgive me, children. I had read it. I knew it would happen. But still . . ." His hands fumbled up to his battered face. "I thought I could resist him. . . ."

Shireen stared at the old man, panic in her eyes. So the monk *did* know. They'd made it so far without anyone coming to get them that she'd started to let herself think that Rashid was wrong. But he'd been right. It was a trap. How were they going to get out? She turned to her brother. "Jared—"

Miranda cut her off. "That's okay. We already knew that. Rashid told us."

"You knew?" The old shopkeeper startled at her words. "Yes, yes," he added, as if remembering something. "Of course you knew. And still, my brave ones, you did not turn back. Still you came to get me!"

"Well, we couldn't very well just leave you behind!" she answered, blushing. "But, signore, just now you said that you knew that Fra Bartolomeo was going to question you?"

"Yes," he acknowledged. "I knew. And yet I thought I could resist him. If only for a little while. To buy you some more time. I am a foolish old man. That is not my role; I cannot change what will happen."

"So it *was* in the book all along? You getting kidnapped. That was meant to happen?"

"Yes," he answered quietly. "That was written."

"But, my signore," Maldini looked up at him. "Why didn't you tell me?"

"Would you have allowed me to give the children the book and the treasures, to begin their adventure, if you had known?" he replied, blinking down at the cat. "Would you have allowed it if you had known that I would be taken to this place?"

Maldini went quiet, unable to respond.

"No," the old man answered for him, "you would not have allowed it. And if you had not, then none of you would be here now. And these other children the monk has imprisoned, they would have no hope of ever being rescued. I am sorry, Maldini, dear friend. I could not let you know. Also, remember, I told you: When the time came to explain, I would be with you."

"And that's now?" Miranda asked.

"Yes," he affirmed.

"But that means Jared didn't mess everything up." Miranda turned to look at her brother. "This *was* supposed to happen. This *was* in the book. You knew it was going to happen, and you let it happen, so we'd come?"

"Yes," he answered simply.

Jared's eyes were widening as the old man's word's sunk in. So he really *hadn't* fouled everything up? They were supposed to come to the island! Dropping the die when he had been sleeping, waking up Rashid, Maria, and Francesca when he had—that was supposed to happen all along. The old man had known what was coming and he'd sacrificed himself so they'd be here now to try and rescue not just him, but all the kids too! But then the next thought came rushing in: What difference did that make? It was still a trap. Fra Bartolomeo was still waiting for them! "Quick!" he urged the shopkeeper. "You've read the whole book. You know what happens next. Tell us. How are we supposed to get out of here?"

"No." Maldini's signore shook his tired head. "I cannot do that."

"What?" Jared stared back at him, startled. "Why not?!"

"It does not work that way," he tried to explain. "I cannot tell you what to do. You have to—"

"Believe!" Miranda broke in before he could finish his sentence. "That's how all of this works, right?" She pushed on earnestly, clasping his fingers and looking up into his face for affirmation. "I think I figured it out. That's why you couldn't tell us what was going to happen when we met you the first time. Because then we'd have known. And what we need to do is believe! That's why all these things only work for kids!" She raised her ring again, her eyes narrowing in concentration as she worked it all out. "Our stuff, the book Rashid took from his uncle. Kids believe in them and adults don't. That's what makes the difference, right? If you know, they don't work. And that's the problem with adults. Except you, you're special—Maldini told me. But most adults, they think they know everything, so they can't believe anymore. They think believing is just for kids."

Now Miranda was standing, talking to them all. "But they're wrong. You have to believe. Or you always keep doing what you already know how to do, what seems possible, and you can never make anything really great happen. And that's what we've got to do now, right? We've got to believe?"

"Yes," he answered quietly. "That is right."

"Believe in what?" Shireen blurted out.

"That you will find a way. That we will be free," he answered simply.

"And what if we don't?" Shireen added with a tremor, looking around the gloomy cell, the dungeon spreading out around them, a thick feeling of dread overcoming her.

"Then . . . ," he started to answer. But there was no time for him to finish the sentence. A roar echoed from the distant shadows, followed by a heavy percussion of boots clattering down the stairwell, pair after studded pair. Twenty hard-faced men were pouring through the doorway into the dungeon. The first dozen were carrying torches and swords; the rest were armed with heavy, long-handled stonemason's hammers. A man with a thick bandage wrapped around his head was leading the second group. Shireen's pounding heart went still. It was the harbor guard. He was shouting a warning to the other men as they began spreading into the lanes between the rows of cells. "The lion, watch out for the lion!"

Before he could say anything else, another fighting roar sounded: "For Saint Mark! For the Republic! For my lady!" A blur of stony white flashed through the dimness and one of the guards went down.

Through the line of bars, Shireen saw three hammers rise in the air and fall savagely. The crack of metal on stone echoed across the dungeon. The lion howled in pain. "Lorenzo!" she cried. She rushed to the door of the cell, sick with panic and guilt. He'd warned her. He'd said the guard would bring others. "Lorenzo!" she shouted again as she took off down the line of cells toward where he'd disappeared at the men's feet. "Lorenzo!" The hammers were rising again.

"Now, faun!" Maldini hissed as Jared and Miranda went scrambling after her. "Now is the time for that spear of yours!"

22

"Kill!"

J ared! Jared, where are you? Get up here! We need you!" Rashid was sprinting down the hall of emptied cells where the children had been held. The silver pen bobbed wildly from the chain around his neck, lines of sweat were bleeding into his eyes, and his voice was frantic. "Jared!" he shouted again, coming to the door at the end of the hall and slamming his way through it. "Jared! We need you!"

What was happening? Where were they? He ran to the dungeon stairwell and skidded to a stop. Ominous sounds echoed up at him—curses and groans and the clash of metal, and then Maldini's voice calling out, "Lorenzo! Silvio! Take up the rear! Keep them back. Jared, to the steps! Shireen, Miranda, follow him! Signore, after them!" Rashid hung in the doorway. They didn't need him down there. He needed them outside, on the courtyard, now! He hesitated. A yelping growl from below shook the air. It was followed by a rough voice shouting commands. "The lion, there, cut him off! Use your hammers! We have him now. Smash him!" Then he heard feet rushing up the stairs, followed by the panting bellow of the faun. "By the grape! By the vat! Take that, you puny human! Bacchus's vines, Lorenzo! Watch yourself! There's one behind you!"

Enough was enough. Things were going terribly out on the courtyard with the fleeing kids. He needed to get Jared, Shireen, and Miranda out there, fast, to help out. But it sounded like they were in danger too. And he'd made a promise. Rashid took a step through the archway and started down, just as a small body scurrying up the mold-stained steps became visible. "Rashid!" Miranda called up to him, her voice breathless and panicky. Jared and Shireen were right behind her, followed by a bearded old man and the cat. There was no sign of the lion or the faun.

"Rashid!" Maldini snapped as he came bounding

up the steps at the old man's side. "What are you doing here? You're supposed to be at the beach with the children!"

Rashid started to answer, but before he could get a word out, the cat had cut him off.

"Never mind—quickly, help my signore!" He flinched at the sound of another roar and the scrape of metal on stone. "He is too weak; take his arm, help him. Silvio and Lorenzo can't hold them off much longer!"

"Do you think you are the only ones in trouble?" Rashid protested. "Jared, please, we need you outside in the courtyard! The monk . . . ," he started to explain. But then he saw that Maldini was right. The shopkeeper was barely able to hobble up the steps, his breathing coming out in gasping wheezes. He could explain as they went along. Right now Jared needed his help. Rashid hurried to put one arm under the old man's shoulder, and Jared braced the other. "We must hurry," Rashid cried. "We need you outside in the courtyard! The monk has found us!"

They started half-carrying, half-dragging Maldini's signore up the final steps and down the corridor toward the hall of emptied prison cells. They were almost to the first turn in the corridor when they heard a sudden squall of noise behind them. Shireen twisted around as Silvio came bursting out from the dungeon stairwell, Lorenzo il Piccolo awkwardly loping into view behind him. A section of his stone mane had been smashed away. There was another chunk missing from his flank, just below his rib cage.

"Lorenzo!" Shireen broke toward him.

"Why are you still here, my lady?" he growled in alarm. "They are on us! Enough of this foolishness. Run!" He turned on his heel and limped back to the stairwell to buy her more time.

"No, Lorenzo! *Lorenzo!*" Shireen shouted, pushing down the hall after him. "Come back! They'll kill you!"

Maldini darted into her path. "He will not come back. Not while your life is in danger. Do you not see that? His honor will not let him. Now honor *him*, and do as he says."

"He is right, *ragazza*," Maldini's signore whispered urgently. "For him to leave, you first must leave. This way, quickly. Miranda, here, help me, take her hand."

"Silvio?" Jared called down the hall. The faun was following Lorenzo il Piccolo back down, pausing just long enough to give Jared a shake of his spear before vanishing back down the steps. Jared had caught sight of a ragged cut on the faun's forehead just below one of his horns. Blood was pouring from it. "Silvio!" he shouted out again.

"Jared, come now!" Maldini purred impatiently. "The faun can take care of himself."

"What?" Jared answered blankly. His eyes were on the framed arch at the top of the stairwell. A violent shudder of swaying light and tottering shadows was pressing through it.

Rashid nervously watched the raging shadows thrown up by the fighting. The guards could come bursting through at any second. "Please, Jared, come now! We need you outside! I've told you: The monk has found us. He must have come the back way from his tower. The children are in danger."

"But what about Silvio and Lorenzo?" Jared protested. "I made a promise! Everyone gets out. Everyone goes free!"

"We don't have time for this!" Maldini broke in. "Your duty is this way. You cannot keep that promise on your own. The lion and the faun have bound themselves to it as well. Let them do their part and you do yours. No one else can command the dragon."

The dragon! Jared's heart leaped. The dragon! He'd forgotten about the dragon.

What was he waiting for? The dragon could save all of them. He just had to get the postcard. One shake and the dragon would spill out and save them all. He took off down the corridor at a sprint, his backpack jostling wildly.

He came tumbling into the courtyard. He'd made it. Silvio and Lorenzo il Piccolo had bought him the time he needed.

The postcard. Where was the postcard? He searched the stone squares. Where was it?

Then he spied it, shimmering in the torchlight where the guard had dropped it when Lorenzo il Piccolo smashed into him.

He bolted across the yard and scooped it up, not hearing the stunned gasp of horror from behind him as his sisters, Maldini, Rashid, and the old man finally came bursting through the door behind him, not yet registering that when they'd passed through earlier the torches mounted on the walls hadn't been lit, not hearing Rashid's shout of warning: "Jared! *Look out!*"

But then there was something he did hear: A cold mocking laugh crawled up the back of his spine and rang in his ears. He whirled around to take in a hor-rifying scene. The dozens and dozens of children were pressed against the courtyard walls, fear freezing their faces, squads of armed guards penning them in. Maria was on one side. Francesca was on the other, her face white, her hands thumbing the beads of a rosary, her lips moving. Everyone was staring in dread at the hooded apparition striding toward them through the flickering light.

"Jared, is it?" the cowled figure asked in a voice completely void of emotion. "I believe the Jew told me that is your name." He took a step toward where Jared was standing, isolated at the center of the courtyard. "Tell me, boy. What is that thing you have in your hand?"

Jared's heart turned to ice. Fra Bartolomeo! Rashid had warned him. He just hadn't been paying enough attention.

He knew he had to respond, but he couldn't stop his mind from spinning with the impossibility that the monk—a monk from eight hundred years ago— really was right in front of him. Somehow this felt

more unthinkable than Rashid, the faun, and everything else; it just didn't seem possible. And yet, here
he was, evil emanating from him in a way Jared had
never imagined.

"Useless boy!" Fra Bartolomeo crooned. "Did you

really think you could come stealing in here and escape me? Did you think you and these infidels and pagans could triumph over me? Did you think I could ever be anything but victorious? Marcello!" He stepped to one side to reveal a small boy crouching behind him. "Marcello, show Jared why we know the victory is ours."

The boy was inspecting an assortment of yellowed ivory fragments spread out on the flagstones of the keep's moonlit entryway. As he looked more closely, Jared realized in a panic that they were not pieces of ivory, but shards of bone.

"Now?" Marcello asked.

"Now." Fra Bartolomeo reached up to finger the object dangling from the thong of leather around his neck. He reached up to touch it. "Do it now, Marcello."

The boy flashed an excited smile at the monk and unknotted the pouch he'd been holding in one hand. He reached into it, withdrew his slender fingers, and threw a great flaring handful of powder into the air over the arrangement of bones.

"No!" Maria shouted. She pushed furiously through the line of guards, ducking under the elbow of one and scrambling past another to reach the leering monk. "No, Marcello, no! It is sacrilege!"

The glowing powder floated down.

Jared froze as the golden flecks hit the bones. The fragments began to shiver and twitch—*unbelievable!*—and inch toward one another. Lines of sinew began to wrap themselves around the hideous shards. Cheeks formed over a hollow skull, a shirt of skin half-curved itself over the rib cage, sheets of muscles stretched along a length of thighbone, and a curl of flesh slunk around the horror's feet. It was flexing its knees and hauling itself upright.

"What do you command of it?" Marcello asked the monk as the creature reached its full, massive height and stood swaying at his side.

"What do you think?" Fra Bartolomeo clasped his hands together—even he could scarcely believe what he saw in front of him. The monstrous thing was nearly seven feet tall. It looked like a giant cadaver that had stepped off an anatomy table, half cut open, the hollow cavity under its rib cage exposed, a gaping hole where the back of its skull should have been, the wet muscles of its legs pulsing with life. "They are enemies of the church. They are enemies of the truth. I have taught you what we must do. This is a war. There is no choice. We have our weapon now. Use it!"

Marcello nodded far more solemnly than one

would expect from a child so young. He pointed at Jared and said to the creature in a clear, determined voice, "Kill! Kill them!"

Jared took a stumbling step backward as the creature lurched toward him, its mouth a nightmarish, toothless hole, its empty eye sockets trained on him. With three huge strides the effigy was halfway across the courtyard, reaching its flesh-wrapped fingers toward Jared. He raised his hands to ward it off . . . and saw what he was holding. "Dragon!" He shook the postcard desperately, shouting out as loudly as he could. "Dragon, come now, dragon, we need you! Dragon!"

The postcard quaked in his hand and Jared threw it on the ground in the path of the approaching horror. The surface of the card shimmered and the dragon hauled his winged mass into the courtyard, blocking the fleshy skeleton's advance.

"Master," he snarled, curling his long sinewy neck around to eye Jared. "You called?"

"That . . . that . . . thing!" Jared pointed a shaking finger. The monster had pulled up. It cocked its head in the direction of the dragon. Behind it Fra Bartolomeo and Marcello were edging backward, shocked looks on their faces.

"I can eat it?" the dragon asked hungrily, sizing up the creature, its scale-lidded eyes locked on the swaying tangle of bone and flesh.

"Yes!" Jared shouted. "Yes! Whatever you want. You are free. I release you. Now please, just help us!"

The dragon flashed its teeth, let out a screeching roar, and with a great beating flap of its wings, launched itself into the night sky.

"My lady!" a voice panted from behind Shireen. "What has that idiot of a cat been telling you? Flee, my lady, flee!"

Shireen tore her eyes away from the rising dragon to see Lorenzo il Piccolo limping into the courtyard. Silvio was at his side, sweat shining on his broad chest, blood pouring from the gash on his forehead. He was breathing heavily, as if he barely had enough strength to keep moving.

"The lion is right, by Bellona," Silvio said with a grimace. "They are on us!" He gestured behind him with the broken shaft of his spear to where a dozen guards were hurtling through the doorway at the far end of the hall, swords and hammers in their hands. "Pluto's gloom! Where is Jared? What are you waiting for?"

Then Silvio saw the dragon in the courtyard. And the pursuing guards did too. They skidded to a halt, blank looks of abject fear on their faces as the dragon, with a giant thud of its wings, lifted into the air. It turned its snout to the open sky above the harbor and beat its wings again, soaring away from the keep. For one terrible moment Jared thought he'd made a last, deadly mistake. *Free,* he'd told the dragon. *You are free.* He'd freed it too soon! The dragon was leaving them! But then the great beast dipped a wing, circled its body round, and came soaring back, rushing in for the kill. Jared darted out of the way as the dragon swept past him, its eyes glittering, its knife-sharp claws stretching out to maul the flesh-tattered skeleton.

"No!" Francesca cried out, sprinting forward. "Dragon, no! It has the arm of Saint George! We stole it for the monk!"

It was too late. The effigy had already grasped its own left arm at the elbow, twisting and snapping off the bone. A dull leer widened its lipless mouth as the dragon swooped in. It pivoted and swung, slashing the ripped-off length of forearm directly at the dragon's head. There was no time to evade the blow. The bone drove cleanly through the thick scales of the dragon's forehead. He shuddered midflight, a great shock of pain rippling down the entire length of his body. He fell like a stone at the effigy's feet, thick torrents of blood gushing from his head. A final, massive quiver ran through his wings. Then he went still.

Jared stared in disbelief. "Dragon…oh no…oh …," he was whispering, stumbling forward to throw himself onto the dragon's still body. He hugged his massive chest. "Oh, no! Oh nooooooo . . ."

Fra Bartolomeo stepped from the shadows, a look of triumph on his face. "Did you believe that creature could stand against the holy relics of Christendom? That traitor of a girl was right." His eyes slittered. "What dragon could resist one wielding the forearm of Saint George? What creature of impurity could resist *me*? Who can resist me now?

"Now, Marcello," he continued, turning to the grinning boy at his side, "tell my creature to finish its work. Guards, round up these wretches."

Marcello waved a hand toward Jared and the skeleton lurched forward, the length of bone still clutched in its hand.

Fra Bartolomeo's guards set to work. The dragon was dead. The faun and lion were exhausted. There was nothing more to fear. They pushed in from all directions, their hard eyes grimly sizing up their prey.

All around the square, children were scattering in panic, sobs and screams bursting from their mouths as the guards moved in and they tried to find some way out. But it was no use. The guards were seizing them by their tunics, throwing them to the ground, backing them up against the walls at the points of their swords. Jared barely had time to grab hold of Francesca's hand and drag her back to join his siblings and their companions. Shireen was spinning around wildly, looking for some way out. It was hopeless. They were hemmed in too. A brace of guards had walled them in from behind, cutting off any path of escape from the approaching effigy.

"Lorenzo!" Shireen begged. "Do something!"

"Behind me, my lady," the lion growled. "Faun!" he rumbled. "At my side." Silvio stepped forward, and in an instant they'd flanked Jared, pressing all four girls behind them.

Rashid pushed his way to the front to take a position next to Jared. "I'm sorry," he said quietly. "I didn't think it would end this way. This is all my fault."

Jared shook his head. "No, it's not. We all chose. No one forced us." He didn't have time or energy to add anything else. He kept an eye on Miranda, making sure he was between her and the hollow-eyed effigy. Five more steps and it would be in striking distance. His sister's face, whiter than white, was frozen with dread. She was watching Marcello. The boy's lips were parted eagerly, almost hungrily. He craned forward, watching the creature shamble ahead, the gore-dripping bone cocked in the air for a killing blow. Fra Bartolomeo, arms crossed over his chest, wore a similar expression of bloodlust, of greed.

Four steps.

"Signore?" Maldini looked up anxiously at the old shopkeeper, who'd taken a position next to Jared, grasping his shoulder as if to steady him. "What is happening? Did I make a mistake? Should I have found some other way?"

"No, my old friend," the shopkeeper answered quietly. "I have told you: It is what had to happen." His blue eyes looked more tired than ever. "I have read this too." Then he began to pull at the zipper on Jared's backpack, forcing it open.

Three.

This is what had to happen? Shireen stared at him incredulously. *This is what he'd read?*

Two.

"Now, Miranda!" Maldini's signore whipped around. He pulled out the thin leather book with Rashid's story in it. He had it open and was forcing it into Miranda's hands, his forefinger pointing urgently at three of the Latin words. "Read, Miranda. If you believe, read!"

Read? Miranda gaped at the old man. But there was no time for an explanation, only time to act. She focused on the page, mouthing the words out loud. *"Parvulus leo rudivit,"* she read. *"Parvulus leo rudivit. . . .* The little lion roared."

Lorenzo il Piccolo shuddered and his head swung round. He gave Miranda a blink of his stone-lidded eyes, as if she'd reminded him of something he'd half-forgotten to do, then turned his muzzle up to the sky and let out a mighty roar that rolled through the night air. Half an instant later the call was echoed. First by one voice, then another, and then another still.

The effigy heard the volleying rumble of sound too, and looked up. Jared craned his head back, searching for the source of the thundering noise. The soldiers were looking. Shireen and Rashid were looking. And Maria, Francesca, Silvio, and Maldini.

But it was Miranda who saw them. She raised an arm and pointed. The air was full of winged bodies, deep points of black darting into view against the star-speckled sky.

"The pigeons," she blurted out. "The pigeons are coming!"

But it wasn't the pigeons. No birds could have tattooed the air with that great a sound. And now, as the moonlight fell on their approaching bodies, there was no mistaking them. No, it wasn't the pigeons. It was the lions. Across the island's harbor they rushed in, a vast speeding pride, their great manes flared, their fighting claws sharp, their mighty jaws roaring in rage. Great and small, marble and iron, gray and white and green they came, soaring through the air to the children's defense: the winged lions of Venice! At their head flew the greatest, the most majestic, the most powerful of them all—the giant lion of Saint Mark, come from his towering pedestal outside the doge's palace.

With a great rushing beat of his wings, the gigantic lion soared through the entrance of the keep, surged into the courtyard, and with one swing of his enormous paw, smashed the bone-wielding effigy into a thousand pieces. Fra Bartolomeo stared openmouthed as the massive lion whirled through the air in search of a new target. He staggered two paces backward, saw the giant mane turning in his direction, and without another word, spun on his heel and fled through the courtyard gates. Marcello followed, panic-stricken.

And then the guards were bolting after them, casting terrified
looks over their shoulders at the surging
pack of lions streaming into the keep behind their
great king.

Shireen was standing in awe, blinking in amazement, trying to take in the scene: the hundreds of

lions roaming the inner yard of the keep; the tunic-clad children weeping in relief; Silvio lifting Jared triumphantly up in his arms, Jared hugging and hugging him; Miranda scooping up Maldini; and above all, that huge, noble lion, larger and more powerful than even Jared's dragon, calmly surveying the scene of his victory. It had all happened so quickly—in a matter of minutes or less. Not a single soldier remained. The courtyard was taken. Fra Bartolomeo was gone. The children were free. Shireen could hardly take it all in.

Lorenzo il Piccolo came padding up to her, an arch look on his face. "You didn't believe I would let you risk yourself on the plans of that cat, my lady? Well, he had his chance, but in the end it takes a lion to settle these things. Now," he purred, a look of sublime pride on his face as he, too, turned to study the great winged lion, "may I introduce you to my glorious father, Lorenzo il Magnifico?"

23
Time to Go

After their rejoicing in the courtyard, Lorenzo il Magnifico had ordered his feline companions back into the sky to search for Fra Bartolomeo, Marcello, and the guards. But they had waited too long. Within minutes one of his lieutenants had come swooping back to make his report. While they'd been celebrating, the monk and the others had made it to the lone boat docked in the harbor. The flying lions had caught sight of it scudding far out to sea, Marcello blowing puff after puff of powder into its sails. They had given chase, but as they approached, Fra Bartolomeo had forced a book in front of the boy's eyes, looking fearfully up over his shoulder at the pursuing lions, and shouting at him to read. A second later Marcello had reached forward and a golden cloth had appeared in his free hand. He'd given a shout of glee, dashed to the front of the ship, and thrown the gold fabric onto the waves. The prow of the ship passed over it and the vessel vanished.

"Vanished?" Miranda asked Lorenzo il Magnifico's lieutenant after hearing his report.

He nodded his great mane.

"It must have been the Aladdin book," she guessed. "There are magic things inside it," she explained. "Just for kids."

He nodded in understanding and turned to his liege for instructions. "Forget them, then," Lorenzo il Magnifico ordered. "They pose no further threat, now that I am here. Justice will find them wherever they flee."

"Are you sure?" Jared asked uncertainly.

"I am always sure," Lorenzo il Magnifico answered. "Now, come," he added, turning his head round to where the dragon lay. "We have work to do. We must honor your companion.

"Antonio"—he returned his attention to his lieutenant—"take the whole pride. We will need stones for the cairn."

"Cairn?" Jared echoed as the entire assembly of lions went flying off to collect a giant pile of stones from the island's beaches.

"A funeral mound," Miranda whispered to him. "It's how they buried people in ancient times."

Jared nodded dully. His heart was aching again as he watched the lions returning in two and threes to lay their stones in the center of the courtyard by the great beast's still form before flying off for more. The dragon was dead. He was really dead.

When Lorenzo il Magnifico deemed that there were enough stones, he inclined his head to Jared and waited for him to proceed. Jared looked around hesitantly. Was there something special he was supposed to do? What if he got it wrong?

But Lorenzo il Magnifico waited patiently for him. So Jared just closed his eyes, breathed a quick prayer, and then picked the roundest, smoothest stone from the mound. The great company of lions was spread in a circle around the courtyard, Shireen, Miranda, Silvio, Maldini, Lorenzo il Piccolo, and all the others scattered among them. Jared forced himself to look as he walked forward—to see the unmoving scaly wings, the blankly staring yellow eyes, the terrible gash in the center of the dragon's forehead. He knelt and gently laid the stone on his reluctant companion's bloodied snout, then stepped back, thumbing away a tear. Shireen picked up another stone from the pile and placed it beside Jared's. Then Miranda took her turn, and after that Maria, Rashid, Francesca, Maldini's signore, Silvio, and all the freed children. They repeated this time and again until the dragon's great sinewy length had completely disappeared under the cairn of stones.

When it was done, Jared stood stock-still with his jaw quivering. Silvio trotted over to him and put his arm around his shoulders, screening him from view as Jared pressed against his chest to let the bitter, guilty tears run down his cheeks. "I promised! I promised everyone would make it home! I promised everyone would go free."

"He died a hero, my boy," Silvio said, hugging him tight. "By Hector's sword, 'twas a noble death you gave him, and there's no better kind."

"A noble death?" Jared searched the faun's eyes. Silvio had a look on his face that he'd never seen before.

"Aye." Silvio nodded. "'Twas for friendship he died. A rare thing. A noble thing." Jared bit his lip, listening. "Don't you recall?" he continued. "That first time on the roof? You said you wanted him to be your friend. Well, you have made it so. The knight was about to slaughter the dragon as an enemy before you called him from that card. Now he must be remembered differently. You humans cannot hate him anymore. 'Twas a noble death, by Hercules! 'Twas a friendship for the ages!" At last he saw a note of understanding in Jared's brown eyes. Encouraged, he went on. "Listen to me, my lad. There is more than one way to be rescued. There is more than one way to be free. He was trapped before you met him. At the end, you set him free."

Lorenzo il Piccolo had watched the dragon's burial respectfully. Not that he cared for the beast, but there was a proper way to do things, and he approved of this. When the ritual was complete, he broke ranks from the enclosing circle of lions and limped over to Shireen. The missing chunk from his hindquarters definitely diminished his proud gait.

"My lady, it is time to go."

Shireen ran her fingers along his mane, swallowing hard. She was heartsick over the dragon's death—she couldn't imagine how Jared was taking it. But Lorenzo il Piccolo was right: They had to go. "You're right," she said. "How?"

"My father and his liege lions offer you their service," Lorenzo il Piccolo responded. "Il Magnifico would be honored if you flew on his back."

"He wants to carry *me*?" Shireen asked. She knew how vain Lorenzo il Piccolo was. How much prouder must his regal father be? She could hardly believe that he had made such an offer.

"You are my lady. He would take it as an honor."

Shireen glanced uncertainly over at the enormous lion. He inclined his great head in a fractional bow. Remembering her first meeting with Lorenzo il Piccolo, she returned him a neat curtsy, then added a broad smile. Once she'd had a chance to gather herself, she hurried through the courtyard, telling Maria and Francesca to collect the children and mount them on the backs of the waiting lions. Then she passed on the news to Jared, Miranda, Maldini, and his signore. The cat nodded, then, remembering one last detail, darted over to Silvio and asked him to quickly gather a few fragments of the monk's shattered creature and put them in Jared's backpack. The faun raised his eyebrows, then set to it. When the preparations were complete and Shireen saw that all the others were safely astride their lions, she hurried back over to Lorenzo il Piccolo and the waiting il Magnifico. The great lion bent down. She put one hand at the base of his wing and pulled herself onto his broad back. Lorenzo il Piccolo leaped up behind her. With one surge of his hindquarters, il Magnifico rose up into the air, all his lions following him. The air shook to the beat of their wings, and in a great dizzying rush they were off.

Dragons are swift but lions are swifter. The hundreds of maned creatures were racing home at an incredible speed. As they flew, Lorenzo il Piccolo explained things to Shireen. He had alerted his father to the danger she was falling into days ago, on that first night when he had gone to pay his respects. "Il Magnifico said that I should continue to hold you in my protection, but agreed that he would come if I thought his aid was needed," he told her. Then, on his last visit early that evening, the little lion had told il Magnifico that the time had arrived. When the dragon had flown them over Venice before making for the lagoon and the sea beyond, Shireen's ring had, as usual, woken the city's lions—but this time their leader had told them to follow her. They had flown silently behind the children and had been circling the island all night, waiting to be summoned into battle by il Piccolo's roar. "I had almost forgotten," he confessed, "in all the hubbub on the square, with that bone-horror advancing and the guards at our backs. But then your sister read, and I recalled, and of course my magnificent father came."

"Oh, thank you," Shireen breathed to the great lion. "Thank you!"

"Think nothing of it," il Magnifico growled in his basso profundo. "It was a matter of my son's honor. I could do no other." The cold wind was whistling past, chasing the long strands of hair from Shireen's face.

"But there's one thing I don't understand," she said after a moment. "I know the ring wakes lions if I go past them . . . but I don't think we flew over your pedestal on San Marco. How did you . . . ?" She cut herself off just in time. She didn't know much about state protocol. But it couldn't be good to suggest that if it wasn't for her and her ring, Lorenzo il Magnifico would still just be a lifeless statue stuck on the top of a column next to the doge's palace.

"I never sleep," il Magnifico responded. "That's just a pose for the tourists. I am Venice. I am the Republic. The Republic never sleeps." He paused for a moment, a troubled look briefly narrowing his noble eyes. "And you see," he continued, "my lions and I, we failed these children once, when they first set off. I made an oath never to fail them again."

It took Shireen a second to figure out what he meant, and then she remembered. The night Maria and all the others set off on their crusade, the lions had accompanied them. But then the soldiers had come on their boats with the list of all the wealthy children and a letter from the doge commanding the lions to return home. They'd obeyed. They'd let the remaining children sail off on their own, into captivity.

"Oh!" she said. "That was you! Way back then! And that's why you came now? Because of your oath?"

Lorenzo il Magnifico held silent. His wings were pounding the air. Together they watched the silhouetted spires and church towers of Venice pulling into view against the first gathering blue of dawn. They were getting close. "Yes, lady," he said at last. "For my oath. And for my son," he added, turning his neck and taking in Lorenzo il Piccolo with regal fondness. Lorenzo il Piccolo returned his look impassively, but Shireen could see his tail swishing a little more briskly as he balanced on his father's back. She reached out and rested her hand gently on the jagged hollow of his thigh.

Off to her side, Maldini was calling out something. Shireen glanced to where the cat was soaring along on the back of a flying lion with Miranda and his signore. He'd shouted out an instruction to Silvio and Jared, who were flying off il Magnifico's other flank on a lion almost as big. Jared was seated in Silvio's lap, his head leaned against the faun's barrel chest, a solemn look in his eyes. There was a smear of blood crusted at Silvio's hairline, but the wound had stopped bleeding. He looked like he'd be okay.

Jared nodded in response to Maldini's instruction and leaned down to direct the lion. They veered off, heading for the northern quarter of the floating city spread out beneath them.

"Where are they going?" Shireen shouted across to Maldini.

"To my signore's store," the cat called back. "We need a book."

Another book? she wondered. Why? Weren't they done? Then it came to her. How could she not have thought of this? In the relief of their escape, it seemed she had left her brain behind. Of course they weren't done yet. They'd escaped Fra Bartolomeo, but now what were they supposed to do with Rashid, Maria, Francesca, and all the children they'd freed? They couldn't just show up in the middle of Venice with a hundred kids from the Middle Ages and act like everything was over! What on earth were they supposed to do? Did Maldini and his signore really have a plan to send them all back to their own time? Was there some way they could really make that happen? She turned and sought out the others.

There they were, scattered among the flight of lions: Maria and Francesca occasionally directing their mounts to fly closer to one of the younger children, Rashid watching Jared and Silvio vanish off into the distance. Rashid looked pensive. As did Francesca. When she wasn't encouraging one of the children, she had that faraway look again. And Maria? Shireen studied her carefully, pushing the windblown hair out of her eyes as Lorenzo il Magnifico began to wing closer down to the surface of the lagoon. The jewels in Maria's headscarf were glittering points of color. Her eyes were still serious, but something had brightened within them, something light and steady all at once. She turned and caught Shireen's gaze. She was beaming, a look of serenity and conviction on her face, her chin held high. It was as if, at last, she'd seen it—seen that they were going to do it, seen herself finally leading the crusade of children back to the Venice they'd left hundreds of years ago. Was she right? Could she see something invisible to Shireen that made her so sure?

The lions flew over San Pietro di Castello and were dropping low on the far side. Lorenzo il Magnifico spotted an uninhabited stretch of wasteland at the edge of the Arsenale shipyards. A moment later his paws were touching the ground and Shireen was sliding off his vast back, the freed children and all the others doing the same. She turned to try to say something to him. Something that would be enough of a thanks.

But he was too noble for that. With one great rumbling farewell and the slightest bow of his head, il Magnifico had already leaped back into the air, his lions following him. A line of pink light was penciling the border of the sky; daylight's full blossoming was less than half an hour away. Shireen raised an arm in a silent wave, then couldn't stop herself. "Thank you! Thank you!" she called out. Il Magnifico and his pride, one lion after another, peeled off east, west, north, or south to return to their bridges and pedestals and harden back into stone before the first round of newspaper vendors, vegetable sellers, and curio hawkers set up shop for the day.

And then, all at once, everything was coming to an end. As Lorenzo il Magnifico vanished, there had been a speck speeding in from the opposite direction, gathering shape as it came in to land. Jared and Silvio were back from the store, climbing off the lion who had flown them there. Jared walked across the weedy ground of the abandoned shipyard with the faun. His face was set beneath the turned-down fringe of his ski cap. Maldini asked the lion who'd flown them to wait and bounded over to Jared.

"You have the ink?" The cat cocked his head at Jared. "And the book?"

"I do," Jared answered. He showed Maldini a small round bottle of black ink and held up an old leather-bound volume. It looked identical to the book with Rashid's story that their dad had been reading to them. Jared took the original book out of his backpack and compared them. He couldn't see any difference. "What do we need this one for?"

"I have rewritten it," Maldini's signore explained, examining the book. "Long ago. In expectation of this day. In expectation that you would not fail," he added, a slight smile parting his lips. "There are a few changes. It is still Rashid's story, but your names are no longer in it. When you return to your apartment, slip this one into your father's room. When he gets to the end, he will find no trace of you in it."

Miranda swallowed down the disappointment that

was gathering in her chest. Dad wasn't going to read about their adventure? No one would ever know what they'd done? She forced her fists into her coat pocket with a sigh. She knew Maldini's signore was right. It made sense. But still, after everything they'd done, no one was ever going to know?

Maldini's signore had put the altered copy of the book in Jared's backpack, double-checking to make certain it was the right one. "Now," he said, zipping the pack closed, "Jared, give me the original." Jared handed him the copy they'd been reading, the one with their names mixed in amidst the jumble of Latin. "And your die," Maldini's signore added. "Please give it to Rashid when he is done with his prayers." He gestured off to a side of the shipyard, where Rashid had found a water pump and was washing his hands and face. "He must roll it."

"Rashid?" Jared asked, his voice ever so strained. "Why Rashid? Why not me?"

"Because he must take the die with him when he goes," he answered. "And Miranda and Shireen, you must give your rings to Francesca and Maria. You have accomplished your task. You have held true. Now these things must return to their true owners."

"Do we have to?" Miranda asked, rubbing the

amazing ring with her thumb. "Can't we keep them?"

He shook his head.

"But why?"

The shopkeeper remained silent.

Miranda's questioning gaze sharpened. Why wouldn't he say?

"You read that, too?" she finally guessed. "In the original version? In the real book?"

"You are very wise, *ragazza*," he said with a smile. "Yes, that is what you must do. And also, if these treasures are not returned to the past, then they will not be waiting for you in my store when you first come to see me."

Oh! Miranda thought, as her mind raced through what he'd just said. Right! It was the time loop they were in. The only way she'd ever have her ring was to give it up now. But then something about the way Maldini's signore was looking at her while she puzzled through this caught her attention. There was something he was holding back. "That's not all, is it?" she burst out. "There's something else! Rashid and Maria and Francesca still *need* the die and the rings! Not just to take them into the past so they'll be waiting for us. There's something else they've got to do! Some other job! The story's not done!"

"Perhaps." The shopkeeper smiled again, the color at last returning to his cheeks. He was looking at her, and at the same time it seemed like he was looking through her, as if he could take in things that weren't there, things he wouldn't have been able to see even if he had his glasses on and the world came crisp and sharp to his eyes. "But let us not speak of that now. It is time to finish what you began."

He beckoned to the faun. "Silvio, say your good-byes. Then you must go."

"Go?" the faun echoed incredulously. "Go where, by Minerva's owl?"

"Back to your painting. To the dance in the woods."

"Why should I do that? The lad and I have barely introduced ourselves!" Silvio wrapped a thick arm around Jared's shoulder as if defying anyone to separate them.

"You do not understand," Maldini's signore said gently. "This is over now. As soon as Rashid and the others leave, everything will be finished. They will take the treasures with them. The power to keep you here will follow. You must go too, or . . ."

"Go on, go on, out with it," Silvio insisted. His voice held its regular bluster, but he was frowning as if he had begun to sense what the old man was saying.

"Or you will not *be*. There are no fauns in this world." The shopkeeper pointed to the city waking around them. In the distance the first vaporettos of the morning were starting their motorized crawls across the mist-laced waters of the lagoon. "You must return to your home while there is still time. The last lion will take you."

Jared had been following their exchange anxiously. "But couldn't we just believe in him?" he suggested. "Didn't you say that was the secret to everything? Wouldn't that work, even without the die? If I just believed in him, couldn't Silvio stay?"

"No." Maldini's signore put his hand on Jared's shoulder. "No, my dear boy. Believing, too, that is not enough. You cannot just believe. Your belief must have a purpose. And you have had that, a high and mighty purpose, you and your sisters: to guide everyone home, to see everyone free. That is what you believed in. That is what you promised. That is what has bound us. That is what has made everything possible."

"But I hadn't sworn that at the beginning," Jared protested, "not when I met Silvio. And the die worked then, long before I made the promise!"

"Yes, that is true," the old shopkeeper responded.

"But your promise, it was waiting for you from the very start. And when the time came you made it. If you had not been capable of that vow, if you had not had it inside you to promise that everyone would be free, and then to act on your vow, to follow it, even when it did not seem possible, then these things," he gestured at the die and rings, "they would never have had any power.

"Shireen." He turned to include her. "Earlier, on the island, you asked me what would happen if you did not believe. I did not have time to answer. So let me answer now. It is the same thing I am telling Jared. If your belief had failed—not in your ring, not in the book, but in this, in the promise you shared with your brother and Miranda, with Rashid, Maria, and Francesca—then, even now, we would not be free."

"But I didn't really believe it!" Shireen objected before she could stop herself. "Not then, not when we were trapped in the dungeon."

"Yes, you did." His gaze lit up. "Yes, you did. You did not think it, but you believed it. Or you never would have been there. Believing is not thinking something is true, Shireen. It is acting for the truth. And before you doubted, you acted. You put yourself there in that dungeon. I know you were afraid.

But that is only because first you believed.

"Listen to me now, all three of you. Why do you think, of all the children who ever came into my shop, put their hands into the leather bag, and sifted through it when they thought I was not looking, why do you think *you* were the ones for whom the die and rings lit up? Why do you think *you* were the ones we have been waiting for? Not because of how you looked, but because even then, when you walked through the door, you had your vow waiting inside you. Because you would risk your lives to keep it. As Maria, Francesca, and Rashid had that promise waiting in them, and would stake their lives for it too. And now," he said, turning his attention back to Jared, "you must finish what you have promised. The purpose you have sworn to is ending. Silvio must go home now, while there is still time."

Jared had listened carefully to everything Maldini's signore had said. It all made sense. It was even kind of great. But still . . . this wasn't how he wanted it to end. He didn't want to send Silvio away. He couldn't stand it.

But one last time he had to square his shoulders. It didn't matter how much he wanted Silvio to stay. He had to go. If he didn't get back to his painting in time, now, while they were still completing their promise, then . . . He couldn't stand to think about that, either.

"He's right," Jared said at last, pressing himself against the faun. "Maldini's signore is right."

Silvio looked like he'd been punched. All the air had gone out of him. "Couldn't I stay just a little longer?" he begged.

Jared took a deep breath and shook his head. "It's not safe. Now come on. I promised: Everyone goes home. You just have to go. . . ." He paused, his jaw quivering as he tried to get control of himself. "You just have to go first. . . . It'll help the kids," he added in a whisper. He gestured around to the throng of children shivering in their tunics, quiet as mice, beyond surprise at their adventures, and waiting, expectantly waiting, for yet another show of magic. "It'll show them that everything's okay now."

"Oh, my captain!" Silvio cried, agony in his voice. He lifted Jared clear off the ground, hugging him to his chest one last time. "Good-bye, my lad," he whispered. "Any time you wish it, come to my forest; I will be waiting for you." Jared nodded as the faun set him down, blinking hard. The hurt was too big. There was nothing else he could say right now.

Silvio turned to Miranda and Shireen. "Good-bye, dear girls." His voice was breaking. "Take care of that fellow for me."

"We will," Shireen assured him as he crushed her to his chest. Miranda gave him a kiss and then he was trotting off, wiping his wet cheeks. Before the faun could mount the waiting lion, Maldini came loping over and asked for one last bit of help.

"Silvio, would you take those relics from Jared's backpack? Leave the bone from Saint George's arm at the door to San Marco on your way back to the Accademia, and then, if you would, when you get back to the gallery, before you go back into your forest, stick those bits of wood back in the paintings where they belong."

"As you wish, Signor Cat!" the faun replied, sinking to give Maldini an affectionate pet before taking the things from the backpack and then vaulting onto the waiting lion. It rose into the air and circled once. Silvio waved madly down at them from its back.

"Good-bye, Silvio!" Jared shouted as they winged off. "Good-bye!" And then the faun was gone, vanishing over the climbing towers and domes of the city. They were glinting pink and gold in the rays of the rising sun.

When there was no more sight of him, Jared set his jaw and turned to Rashid, who was just getting to his feet, his dawn prayer complete. "Okay," Jared said, holding out the die. "It's going to take both of us again. I think you're supposed to do something with this."

24
The Secret of the Pen

Rashid rolled the die. It tumbled three times and came to rest on the hard rocky ground, a shard of light bursting through the one blank side. Jared's dark eyebrows shot up. That side? Why that one?

"Now what?" Rashid asked.

"Open this," Maldini's signore answered. He pressed the leather-bound volume into Rashid's hand, the original book kept for so many years in the Ghetto shop. Rashid turned to the first page. It was blank. And the next page. And the next.

"What happened?!" Shireen asked, shouldering in to get a look. "Where'd all the writing go?"

"The die erased it," the old man answered.

She stared at him. "Why?"

"Why do you think?" he answered gently. "A book cannot write itself. It needs to be penned. Who do you think wrote this one? Now, Jared, the ink, please."

Jared was just as confused as Shireen. That's what the blank side was for? To erase the writing in the book? He was still puzzling it over as he handed Maldini's signore the bottle.

The shopkeeper turned back to the green-eyed boy. "Rashid, your pen?"

Rashid blinked uncertainly and then, all at once, his eyes widened with understanding. His hand fumbled under the collar of his robe and he pulled out the silver chain. "So that is why I chose this that very first time I entered Ala ad-Din's cavern. That is why I chose the pen! It is not worthless after all."

"No," Maldini's signore answered. "A pen is never worthless. In the right hand, it holds a whole world and all the treasures you could ever want. Now write your story. All of it. From the beginning until you are here, with all of us. Then you may write your own ending, for yourself and all these others." He gestured toward Maria, Francesca, and the crowd of children nervously milling around them. Behind their shoulders, the sun had cleared the tips of the church towers and was throwing long shadows over the clearing. "There is little time. Come, Rashid, begin. Take them home. Make them believe, too."

Rashid held the shopkeeper's look for a score of heartbeats. "My uncle's friend in Venice," he finally spoke, "Signor Isaac . . . he is your ancestor?"

"Yes."

"Very well." Rashid smiled. "I will write it. I will make them all believe. And when we are home, I will send this book to Signor Isaac, to his shop, so that it will be waiting for you. Then no one can ever say that I am a book thief!" He grinned and sat himself cross-legged on the ground, dipped the nib of the pen in the mouth of the bottle, shook free an excess drop of black ink, and prepared to write. As he was about to pen the first word, though, he paused and glanced up at Jared. "You do not read Arabic?"

"No." Jared shook his head.

"Latin?"

"Yeah! Well, actually, not too much. My dad's been teaching us. But he's the one who really knows—he was translating the book from Latin when he read to us."

"Then I will write in Latin, so that when the time comes he can read to you. My uncle Mounir taught me," he added proudly. "He is a great scholar." He returned his attention to the blank book, thought for a second, and then began. The nib scratched against the page hesitantly at first, and then it began to fly. It was moving across the page with incredible speed, writing line after line. Within moments he had filled a page and then a second, and then he was turning to a new blank surface and the pen was darting over it at a lightning pace.

As the lines of black print filled the pages, Jared could make out something strange about the words. The black ink was shivering and gleaming, like it was made from an ebony stream of light. As his gaze raced to keep up with Rashid's speeding hand, the letters seemed to lift off the page in front of his eyes and change their shapes, refitting themselves into combinations Jared could grasp, translating themselves so that he could follow along with Maria and Francesca as their eyes also drank in what Rashid was writing and read it out to the other children.

᪰ ᪰ ᪰

"Lorenzo!" Shireen spun around, startled by the warm puff of breath at her side as the little lion ambled up to her. "What are you still doing here? You've got to go!" She'd been about to slip the ring off her finger to give to Maria when the lion's approach had made the problem suddenly, startlingly clear. Lorenzo il Piccolo hadn't left with his father. He was still there, standing guard at her side. And if what she thought was about to happen really did happen, then he had to get out of there. Fast. Rashid had already filled dozens of pages. Maria and Francesca were peering over his shoulders, reading aloud what he'd written to the throng of children behind them. His pen was moving with magical fastness and so were the girls' lips as their eyes skimmed across the pages, desperately trying to keep up with the words streaming out of the silver nib. It was as if they were all inside a cone of accelerated time—the pen moving faster and faster, the words sounding out of Maria and Francesca's mouths at a frantic pace, a distant gleam coming into their eyes and the attentive eyes of all the listening children. The die was shining. The ink was glowing. They were about to follow Rashid back into the story. And when Maria went, and took the ring with her, and they'd finally all kept their promises, the ring's power over Lorenzo il Piccolo would be gone. He had to get out of there and back to his balcony, fast, or he'd end up frozen on this wasteland. There couldn't be much time.

"Lorenzo!" Shireen exclaimed again. "You have to go home!"

"No, my lady," he responded, his eyes as unblinking as ever. "I have thought better of it. I have spent enough years on that balcony where you found me. My duty to you is done. I have preserved my honor. Now it is Maria who needs my assistance. I will accompany her, so long as she has need of me. Her purpose will be mine." He looked up at Maria, who'd turned away from the book at the sound of her name coming from the small lion's mouth. She looked stunned by his announcement. Lorenzo il Piccolo swung his stony gaze back to Shireen and peered deeply into her eyes.

"By your leave, my lady?"

Her pulse was hammering. How'd he do it? She hadn't even known he'd existed until a couple of days ago. So how did he make her feel like this when he said he was leaving and she knew she'd never see him again? She shot a look over to Maldini's signore to make sure this would work—that Lorenzo il Piccolo would be safe, that he'd stay alive if she let him follow Maria. He nodded quietly. She knelt down over the little lion, took him in her arms, and clasped his stone body to her. "Yes, Lorenzo. By my leave."

"Very well," he growled. For just a moment she could feel him leaning his weight back into her, accepting her hugging arms, and nuzzling his snout against her chest softly, to make sure he didn't hurt her. And then he was all stony and proud again. He turned to Maria. "My lady, you will permit me to accompany you?"

Maria nodded her agreement and reached out to squeeze Shireen's hand. "Thank you," she breathed quietly. Shireen swallowed, slipped off the ring, and slid it over Maria's finger. Maria rubbed it once, rested her palm on Lorenzo il Piccolo's mane, and then returned her gaze to the book. Shireen glanced at the words Maria was reading. They somersaulted in front of her eyes just as they had for Jared, turning themselves into English for her: "A mist appeared around the island while we slept, hiding it from the world, hiding it until our friends came to help us. . . ."

Maldini had watched the exchange between Shireen and Maria silently. He knew what had to come next. He purred quietly to his signore and the old man stepped away from the host of children jammed around Rashid. "*Ragazzi*," he said. "My *ragazzi*. You do understand? This did not have to be. It needed you. You and Rashid, Maria, and Francesca. It needed all of you. You have made it true." He held them in that measuring look Jared had noticed the first time they'd gone into his shop, but now with something different in it, something that wasn't just hopeful. Something proud. Then he turned and began to walk toward the entrance of the *calle* that led back into the city.

Jared crouched down to look the cat square in the face. "Maldini, are we okay?"

"'Okay'?" Maldini echoed, a mischievous glint in his golden eyes. "Why would we not be 'okay'?"

"Well, um, you know," Jared mumbled. "Even if it was all in the book, waiting for us to make things happen, I'm still the one who got us all into such a mess. I still just kind of let the die fall out of my hand and got your signore kidnapped. And . . ." He hesitated before forcing it out. "You've been mad at me."

"Jared." The cat smiled. "I have never been mad at you. I was only waiting for you to be who you are. The boy my signore read to me about. The one who would find a way. The one who brought us all home. And look . . ." He gestured around. "Here we are." He held Jared's eye. "You have done it." Then he turned to Jared's sister. "Miranda . . . ," he began.

"Don't go!" she pleaded, her face wretched with grief. "Please don't go!"

"I must go," he said, "but I will not forget you. And you will not forget me."

"No!" she begged.

"Write me a story," Maldini purred. "Write a story about you and me. Then we will be together again." He pressed his muzzle against her, and before she could stop him he had leaped from her arms. He bounded off to join his retreating signore, hurrying to leave before she had the chance to give her ring away and find him standing speechless before her.

Miranda stared after Maldini, blinking back tears as Jared gently pulled the ring from her finger and put it in Francesca's palm. Francesca barely glanced at the ring. Her gray eyes had a distant look in them as they ran across the shimmering black letters Rashid had shaped on the page. So now there was just the die. Jared picked it up and dropped it in Rashid's pocket.

Rashid turned, his hand momentarily pausing. "Wait," he said. He set the nib to the page and dashed off a final paragraph, then returned his attention to Jared and handed him the silver pen and bottle of ink.

"Here," he said, nodding at the pen. "I am finished. Keep it. On one condition."

"What?"

"Even after we are gone, when there is no sign of us, you will not forget us?"

Jared didn't hesitate. "No. Never."

"Then it is yours." Rashid bit at his lower lip before hurrying on. "This last section, the words I just wrote . . . Can I read them to you so you can hear how it all ends?" Knowing what Jared's response would be before he had the chance to answer, Rashid began to read the same words that Maria and Francesca were speaking, their eyes growing more and more distant as the magic began to throw its ropes around them.

"'I set the pen aside. The book was written.'" Rashid stole a quick glance at his friend, then he continued.

We were on the edge of a wasteland in Venice. Jared, Shireen, and Miranda were beside me, and the words I had written told me that I was coming home. The words showed me my father's house in Grenada. It was evening; my uncle was sitting on a pillow in the courtyard. A book was in his lap. A story was falling from his lips, and as I read I could see the courtyard there before me, could smell the scent of lemon, could feel the summer heat of the Andalusian night on my skin. I could see my home opening before me, and my thoughts went running into it. And all around me the others—Maria, Francesca, and all the children who had followed them—they too had seen their homes again. Venice—their Venice, the Venice they had left— was opening before them and they were running into it, running home. Just as in my mind, as I read these words, I too had come home. . . ."

Rashid's voice stilled but his lips continued to move as he read. A look of fierce joy crossed his face as his eyes ran across the page. He seemed to take a half step forward.

And then he was gone.

They watched, stunned, as his body melted away. All around them the others were vanishing too: Maria, Francesca, all the wandering children, Lorenzo il Piccolo. One second Rashid had been right there in front of them, the book open in his hands, reading, the two girls peering over his shoulder, the stone lion at their side, the mass of children behind them, listening intently. And then, as simply as the world inside a book opens up when you turn the first page, as simply and as quickly as that, they were all gone.

The kids stood there breathless for a moment, the rising winter sun pouring its cold bright light over them. Just the three of them.

Jared shook his head to clear the sparkle of light from his eyes, then reached into his backpack one last time and retrieved the apartment key that Maldini had remembered to have Silvio put there. "Shireen, Miranda," he said, "come on. It's over. We've done it. Let's get home."

The rest of that remarkable day had come and gone. They had crept silently into the apartment just before their parents woke up, hauled themselves into bed, and collapsed into sleep for a few hours before their father came to get them up. How they got through the rest of that long Sunday they didn't know, dull-eyed with fatigue as they were. Even when Dad came home with a newspaper bearing the astounding news that all the relics stolen from the city had suddenly reappeared, they did little more than nod silently to each other. Good, Silvio had done as Maldini had asked.

After supper, when their father offered to read the next bit of Rashid's story, their breath caught in alarm.

Jared had found a way earlier in the day to make the switch. The book their dad was holding now wasn't the real one—it was the new copy Maldini's signore had given them, the one with their names taken out. But still, what if he noticed something different and asked them about it? He didn't seem to detect anything, though, and after he'd read just a page or two and they were sure everything was going to be okay, Jared cut him off. All that stuff had happened so long ago, Jared had explained. It was interesting at first, but after a while it got boring. Who cared about the crusades these days?

Tuesday was the long-awaited Carnevale. Dad canceled his classes and Mom was feeling a bit better so they spent the day together, wandering through Venice, trying new pastries, taking in the teeming mass of people in costume. Jared had brought his skateboard along and kept zipping up ahead of the others. He needed a rush. Deep in his bones and in every muscle in his body he needed a surge of energy. After everything that had happened, going back to normal life just didn't seem possible. Feeling the wheels of his skateboard spinning against the pavement and his deck lifting into the air when he pushed his heel hard against it to jump wasn't much, but it helped.

And then, as he angled into Campo San Zaccaria, with his family trailing twenty yards behind, his heart leaped. A great shaggy-legged creature was ambling through the crowd of harlequins, Spanish dancers, and endless men and women in sun-and-moon masks. Silvio? He ground to a halt, his pulse racing. He pushed off to get the board moving again so he could get a better look, but before he could find a gap through the press of bodies, Shireen had hurried through the entrance of the square behind him.

"Jared!" she shouted. "What are you doing?"

"It's Silvio!" He turned back at the sound of her voice and then gestured ahead through the crowd.

Her eyes widened for a second as she followed his pointing finger, then she shook her head in disappointment. "No, it's just some dressed-up stranger."

Stranger? The word echoed in his head as he looked again. *That's not a stranger, it's . . .* But it wasn't Silvio. The siblings' shouting voices had caught people's attention. All around the square, costumed revelers were looking at them, including a man with fake goatskins wrapped around his legs who paused for a second to peer back before disappearing through the covered alleyway leading onto the Riva degli Schiavoni. It wasn't Silvio, Jared realized, his heart sinking. Just some tourist dressed up like a faun for Carnevale. There was no use wishing. The die was gone. Their adventure was over. Silvio must be safely back in his painting by now.

"All right, all right." Jared shook his head glumly before Shireen could light into him. He'd stepped off his skateboard and was holding it awkwardly at his side. "You don't have to tell me."

"Tell you what?"

"That I'm an idiot."

"You're right. I don't." She shook her head in agreement. "Because you knew that already. And besides," she whispered quickly as Miranda and their parents entered the square, "so am I. Who do you think I've been looking for all day?" She raised her eyes to the recessed space above the doors of the church flanking the campo. A small winged lion was carved into the stone, staring back at them unmovingly.

Shireen gave Jared's shoulder a quick sympathetic squeeze as their dad joined them. "Where are Mom and Miranda?" she asked innocently.

"Over there," their father answered vaguely, pointing at a brightly lit souvenir shop at the entrance to the square. "I think Miranda's buying something for my birthday. I'm not supposed to notice." He gave his glasses a quick polish with the end of his tie. "Hey, look at that!" he said excitedly as he settled the glasses back on his nose. A man in a long-beaked black mask wearing a billowing ebony cloak covered in raven feathers had just come flapping into the square. "Have you ever seen anything like that? What an incredible costume. That's something you can tell your friends about when you get home. They'll never believe how amazing this place is."

"You're right, Dad." Jared fought back a huge grin. "They won't."

By Thursday they were starting to feel a little better. It helped that it was Dad's birthday. Late the night before, Miranda had shown Jared and Shireen what she had picked out for him at the souvenir shop back in the square. It was a small lined notebook, covered in the thick marbled paper that was one of Venice's specialties.

"That's nice," Shireen had yawned sleepily from her bed.

Jared had given it a quick look, then rolled back over on his stomach and closed his eyes. He was flying over Venice on the dragon's back again. But this time the dragon wasn't bleeding from the snout, and he wasn't angry, and Jared didn't have to shout into his ears to tell him where to go. Jared was on his feet, balancing his weight on the dragon's shoulder blades, with his arms stretched out into the cold night air rushing past. Whichever way he bent, the dragon's body followed, the rise and dip of his mighty wings echoing the tilt of Jared's body, like they shared each other's thoughts, like they were made for each other.

Miranda had waited until Jared and Shireen were all the way asleep, then she had snuck quietly out of bed, grabbed the notebook, searched through the pockets of Jared's coat until she had found what she was looking for, and started working, her hand moving faster and faster.

The next morning, as a birthday breakfast, their mother made pancakes, and when they'd scarfed them all up, she brought out the present she'd chosen for Dad in the old man's shop. As the wrapping paper peeled away from the surface of the framed map of the Santiago pilgrimage route, his eyes brightened. He held it up for them all to admire. "Kids," he said once they'd all had a chance to get a good look at it, "we've also got a surprise for you." He looked over at their mother to make sure that he should go ahead. "You know how

Mom's been feeling a little sick?" he asked. "Well, there's nothing really wrong with her. It's just that—"

"You're going to have a baby!" Shireen exclaimed before he could finish the sentence. She looked excitedly over at their mother to see if she'd guessed it right. Of course! What else? That's why Dad had been giving Mom all those goofy looks whenever she said she was feeling sick. Her mother smiled back at her. "Mom!" Shireen shouted gleefully, rushing over to give her a hug, Miranda at her heels. "I get to help raise this one, okay? You know"—she nudged Miranda playfully in the ribs—"the right way! It's a girl. I know it. She'll be just like me!"

Just what we need! Jared thought, but he was also grinning. So they weren't going to go back to normal life after all—not to the way everything had always been. Who knew? Maybe Shireen was wrong. Maybe it would be a boy. It was about time he had a brother.

They were climbing into their beds that night when Miranda called to their father. "Dad, remember how that other book got boring? Well, I figured out what was wrong with it. It needed some real kids. You know, from now. That's the kind of stuff people like reading about. So we've been working on something. For your birthday." She reached under her bed and pulled out the notebook she'd been scribbling in all day.

As she pushed herself back up, Jared saw a flash of silver chain at the edge of Miranda's pajama collar. His eyes darted to the closet where his coat was hanging. Rashid's pen! She'd taken it?

"What is it?" Dad was asking, taking the notebook from her.

"A story," Miranda told him, shooting Jared a be-quiet look. "We've been working on it together. All of us. It's just the first part. We thought maybe we could start it for you, and then we can give you ideas about what else should happen, and then you can finish it. It'll be like we all wrote it together. Maybe when the baby's older we can share it with her, or him."

"Miranda!" Their father was smiling delightedly. "Kids! That's a great idea. Can I read how it begins?"

"Sure," she said. "It's set in Venice. We're the characters." She lay back against her pillows, folding her hands behind her head and looking up through the skylight. Jared shook his head in disbelief and then started to grin. He flashed Shireen a quick wink and mimed the stitched-lips sign before she had a chance to say anything. Their dad flipped open the notebook, scanned the first sentence, and began to read.